Twelve Days
to Save
Christmas

BOOKS BY ELIZABETH NEEP

The Spare Bedroom
Never Say No
The New Me

WRITING AS LIZZIE O'HAGAN
What Are Friends For?
The Visa

Elizabeth Neep

Twelve Days to Save Christmas

Bookouture

Published by Bookouture in 2021

An imprint of Storyfire Ltd.
Carmelite House
50 Victoria Embankment
London EC4Y 0DZ

www.bookouture.com

ISBN: 978-1-80019-8487
eBook ISBN: 978-1-80019-847-0

To all the friends I have met at Trent Vineyard and KXC, thanks for showing me how fun a life of generosity can be.

Chapter One

Wednesday, 24 November

'George, *please* put it on.' I can just about glimpse his amber eyes looking back at me over the vast expanse of fabric that I'm holding between us.

'I wouldn't even know *how*.' George sighs heavily, his broad shoulders stiffening as he takes a step back from his knitwear nightmare.

'Oh, it's *easy*,' I say, shaking away his cynicism, refusing to let it steal my cheer. Mere minutes ago, I was in our bedroom, FaceTiming Dee and walking her through the winter wardrobe I have bought for our trip to the Cotswolds next month, the one I've planned for all our friends. *Dee* thought the two-person Christmas jumper was funny.

'I put my arm through here…' I explain, diving into the fabric and emerging with a Mrs Claus body on my own.

'Poppy, *please.*'

'And you put your arm through here…' I say, gesturing for George to become my Santa Claus. He just stands there. 'Come on, this is meant to be fun. There were no complaints when I dressed up as Mrs Claus last year. I guess this isn't *quite* as sexy as that.'

'Can't we just…'

'I need you to be my Santa Claus.'

'I don't want to be Santa Claus.'

'No,' I say, reaching my hands to his hips, the spare arm of our two-person jumper flopping lifelessly by my side. 'Clearly, you want to be the Grinch.'

'Poppy…' George whispers my name softly, kindness in his eyes. But I know what he's doing. He's trying to distract me from my one-woman mission to get my man in a two-person jumper.

'George, I won't tell you again,' I narrow my eyes in fake disdain, putting my hands to my hips, both of us watching the spare jumper-arm dangle by my side. 'Put the jumper on.'

'I don't want to put the jumper on.'

'It's just a jumper.'

'It's *November*.'

'Yes?' I say, hands still on hips.

'It's not even *close* to Christmas.'

'Tell that to London.'

George shakes his head. I know from the five Christmases we've been together that he's one of those *don't play me a Christmas song before the first of December* people. I've never understood those people. If something makes you happy, why wouldn't you want to extend the celebrations? It's the reason I still buy George a coffee every second Monday of the month, to mark the first cautious coffee we ever shared together. Yes, some people may think that's overkill, that once you've shared a thousand coffees together you don't really need to commemorate the first. But I like remembering how two relative strangers can become the kind of close-knit couple that squabble over knitwear.

'Plus, it's only a *month* until Christmas,' I go on, mustering the excitement I had felt when talking to Dee on the phone. Our trip is going to be perfect: five full days, four couples, three day trips, two hot tubs (two!), one wonderfully wintery getaway.

'No.' George looks from Mrs Claus to my face. 'It's a month until Christmas *Eve.*'

'Everybody knows that's when Christmas begins!' I throw my arms out but only one of them is visible under the weight of the fabric. 'Now. Put. It. On.' I push one arm into the air, followed by the other, becoming the cheerleader I always am for George. Even when what I'm cheerleading him into is way out of his cool-guy comfort zone.

'But I need to talk to you about something,' George says softly. That old chestnut. But I shall not be deterred. He's been so busy with work lately, not to mention his band, which started as a side-project but is now making its way onto centre stage.

He needs cheering up and 'tis the season for cheer. It's a month until Christmas. Less than four weeks until we go away. And I know George wants to get on this holidays-are-a-coming train with me, he just needs a bit of coaxing to get on board.

'Well, we can talk and look *dashing* at the same time.'

'Is that a reindeer pun?'

'It's not *not* a reindeer pun,' I say, and I see his face dimple at the cheeks. There it is. The smile I love most in the world. The one I always manage to probe and poke and kiss out of him, no matter how busy or stressed or tired he's been.

'I'm not sure I…' George begins as I twiddle Mrs Claus' pigtails on my front, which are unfortunately positioned in the exact same place as my nipples. 'Poppy, are you even listening?' he asks. 'If I put the damn jumper on, will you listen to me?'

'Deal,' I say, as George disappears underneath the jumper until his messy mop of dark hair pops through the neck and he becomes the Mr to my Mrs. He turns to me with a smile so soft that I fear that if I hold him too tightly, I might just scare it away.

'Happy now?'

'Almost.' I begin to shuffle in the direction of the mirror. George follows. He has no choice not to. Together, we look at our reflection. We look ridiculous. Gloriously ridiculous. I study our shapes, the way his big frame towers against mine. Mr and Mrs Claus dangle from our fronts, almost as good a double act as *us*.

'*Now* I'm happy,' I say, turning my body around to face him as the fabric holding us together forces George to do the same. He looks down at me, his eyes widening as if to take me in, flicking through my features, from my eyes to my nose to my mouth, lingering on my lips for a moment that seems to stretch on forever. The fact that I am still desperate for him to kiss me after five years of kisses feels like a dream come true.

'But I'm not,' George says slowly. 'Poppy, I… you're…'

'Fine, you can take it off now,' I laugh, reaching to pull the jumper up.

'No, Poppy,' George objects as I wonder whether he just likes disagreeing with me. 'It's not the jumper. Well, it's kind of the jumper,' he admits, catching another glimpse of himself in the floor-length mirror. 'Look, shall we sit down?' He smiles again but for some reason it doesn't feel like all the smiles that have gone before.

'No.' Now it's my turn to object. 'If it's not the jumper thing...'

'It's the *whole* thing,' George interjects, the volume of his voice inching louder.

'What thing?' I say, my heartbeat quickening to match the urgency of his tone.

'Us. You and me.' The way he refers to us together before breaking us into two parts feels ominous, like he's trying to warn me of something I can't quite comprehend.

'We're not a thing,' I object breathlessly. We're a couple. We're in love. We're best friends. How can five years of shared life and growing up be bundled into a single *thing*?

'What I'm trying to say, Poppy,' George says, still standing before me as the fabric holding us together begins to itch. 'Is that you're wonderful...' Okay, well, that's not bad. 'And gorgeous...' These are all good things. So, why is he looking at me like he's about to punch a puppy? 'But... I think we should break up.'

Everything stops, from my breath to my heartbeat, as I wait for the punchline. Come on, George, where is that smile? The one that tells me that everything will be okay. George tries to take a step backwards but still attached, I come with him. I always come with him. Ever since that first coffee date on the second Monday of the month, we've rarely left each other's side. We've woken up every morning together, gone to sleep every night together. First at his place, then at ours. I look from Mrs Claus to my Mr Right and everything feels wrong.

'Poppy, shall we sit down?' George echoes again, eyes darting to the sofa, the one we picked out together to go perfectly with the one-bedroom flat we rent together. He motions to lift the two-person jumper up so that we can become two separate entities. But I can't move.

'Wh…' I manage to make a sound, neither one of us knowing where it's going next. We both know it's a question though. What? Where? *Why?*

'Poppy, let's take this jumper off…'

I watch as George wriggles his way out of the jumper, the one he never wanted to put on in the first place. I keep it on, letting the arm that George was filling once again fall limp. My whole damn body is limp. My eyes follow his frame as he moves to sit on the sofa, not looking back to see whether I'm following. I'm not following any of this. Somehow, I move from the mirror to stand mere metres in front of him but unable to stomach sitting down, I stand there, still drenched in a jumper made for two. I feel like a melted snowman.

'Poppy, I know this may be a bit of a shock…' George begins, his voice still butter. He can't even bring himself to say that I probably saw this coming too. We both know I didn't. Not even an hour has passed since Dee was laughing through my phone screen commending my cashmere, telling me which outfits to share photos of on social media, promising I'll look every inch like Cameron Diaz in *The Holiday*. *'Who does that make George?'* I had asked, already knowing her answer: *Jude Law, who else? You guys are perfect together. I wish Charlie could be a bit more like him…'* Not even an hour ago I felt like the luckiest girl in the world. Now, I'm standing here before the man I love, jilted and shivering. If Baby thought it was cold outside, she has no bloody idea how icy it is in here.

'I've been feeling this way for a while,' he says, looking too sad for me to hate him.

'How long?'

'A few months.'

A few months? We've been together for years. Surely, a few months isn't worth throwing five years of love and friendship away? I search his face for signs I should have seen earlier, the ones that would have warned me something wasn't right but there are none. We were perfect. We *are* perfect. I've made sure of it.

'Yeah, a few months,' he repeats, eyes drifting into the middle distance as he tries to pinpoint the precise moment he started to feel differently. 'Around the time you lost your—'

'I didn't lose my job,' I don't let him complete the sentence I know is coming next.

'Okay, yeah, sorry,' George continues to speak softly but more quickly, like he just wants to get this *thing* over with now. 'When you took voluntary redundancy.'

I know from the way he says the word 'voluntary' that he's struggling not to make air quotes with his fingers, struggling not to make a mockery of my decision to abandon the sinking PR start-up I was working at in favour of a freelance lifestyle, one that has started so slowly that you'd be forgiven for thinking it hadn't started at all. But I've been busy. It's not my fault that the exact moment my career started to stall, George decided to turn up the volume on things with the band.

'I guess since then you've been… well, *we've* been a bit…' George hurries to correct his misplaced word but we both know he means it. I've been a bit something, a bit what? Loving? Supportive? So scared that I'd look like I wasn't happy about him finally trying to make his boyhood fantasy become a reality that I pushed aside job-hunting to meet him on his lunchbreak or clap along front-row at every single one of his gigs?

'Needy?' George says reluctantly, like he knows it's a mistake even before he's muttered it. Even so it floors me, my legs chattering together at such speed that I decide it's better to sit on the carpet, kneeling by his feet for a second before I try to muster a more powerful pose. I cross my legs, feeling like a child. A bit needy. *Needy?*

'Well… I don't know if that's the right word,' George goes on, reaching for my hand. Words were my thing before I took that redundancy. Despite being a musician by night, George is an accountant by day, and I know he still thinks in numbers. Five years of happiness plus three months of doubt and this still isn't an outcome I can compute.

'But ever since you lost… since you decided to go freelance…' I feel the invisible air quotes again. 'You're always…' He searches for the right word again. '…here.'

'In the apartment?'

'No, not *here* here.' He shakes his head hurriedly. He's not making sense. None of this is making sense. I study the symmetry of his face, from his strong jaw to his crinkled brow, searching for signs of exhaustion or mental breakdown or something else going on that his confused brain has decided to pin on me. 'Just here, as in, where I am. You're wonderful…' I wish he'd stop saying that.

'*But…*' I'd wish he'd stop saying that even more. 'I wake up and you're here, I go to sleep and you're here. I go to work and you're there, waiting to take me on my lunchbreak or surprise me with my favourite coffee…'

I watch on, stunned, trying to see how adding any of these things together can equate to a mistake. These are nice things. And you do nice things for the people you love. Not that my family taught me that, but George did, right around the time *he* became my family.

'I play a gig and all the guys have this, like, air of mystery around them,' George says, and I want to shout that if it's mystery he's after then bravo because he's sounding as clear as a flipping raincloud. 'But no, not me; there's my girlfriend standing front row, shouting my name.'

I thought he liked that, that we've always been each other's biggest fans.

'I thought that's what you wanted.'

'Yes, I…' George softens, but then his body stiffens again as if he's mustering the strength to break my heart in two. 'What I want,' he breathes and it's like he's been holding onto this for years. *A few months*, I remind myself. He's only been feeling this way for a few months. 'Is to be with someone whose whole world doesn't revolve around me. It's too much pressure. I want to be with someone who takes risks, tries new things…'

Like being the first person to ever cry cross-legged in the centre of their living room wearing a two-person Christmas jumper in November?

'I want to be with someone who knows what *they* want and maybe you just need some time to work that out and…'

'I want you.'

'Poppy…'

I knew as soon as I'd said those three words that they were basically George's case in point, but the way he's saying my name now tells me that for sure. And yet, I can't help but say the next three words that come to my mind, the only ones with enough power to fix this.

'I love you.'

'I know, me too, I just…' George shakes his head. 'I think we need this.'

How the hell could I need this?

'What are we going to do now?' I say, hating myself for needing George to have the answers. But he always has. Or at least, I stopped asking so many questions about my past around the time I started planning my future with him.

'One of us needs to move out,' he says, reaching for my hand again. I pull away.

'With what money?'

'I guess, maybe… you need to get a job…'

I thought I had a job, a freelance one. But the way George says this tells me he thinks I'm as employed as my redundancy was voluntary.

'I have a…'

'A *steady* job.'

'I need time.'

'We've paid the rent until the end of the year, you can stay here until then.' He forces a sad smile, trying to keep strong for the two of us. Is this the kind of pressure he is talking about? The pressure to be the leader, the decision-maker, the one that makes things happen?

'Then what?' Damn it, Poppy.

'Then we'll find somewhere new,' George says, treating the word 'we' with a light touch seeing as we're not really *we* anymore. 'Or I'll stay on here.'

'In our place? That's not fair.' Now I don't just look like a child, I sound like one too.

'If you can afford to cover the rent by yourself then by all means…' he says, the end of his sentence drifting off at the sight of my widening eyes, staring back at him now. If I didn't love him so much, I'd hate him. But the man has a point.

'But where will *you* stay?' I say, tears making tracks down my face.

'I'll stay here too,' George says, and a glimmer of hope fills my heart. He's not ready to move on either. 'But I'll sleep on the sofa bed,' he looks to the cushions beneath him, the ones that have made so many of *our* guests feel welcome at *ours*.

'And I'll be at the office three days a week and out most evenings anyway,' George goes on, mentally mapping through his routine even though I know every inch of it by heart. I used to love Mondays and Fridays when George was working from home, sleepy Sundays where he had no band practice to run off to. Now these days are going to be excruciating.

'You'll have plenty of space, I promise. Then I'll be back at my parents' for Christmas,' he adds, and this feels like the most excruciating thought of all. I've only had five good Christmases in my life and each one of these was spent with George and his family.

And, though he hasn't explicitly asked me to spend Christmas with his family this year, after spending the past four festive seasons embraced by the whole clan as if I was one of their own, I assumed it was a given. There is a lot I've assumed.

'So, you're saying we should stay together until New Year?'

'Well, in the flat until New Year… not *together*-together.'

Yes, thanks, George. I got that part, at least.

'Oh crap, I'm going to be late for practice,' George says, looking up from his watch to me, as if he's waiting for me to stop him from leaving or follow him out of the bloody door. I just sit there, in the middle of the floor, drowning in ugly knitwear and even uglier tears.

This can't be happening. The thought runs on repeat as I watch George grab his guitar and head towards the front door to our apartment. I look down to see Mrs Claus smiling back at me, mocking me, and up to see my should-be Santa Claus leaving his baggage behind.

Chapter Two

Twelve Choir Members

Waking up on the sofa, I can't breathe and it only takes a moment for me to realise why. I look down to see the festive-green arms of the couple's jumper tangled around my neck and peel off the comedy knitwear. Turns out I'm the joke.

I look up at the clock on the wall, the one we bought on our trip to Paris this time last year. Back when everyone thought George was preparing to pop the question. Only an hour has passed since he left. One blissful hour of release but now I fear I may never sleep again. This can't be right. I scan our shared apartment for clues, mentally replaying the last few hours. Rewind one hour and I'm asleep on our sofa. Rewind three and I'm dancing in our bedroom. But rewind *two* and the love of my life is breaking up with me for being too needy.

I want to be with someone who takes risks, tries new things… The injustice of his words pushes me to my feet. I take risks. I try new things. Just three hours ago I was trying on *multiple* new things for Dee. I walk into the bedroom and it's exactly as I left it even though by now, everything has changed. I pull on a bright white jumper, hoping to feel something of the joy I had felt just hours ago, but it doesn't work. I flick through the lifestyle magazine I was reading before, but the same headline catches my eye – *Giving Back is the New Going Out* – and it just makes me feel as angry as it did earlier.

Dee: did George like the jumper? I read the message that has just popped into my phone as another wave of sickness washes over me. What should I tell her? What does she already know? I leave her question unanswered whilst more of them flood my mind: Will George stay out all night? What do I say when he comes home? What do I do now? Every inch of this apartment reminds me of him. We share everything together.

Well, except our love of Christmas in November...

The cold winter air slaps me around the face as soon as I step outside. I'm too tired for this, too emotional, but I can't stay in waiting for George to come home. Plus, if anything can make me feel better, it's the Christmas markets. From the smell of a thousand different street foods filling the air to the twinkling lights and happy pink-cheeked faces of friends and tourists mooching around aimlessly, it's the kind of barrage to the senses that can just about make you forget yourself. And God knows, I need to forget today.

Tracing the short walk from Elephant and Castle to South Bank, I hear the sound of music and chatter before I see the market coming into view and try my best to shake off my sadness. George is always talking about travelling the world, touring with the band, but it's the one thing I won't budge on. London has everything we need; well, it *did*.

I head to the first stall I pass, allowing my eyes to feast on the stacks of multi-coloured fudge before me. But then I see a banoffeeflavoured block and remember the time that George and I tried to make a pie for Dee and Charlie only to accidentally order one hundred and fifty *kilograms* of digestive biscuits to our apartment. Next, I come to a hut selling scarves, allowing the very many colours to momentarily wrap around me, making me feel warm. But then I see a simple grey one that George would love. I walk past a stand selling coffee and see the slumped figure of an elderly gentleman, with the kind of grubby hands and unkempt beard that tells me he has been sleeping rough for weeks.

'My boyfriend just bailed on me,' I say, handing him the second cup of coffee I have just bought, mustering a lie to give him some dignity along with his drink. Then, I realise it isn't a lie at all. My boyfriend *has* just bailed on me. He smiles back at me before the sound of singing distracts us both from the moment. I follow the music until I come to stand outside the heaving Cider Lodge, packed full of smiling faces that somehow manage to make me feel even worse. There, I see a twelve-piece choir swaying from side to side in front of it.

'On the first day of Christmas my true love gave to me...'

I look between their shiny faces. Half of them are in their fifties, but I'm surprised to see there are some younger members too. One choir member offers me a massive smile that goes straight to my stomach. He must be in his late twenties, with floppy dark hair, a thick black beard and dark olive skin, even though almost every inch of it is wrapped up in worn denim. He holds my gaze as the choir take a collective and exaggerated intake of breath before listing off the increasing amount of presents they're receiving from their true loves.

'On the sixth day of Christmas my true love gave to me…'

The stranger smiles at me again, a twinkle in his eyes, before he starts to bob up and down on the spot. Oh gosh, they're bobbing. He rolls his eyes as if he knows it's cheesy and I can't help but laugh. Then I notice another member of the choir: an auburn-haired woman dressed in a multi-coloured coat is looking at me. I watch as she turns to look at my new bobbing friend. For some reason I feel like I've just been caught checking the poor guy out.

'On the eighth day of Christmas my true love gave to me…'

As the choir sings on, I try to imagine my life with anyone other than George. Could I just walk up to this handsome stranger and start talking and never stop, just like I did with George all those years ago? Where one coffee had turned into seven, then eight, then…

'On the ninth day of Christmas my true love gave to me…'

I can't do it. I can't see myself with anyone else, can't see myself laughing and joking and spending Christmas with anyone but him. As the choir builds to the crescendo of one of the happiest songs in the world, I feel a rush of emotion run through me. *On the twelfth day of Christmas…* tears begin to make their way down my cheeks. *Eleven, ten…* more follow suit. And by that one bloody partridge in that effing pear tree, I am sobbing, shoulders shaking, audibly wailing into my gloved hands. And there is nothing I can do to stop.

After what feels like an age, I sense a hand on my shoulder and I hate the not-so-small part of me that hopes it is George, finding me in the one place he knew I'd be and telling me that he's making a stupid, seismic mistake; that of course, he could never let me go.

'Honey…' I follow the sound of the voice back to the auburn-haired woman from the choir. 'Are you okay?'

'Yes,' I say, barely audible among my sobs.

'Yeah, well,' the woman begins tactfully, as I notice her loud feather earrings. 'I might just believe that if you didn't look like Alice Cooper just found out Christmas got cancelled.'

'Who's Alice? Does she like Christmas?'

'*He* has make-up down his…' she begins, shaking her head as my face falls. 'It doesn't matter,' she rallies a smile. 'You look like you could do with a drink?'

'I…' I begin, taken aback by her offer. If only a random middle-aged stranger asking me for a drink was the strangest part of my day. I should say no. What kind of person accepts a drink from a random stranger? But then, George did say he wants to be with someone who takes risks, tries new things. Is this the kind of 'yes' person he wants to be with? I force myself to nod before I can think better of it. After today, what have I got to lose?

'I'm Marie, by the way,' the woman says as she steers me into the Cider Lodge and seems to effortlessly make her way to the front of the queue. There was an article in that damn lifestyle magazine that said that fifty is the new thirty; that there's a confidence that comes with living in your body for that long. I wish I knew how that feels. Right now, having spent years twenty to twenty-five with George, I feel like my body is one half of his.

'I'm Poppy.'

'And you're having a bad day?'

I look back at her blankly.

'Mulled wine okay for you?' She goes on, unperturbed. I accept the steaming cup she's handing me and will my face to look more thankful than I feel.

'Bad week? Month? Year?' Marie quizzes me further, increasingly concerned. It feels like the kind of count-up climax she's just been singing about – except lamer.

'No, no,' I say, shaking my head and following her to a nearby bench. I see her shoo a group of boys so that we can sit down but I sense their scared faces are less to do with her and more to do with the state of my face. 'I was having a good year, at least I thought I was.'

'And then what?'

'I, er…'

'Sorry if I'm being nosy,' Marie steals the thought from my mind. 'But having just gone through a second divorce, I know heartbreak when I see it. And crying to the bloody "Twelve Days of Christmas" is a code red in my eyes.'

'It is.'

'It is what, love?'

'A code red… erm… a heartbreak.'

'Honey,' Marie says with code red levels of sass. 'At least you're not fifty-two, twice-divorced and singing in a twelve-piece choir.' She grins so broadly that I don't know whether to laugh or cry. 'But if you wanna talk, I don't have anywhere better to be.'

The low hum of her phone vibrating on the table tells me she has a thousand places she *could* be. But given that I really need to talk to someone – *anyone* – I start to share.

'He said *what*?' Marie exclaims, over an hour later, throwing her hands into the air before reclaiming her third glass of mulled wine with care. I take a dirty great sip of my own.

'That I'm needy.'

'And are you?'

'No!' I say quickly, though the fact I'm drinking with someone I've only just met tells me otherwise. 'But ever since we started dating, my life got better and I'm scared that without him...' I allow my sentence to trail off, not wanting to tell a relative stranger the scariest thought of all. 'I guess since I went freelance, I've tried to be there for him as much as possible...'

'Maybe you need a hobby?' Marie says, her neat eyebrows raised.

'I'm *not* joining the choir,' I object for the third time since we started drinking.

'Just saying,' Marie puts her hands in the air. 'It's a good way to meet people.'

'But I don't *want* to meet people,' I say as she pretends to look offended. 'I mean, I don't want to meet guys – I just want George.'

'Is he your *true love*?'

'I don't think he's going to buy me a partridge any time soon.'

'I'm serious,' Marie says, lowering her voice, leaning in a little closer. 'Is it love?'

'Yes,' I sigh, never meaning anything more. 'I'm sure of it.'

'Then what are you waiting for?' Marie says with a sly smile. 'Show him that he's making a huge mistake by breaking up with you.'

'But how?'

'Well, that depends...'

I wait on the next words out of her mouth as if they might solve everything. I need them to solve everything.

'How long have you got?'

'He'll be back with his family from Christmas Day,' I say, and just whispering the words *his family* reminds me they're not mine.

'Okay, so you have a full month to work with.'

'Not exactly,' I say, remembering George's assurance that he'd rarely be in the apartment. His words sting all over again. 'He'll be out a lot so really, I have every Monday, Friday and Sunday between now and then.'

'Great, well…' Marie says in a way that doesn't sound all that great, but I can tell she's trying. 'That means you have twelve days to show him you still belong together.'

Just twelve days to fix this, fix *us*, before Christmas.

'Do you think that's enough?'

'If you're as in love as you say you are…' Marie begins as my mind drifts to my conversation with George earlier. I had told him I loved him. What did he say back? I rack my brain for his response but know it's already stored in my heart: *I know, me too…*

'He said he loved me.'

'Honey, you had five years together. Of course he said…'

'No, he said he *loves me*, today, when he was breaking up with me.'

'Oh well, then twelve days is more than enough time to remind him why.' Marie's eyes glisten, before searching the room. 'But just in case, better to start with a bang. Aran!'

My mouth hangs open as I watch Marie get to her feet and call the name across the room. From the other side of the makeshift Cider Lodge the handsome, dark-haired man from the choir stands up and begins to make his way across the room.

'Marie, no. He's coming over. I don't *want* to bang him…'

'Who said anything about that?' Marie whispers back to me quickly.

'You just said, "best start with a bang".'

'I meant a *date*,' Marie laughs. 'Any "banging" is up to you.'

'A date?'

'Yes,' Marie hisses as Aran's figure gets closer and closer to our wineglass-scattered bench. 'It sounds to me like George loves you as much as you love him,' she says. 'But people also want what they can't have, especially men…'

'I'm not sure I—' I begin but before I can form the sentence, Aran appears by our side.

'Hey, trouble,' he says, smiling from me to Marie. 'What can I do you for?'

'This Sunday. You free?' Marie asks, no time for small talk.

'I am,' Aran says slowly, trying to work out where she's going with this.

'Not anymore,' Marie beams between us. 'You're taking Poppy here on a date.'

Chapter Three

Thursday, 25 November

The first thing I notice is that it's still dark outside, the second thing is my dry mouth. I guess George was wrong about the 'gimmicky festive pop-up bars' always watering their mulled wine down. For a second, I can't wait to tell him, to tickle him in the ribs until he puts his hands up in surrender, sighing, *'Okay, fine. You're right, Poppy.'* But then I roll onto my side and realise that *his* side of the bed is empty.

I riffle through every item on my cluttered bedside table until I finally land on my phone. It's five. And not the good *it's five p.m. somewhere* kind, but the one I never, ever see. I must have fallen asleep waiting for George to come back from band practice. The fact that my body gave up waiting makes me wonder whether he even came home.

As soon as the thought has entered my mind, I know there's only one way to get it out again. Creeping to our bedroom door, I push it open, preparing myself for a vacant sofa, an empty apartment – or worse, the misshapen lump of the man I know most in the world with a stranger he's just brought home. It takes a millisecond to recognise the steady beat of George's breath, deep and slow and importantly, *alone*.

Tiptoeing over to the pulled-out sofa bed, I see the shape of his body curled up to one side, as if he knows the empty space is meant for me. I perch on the edge of it. My *true love*. Surely, he must know that's what we are? That he'll wake up today and realise that yesterday was a mistake, that we're perfect together?

I watch the steady rise and fall of his chest, studying the freckle that sits on top of his slightly parted lips. This Christmas was going to be perfect. I had it all planned out. I still have it all planned out – and more besides, thanks to that Marie woman last night. Drinking with a stranger is one thing but can I really go on a date with one?

I was so confident last night that she was speaking sense; that true love always finds a way but that sometimes you need to give it a little push in the right direction. But now, watching George sleeping like this, I'm not so sure. Surely, he'll realise that he's made a mistake without me having to manipulate him. I just have to carry on. Act normal.

'Shit, Poppy, what the hell?' George's eyes open to find me inches from his face.

'Good morning, George…' I begin woodenly, like I've just bumped into someone I used to know at the bus stop. So much for normal.

'Were you watching me *sleep*?'

'No, er… I just need…' I begin as George sits up, rubbing his eyes. 'Here it is!' I say, like I've just found the very thing I've been looking for. Evidently not my marbles.

'Here *what* is?' George asks, now fully confused and on the far edge of the sofa bed.

'My pillow.' I grab one of the decorative cushions he's pushed to one side. 'Can't sleep without it.'

'Poppy, I've never seen you sleep with that cushion in my life. Are you okay?' he asks, eyes searching my startled expression for signs of madness. 'What time is it?'

'It's half five.'

'Four hours sleep,' George groans, counting up the hours on one hand as the sheets around him fall and I see his gorgeous body in the dim morning light.

'What were you doing until half one?' I say before I can stop myself.

'Poppy, please,' he whispers from somewhere beneath the sheets. 'I need a couple more hours before work,' and then, sleepier still, 'Some of us can't just sleep in.'

Some of us can't just sleep in. I replay his final words as I head back to our empty bedroom until they sound an awful lot like *some of us have jobs.* I roll the rewrite of his whispers around my mind until I hear George leave for work hours later and I wander lifelessly into our living room, trying to remind myself how I would usually spend my day.

Back when I was working at Great Relation Expectations, I would leave the house at the same time as George, him always bemoaning the start-up's name – *It just doesn't work. It should be Great Relations, or Great Expectations* – before I could kiss his complaints away and he would kiss away my concerns. Then, I'd head into a day of planning promotions and working on our clients' digital campaigns. Lately, I've spent my mornings looking for work and falling down YouTube holes, surfacing around lunchtime before going to meet George for food, something he said he was looking forward to when he got a new job so close to home. Maybe I don't need to show George what he's missing, I just need to secure what's missing from my life. A job. A real one.

I pull on my puffer jacket and head out of the door, blasting some music into my headphones in the hopes of mustering some type of movie-montage energy, the kind that would see the hero of a film turn everything around. I walk past the coffee shop on the corner of our street, the one George and I go to at least twice a week. I wind past the bakery we buy our bread from and the off-licence where we get our wine and realise that George is written on every page of my story. I also realise that I've been wandering down the exact same route to his office at the exact same time I always do. What was I thinking, believing I can turn this around in three minutes of motivation when it took every ounce of my strength to turn my life around the first time? Just before I met George.

The memories flood my mind, draining my reserves until there is nothing left, and my legs stop outside a dark stone church on the corner of the street. I look up at the stained-glass window, a multi-coloured angel illuminated by the winter sun. I must have walked past this building a thousand times but have never once looked up. *Am I meant to go in there?* I wonder, just looking for something or someone to tell me whether I should take a random stranger's advice, whether I should wait to see if George changes his mind or if I should use our last twelve days together to see to it that he does? Is this a sign?

It's then that I notice an *actual* sign outside the church. Flipping 'eck, is there meant to be a noticeboard underneath all that crap? I wander closer towards the wooden frame haphazardly covered in papers and posters as multi-coloured as the stained-glass window that had first caught my eye. Well, *this* is an eyesore. In quick succession I read the conflicting messages layered over one another, vying for my attention: *Welcome to Church Street! Coffee shop inside! Welcome to Book Club. Movie night every Thursday. Jesus Saves. Alcoholics Anonymous Every Wednesday! Wine-Tasting Night: Free for All.*

And I thought I was confused. *What is this place?*

'Can I help you with something?'

A gruff voice makes me jump out of my skin and I turn around to see a quizzical expression staring back at me. I take a step back to take in the size of the man's frame, all six-foot-something of him, from his worn jeans to his grey zip-up fleece. His pursed lips are surrounded by a light dusting of stubble, which climbs up his angular jaw to meet a messy head of strawberry-blond hair. His green eyes narrow at me in suspicion.

'What is this place?' I ask, his earthy, country-boy ruggedness making me feel like a prissy princess in comparison. I pull my puffer closer around my body in protection.

'Church Street,' he says back to me, still straight-faced.

'No...' I reply slowly, taking a step back from the noticeboard, feeling every bit like I'm trespassing. 'I'm *on* Church Street.'

'Yes, you are,' he says, still not cracking a smile. 'But you're also *at* Church Street.'

'How can I be *on* and *at* somewhere at the same time?' I ask, instantly regretting it. I have a job to look for, a relationship to fix,

I don't need to be wasting my time trying to understand a place that clearly doesn't understand itself. Or talking to a stranger who is about as welcoming as a broken window on a blustery day. But something about the way he's sizing me up makes me want to cut his silly noticeboard down to size.

'Do I know you from somewhe—'

'And what do you actually do here?' I go on, my sentence slicing across his before I can stop it. 'Are you a book club or a coffee shop or a church or a wine bar?'

'Yes,' the stranger says, eyebrows raised at the intensity of my questioning. I just want to work *something* out today. 'All of the above.'

'Well, which is it? You can't have it all.'

'No, but you can do a lot with a little.'

Okay, now I really don't have time for this. The man is talking in riddles.

'Yes, we're a book club,' the stranger goes on, taking another step closer to me and I feel a spark of anger or energy or *something* shoot through my veins. 'And a coffee shop and a church and a wine bar as well; this place is whatever it needs to be.'

And then he smiles, disarming me completely. It's probably just because I wasn't expecting it. Or maybe because it lights up his face in a way that makes him look Hollywood handsome even though he's standing in a graveyard wearing a fleece from the eighties.

'Well, you're in need of some snappier branding.'

'And if you need to know where you are, you're *at* Church Street Community Centre *on* Church Street and do I erm… know you from somewhere?'

'Poppy?'

I turn around to see George standing there, looking from the man to me like we're both strangers to him – or aliens, like we shouldn't be here at all.

'George,' I say, hating myself for still being happy to see him. 'What are you doing?'

'Did you *follow* me here?' He ignores my question completely, clearly concerned; he thinks I'm having a break-up breakdown and that it's all his fault.

'Follow you where?' I ask, trying to stop my cheeks from flooding red.

'Church Street on Church Street,' the stranger looks at me, smirking.

'Yes, *thanks*,' I say, narrowing my eyes back at him. 'I got that.' I turn back to George, who should be in the office right now. 'Are you going to a meeting?'

'Yes,' he begins slowly. 'Well, I'm meeting somebody. A friend…'

Which one? I know all of George's friends. I feel my heartbeat picking up pace, panic rushing through my veins. Unless he's not meeting a friend at all. What if he's meeting a something-like-a-friend or a more-than-friend when just yesterday I thought I was his best friend and girlfriend all wrapped into one stupid, ugly jumper?

'Were you coming to my office?' George smiles sadly, seeming to ignore the strawberry-blond stranger beside us.

'No!' I object. *Well, not intentionally. I drifted here, just like I've drifted for months.* 'I am here, at…' I try to form a sentence and the stranger mouths 'Church Street', like these two little words and the sheer amount of times we've said them to one another during the last ten minutes is now a private joke between us. But there's nothing funny about this.

'At Church Street, to…' I'm standing here in front of the man I love looking every bit as needy as he thinks I've become. But I'm not needy. I'm not that girl. I've just had a blip. Marie is right: I need to use our remaining twelve days together to show him that before it's too late. 'I'm here to volunteer,' I say as both George and the stranger look back at me in surprise. But George had better get used to surprises, risks, new things, because the blood coursing through my veins tells me I'm not letting this – *us* – go without a fight.

Chapter Four

Eleven Volunteers

'The coast is clear.'

I look up from my position perched on a wooden bench inside the stone-floored entrance to the community centre to see the stranger towering over me.

'Ex-boyfriend?' *No, not an ex. My boyfriend, my best friend.* I shake my head, unable to voice a compelling answer out loud. But soon, soon George will be my future again.

'Well, I guess you should be getting back to your day?'

Clearly, I haven't convinced him that I am here to volunteer. But what about George? I glance down at my phone to see whether he's messaged. But no, he's occupied with his friend. And I'm really not in a rush to go back to our empty apartment and my empty inbox.

'Because I need to...' The stranger goes on, his eyes gazing through the glass double doors into the body of the building, which I've walked past countless times but never stepped foot inside until now. The hall looks alive with chatter and activity as bodies gather around tables and criss-cross each other along the width of the church hall. 'I'm busy.'

'I'm Poppy.'

'I know,' the man looks taken aback. 'I heard your non-ex-boyfriend say.'

'Are you this welcoming to all your volunteers?'

I see his eyebrows soar as if to say: *are you actually going to volunteer, then?* I'm asking myself the same question. But what better way to show George that my life doesn't revolve around him?

'Theo,' he says, putting a strong open palm between us. I look at it, grubby and scarred, nothing like George's moisturised mitts. 'Where I'm from, you shake it.'

'Pardon?'

'Hands, you shake hands,' Theo holds my gaze, trying not to smile.

'Sorry,' I say, shaking my head before shaking his hand.

'Let me show you around.' He tilts his head to one side before I realise I'm still holding his hand. His eyes explore my expression inquisitively like he still can't work me out, our fingers wrapped tightly together. Then he gives my hand a little tug, pulling me to my feet. He proceeds to push one of the glass doors open and I am hit with sights and smells and sounds. It's the same assault on the senses I got at the winter markets yesterday, only this time, the cheer doesn't feel magical: it feels chaotic.

To my left I see a long row of paper-covered tables, the kind with metal legs that fold beneath them so that they can be stored around the back of school stages until the next bake or bric-a-brac sale. Steam rises from deep silver urns, covering the people standing behind them who are serving a long line of people dressed in heavy coats and multi-coloured clothes; I instantly feel overdressed, uncomfortable. To my right there are yet more tables assembled with people gathered around each of them, some holding playing cards, one man in an anorak craning to look over the next lady's hand.

'Stanley,' Theo says with a stern voice. 'Don't think we can't see you.'

'What?' The man turns around to look at us with a smile so broad and mischievous that it makes up for the two front teeth he is missing. 'I'm not doing 'owt.'

Theo laughs, shaking his head in feigned despair before turning back to me.

'Any good at poker?'

'I've never played,' I say, feeling every bit like I don't belong here. Unlike Theo, who looks more and more in his element with every step we take into the hall.

'I'll learn ya, pet.' Stanley whips around to look at me; he's clearly from Yorkshire but he looks at home here too.

'*Teach* her.' Theo manages to correct him without sound patronising, something George has rarely mastered when mansplaining to me. 'And like heck you will.' Theo laughs again, and I feel something inside me flutter as he fixes his eyes on me. 'Get Linda to teach you,' he explains, both of us pretending that this tour isn't a one-time thing. 'We still can't work out her tell.' Theo looks at an elderly woman, hunched over her cards and beaming back at him. Clearly, Theo is a hit with the ladies – the over-sixties, at least.

'What's mine?' Stanley asks loudly; there is nothing subtle about him.

'Poppy?' Theo says, ushering me to guess.

'Er…' I stall, looking around the crowded room, feeling increasingly like a fraud. I don't know anything about poker or these people. 'You look at other people's cards?'

'And we have a winner!' Theo says, putting his hands up in the air in celebration before steering us past more people, all looking up at him and smiling, until we come to the back of the hall.

I look up to see the stained-glass angel towering over us. On the wall below her, an array of clip frames is mounted on the wall, each one displaying a photo of people with arms wrapped around each other. Some photos are black and white, others full colour and some look like they were taken just weeks ago.

'Who are these people?' I ask, looking into one, searching every smiling face. They look like no friendship group I've been a part of – all different heights and colours and shapes and styles. Well, no friendship group I've been in recently. The people in these photographs, in this room, are a far cry from the carefully curated group of millennials I'm in now.

'These are the people that have spent time here at Church Street,' Theo explains, turning to me with a soft smile. 'I know our "branding" may not be quite to your taste…' Unlike George, Theo doesn't even try and spare the air quotes. 'But we're here to help people who have fallen on hard times get back on their feet again. So, sometimes we're a book club and sometimes we're a food bank or a soup kitchen and even though that might not fit into a neat brand…' he continues, increasingly agitated. I would tell him he's got nothing to prove if I didn't feel like I was trying to prove myself too; if I didn't feel miles away from the girl I once was. 'Turns out different people need different things because, well, people are different.'

'I know that,' I mutter, allowing myself to fall further into one of the photographs, studying every broad smile and year-lined face. I've always felt different, no matter what school I was shifted to next, I always felt like the *different* one. A silence stretches on and I feel like Theo is waiting for me to say something but all I can think about is the lump in my throat and the tears forming in my eyes and the fact that George has always been my home.

'You making girls cry again?' A woman's voice breaks me from the thought and I turn to see her weave her body underneath Theo's arm, nestling close to his side.

'I didn't think I was.' His head jolts to me, wondering whether he's missed something.

'No, he's not,' I confirm, shaking my head and, I hope, shaking my sadness away too. 'Just dust from the photograph.'

'I told you, you need to clean them,' the woman looks up at Theo teasingly, her eyes wide with affection. Well, I say 'woman', but she looks about seventeen, eighteen at a push. And Theo has to be a good ten years older than that. Is this the kind of 'someone' that George is after now? A younger someone?

'I'm Avery,' the pale, red-haired girl thrusts a hand out towards me. 'Theo's sister.' Oh… his *sister*. 'Ohmigod, I love your coat, and your *shoes*…'

'They're Kurt Geiger,' I say before catching Theo trying and failing to stifle a scoff. 'They were a present,' I add quickly. I imagine he doesn't need to ask who from.

'Cool,' Avery says, elongating the word, reverberating with enthusiasm in a way that makes me wish I could be seventeen again. Well, someone else's experience of being seventeen. 'Are you volunteering here now?' She beams, eyes wide.

'Just today,' Theo says a little too quickly as I try to work out why he's making it so damn hard for me to join his team; do I just repel men nowadays?

'Oh, you should *definitely* volunteer regularly,' Avery chatters on. 'You've won Stanley over already.' She winks, looking back to the old man who waves across the room. Okay, so I haven't managed to repel *all* men – just the ones under thirty.

'I'm sure Poppy has more important things to do with her time,' Theo says again, looking from my Kurt Geigers up to my Lululemon puffer until I feel suitably judged.

'I don't actually,' I say quietly, reluctantly, before recovering my smile. I should. I should have a job by now. But I've been trying to get work for weeks. And I can't risk spending the next month waiting for an opportunity to fall into my inbox. Not when George needs to see that I'm still the perky, positive Poppy that he fell in love with. 'I mean, it sounds quite fun.' I see Avery shake her head slightly, warning me that 'fun' is not the right word to convince Theo that I'll make a good addition here. 'Quite *worthwhile*, I mean.'

'Amazing!' Avery claps her hands together in glee.

'That's great, Poppy,' Theo says slowly, his hands in his pockets. 'But this isn't really a pop-in, pop-out situation. We do require a level of commitment from our volunteers…' If only Theo knew how committed I am. The only reason I'm here is to show George that our commitment is worth it. To show him that I can take a risk, that I can try new things.

'We can't have people show up once every two months for the glory points.' The way Theo says this makes me feel like he's speaking from experience; that he's seen countless volunteers start purposefully only to have their passion for the cause fizzle. 'These are real people with real feelings and they get attached pretty quickly.' Theo stops talking, hands still in pockets, and instantly looks remorseful, like he's not sure whether he's meant to be convincing or deterring me, like he isn't quite sure which way is right. *Join the club, mate.*

'He's just saying that because all our volunteers have ditched us lately.'

'That's not true,' Theo shakes his head, but his worried expression says otherwise.

'It is,' Avery ignores him, looking to me. 'Christmas is a hard time for us here. The volunteers get lower but the need for this place gets higher.'

'We want to open on Christmas Day,' Theo says, softening. 'To serve dinner for those who have nowhere else to go, but we need eleven volunteers to do that safely for the number of visitors we'd be expecting…'

'And right now, we're nowhere close.'

'Well, I can't promise about Christmas Day,' I begin, knowing in my gut that by then everything with George will be back on track. 'But I'd like to help out in the lead-up.'

'Really?' Theo asks, that winning smile back again. 'What days can you do?'

'How about Mondays and Fridays?'

'You can start next Monday,' Theo says after a long pause.

'Okay,' I breathe, feeling like it might be. Every Monday and Friday. That's seven out of my twelve days to fix *us* before Christmas. Seven days where George will be able to see that I have a thousand things going on in my life other than him. And more importantly, that he has a thousand reasons to want to keep me a part of his.

Chapter Five

Sunday, 28 November

Ten Mins of Dating

I look in the mirror at the made-up face looking back at me. I look like myself again. Not the broken mess I was five days ago, back when George told me we should break up. Not the hungover lover hoping that time would heal this. I don't have time. And George hasn't given me any of his since he thought I'd stalked him all the way to the church. He's trying to be respectful, kind, to give me space. But I don't *want* space. And now, I only have eleven days with him here in the apartment to make him see sense. But tonight, the plan begins.

'Crap,' I whisper as my phone buzzes against the dressing table and the mascara wand I'm holding shoots across my face. I look down to see an unknown number but given what I'm going to be doing tonight, there's only one person it can be.

'Aran?'

'Not nearly as sexy, I'm afraid.' Okay, so maybe there are two people.

'Marie?'

'Guilty,' she says and I can practically hear her smiling down the line. 'But glad to hear that Aran is on the brain, I thought you might have forgotten.'

'My first date in more than five years with a guy that's not my boyfriend?'

'Or thought better of it?' she goes on. We both know this is more likely. But she didn't see George's face in the churchyard. Like, even my body knew to subconsciously follow him anywhere. I need to prove him wrong, to show him that us being together is *right*.

'I need to do something. I can't just let him slip away.'

'No, not your true love,' Marie confirms. 'Not at Christmas.'

'You sound like a Charles Dickens character.'

'Just call me your Ghost of Christmas Future,' she laughs down the line. Like last time, it feels good to have someone to talk to. Dee hasn't called me once since jumper-gate. Part of me wonders whether George has already told her about the break-up and she's avoiding me, whether five years of friendship can't cover over the fact that they were George's friends first. 'Aran will be there in forty-five minutes. How long does it take you to get there?'

'Thirty-five?'

'Ten minutes to play with, then,' Marie mutters mysteriously. 'Use them wisely.'

Hanging up the call, I take one last look in the floor-length mirror, scanning my outfit from my semi-sheer shirt and dark skinny jeans and down to the same heeled boots that I was wearing at Church Street. After the week I've had, I look quite good and yet, I *feel* awful. I haven't dressed up like this for someone other than George in well, forever. But that's what this is about. To show him that he's not the only thing that matters.

Pushing the door into the living room open, I hear the low hum of sport on the television immediately. George is stretched along the full length of the sofa, remote in hand. It's such a familiar sight that I wonder whether I could simply sit down beside him and our bodies would know to morph us back together again. But no, our normal routine wasn't working for George. He's been damn clear about that. And it's time to shake things up.

I walk into the room, slower than feels comfortable – like a nervous bride walking down the aisle, knowing to savour every step. I don't look at him once. Instead, I walk past him and in the direction of our small kitchenette at the back of the open-plan room, my purposeful strides beckoning his eyes to follow my frame from behind. Finally, I turn, heart hammering harder, to look in his direction, only to see the brief movement of his head returning to the screen. *Ha. Made you look.*

Reaching to the top cupboard for a wine glass, I then grab a bottle of red, a special one we said we'd share together. I'll leave the rest for him, of course I will, but right now he needs to know that he's my starter and that my main course for the evening is happening nowhere near him. I pour myself a glass and swirl the drink around my mouth, savouring the taste of knowing his eyes are on me. Then, he reaches to turn off the TV before walking into the empty bedroom, robbing me of my chance to make him watch *me* walk away.

*

Walking into the low-lit entrance to the restaurant, I see Aran sitting on a high stool pulled up against the bar, exactly where he said he would be. What the hell am I doing here, going on a date with someone other than George? I watch him for a moment, studying his smile, how he's making small talk with the barman who is currently pulling his pint. He looks nice, his long-sleeved white T-shirt smart but relaxed, his jeans and boots combo looking every bit as cosy as when he was wrapped up and singing the 'Twelve Days of Christmas'. For a moment, I wonder whether I should take a photograph, or orchestrate a subtle selfie, just some evidence of this date for George to uncover on my phone. Deep down, I know that's not necessary – or normal, for that matter. And though seeing me getting ready for a date might not have left much of an impact on him, that doesn't mean the aftermath won't knock him for six.

'Poppy!' Aran says, eyes alive with recognition. There's no going back now. 'Drink?'

'Definitely.'

Following Aran and our drinks over to a table by the window, I try to slow my racing heart. The first and last time I dated a stranger, that stranger was George. I know this was meant to be about fixing things with him but as Aran pulls out my chair from beneath the table it feels a lot more like *cheating* on George. I glance at my watch. It's seven forty-five p.m. If I can just last until nine then I can make my excuses and head back home to him.

'So, pretty random, Marie setting us up like that,' Aran says, taking a sip of his pint.

'There's a thin line between random and meticulously calculated.'

His laugh makes me think this isn't the first time Marie has meddled. 'So how long have you known her?'

'Since I joined the choir,' Aran brushes a hand through his beard. 'Three years?'

'You've been in the choir for *three* years?'

'Is that so surprising?' Aran looks a little taken aback.

'You just don't really look like the choir type.'

'And what *type* would that be?' His eyes explore my expression teasingly.

'I don't know,' I begin, not wanting to dig myself a bigger hole than I already have.

'I joined because I knew it would help with my vocals,' Aran says, raising more questions than answers. 'But then I loved the community part of it too. You should join—'

'Your vocals?' I interrupt yet another offer to become the unlucky thirteenth member of the twelve-piece choir. I check my watch again.

'I'm a musician,' Aran explains like this should impress me. Like I haven't been living with one for two years. In love with one for five.

'My boyfriend is in a band. Ever heard of Side Hustle?'

'Your boyfriend?' Aran's handsome features crinkle in confusion.

'Ex-boyfriend, sorry,' I say quickly, looking to my watch again.

'So, how long have *you* known Marie?' Aran asks.

'Erm… four?'

'Years?'

'Days.'

'Four *days*?' Aran says, his mouth hanging open for a moment before he lifts his pint to his lips, perhaps hoping his beer will make this revelation more palatable. 'I knew this was sort of a blind date, but I didn't know Marie would be going in blind too.' He shakes his head, trying to pull this off as a joke. It doesn't quite land. I glimpse the time. *Ten to eight.*

'Am I keeping you?' He notices me looking at my watch for a fourth time.

'No, sorry,' I begin quickly, caught in the act. 'I was just waiting for…'

'Someone else?' Aran's face falls before me.

'No, no, not that. Not someone else. It's just… I'm sorry,' I reel off the words at speed, hoping to find the right ones. But in my defence, nothing about the last five years has prepared me for dating anyone else but George and right now, my attention, my thoughts, my whole bloody heart belongs to him. 'Can I be honest with you for a sec?'

'Please,' Aran drains the last of his beer, preparing himself for what is coming next.

'I think you're great, and really good-looking, but…' I begin. I sound like George.

'Oh God, you're breaking up with me eight minutes into our date.'

'So, you've been clock-watching too?' I say, shocked by his accuracy.

'More subtly than you,' Aran quips back. 'I knew I would be rusty at dating, but I thought I could have lasted longer than *eight* minutes.'

I bite back a comment on the innuendo. We both know that's not how this date is going to end. Not even for eight minutes.

'My long-term girlfriend and I broke up recently.'

'Define recently?'

'Two weeks ago,' Aran says, unable to stem his sadness any longer. 'Are you *smiling*?' He raises his eyebrows in my direction accusatorily.

'No, it's just…' I begin, feeling my shoulders beginning to soften. 'I can beat that.'

'You can?'

'Four,' I repeat. 'I broke up with my boyfriend four days ago.' It feels strange to say the words out loud, even stranger to be sharing them with Aran.

'Then what are we actually doing here?' He laughs across the table as the last of any first date formalities dissolve between us.

'I don't know,' I say, laughing too. 'Marie made me.'

'I guess that's one thing we have in common,' Aran grins. 'That and the fact that neither of us are ready to date.' He breaks away to look at his watch, not even bothering to hide it now. 'It's five to eight. Fancy another?'

'His name is George.'

'I meant another *drink*.'

Aran throws his head back in laughter, but now that our ten-minute date has come to an end, now that any tension between us is suitably thawed, I could really do with a friend.

'How did it go?'

I call Marie the second I'm a safe distance from the restaurant and feel momentarily soothed by hearing her voice. That is, until

I remember that the date portion of my evening with Aran was a complete disaster.

'We decided to just be friends,' I admit as I approach London Bridge and turn my head to see Tower Bridge illuminated in all its glory. I feel bad that Marie's matchmaking efforts have gone to waste but I'm glad to have made another friend in a city so big that it can sometimes make you feel like no one would care if you weren't in it.

'Well, of course you did!' Marie says this like the idea of anything more is preposterous. 'Neither of you are ready to date.'

'Then what was the point in meeting up?' I look out across the river, not able to stop the emotions I've been pushing down the past few days from spilling into my voice. I only went on this date for George. To make him feel jealous or uncomfortable or *something*.

'The point is, George doesn't know it wasn't a *date* date,' Marie goes on like this is obvious. 'And it doesn't really matter, provided he's spending time trying to work it out. Provided he's spending time mentally replaying all the dates you and he shared together…'

I pace along the edge of the water, trying to tell myself that everything will be okay. That I haven't just lost George forever. That there are more dates ahead of us. The past five years have seen us share some good ones. There was our first, the coffee that stretched into four, until we were both buzzing with endorphins and caffeine. The one in the Italian restaurant where we had no idea that the waiters were paid to spontaneously break into song. There was the one where we went axe-throwing because I had had a bad day in the office and George said it would be the perfect way to blow off steam. Then there were the dinners with his family, with his mum and dad and brothers, laughing and joking late into the night. And the dates at home, just the two of us; just me and George in our own little world. Like on our nine-month anniversary where we spent the entire evening dancing to the nine-track mixtape I made for him, each track curated to capture one of the months we'd shared together, both of us feeling like there were infinite months to come.

'Poppy?' Marie's voice breaks me from the thought just as another pedestrian cuts in front of me, diving into the entrance of London Bridge station. 'Are you still there?'

'I think I've had an idea,' I say, memories of that overused mixtape playing in my mind. 'I've only got twelve days to get through to George, right?'

'Well… eleven now…'

'So, I need a shortcut,' I say, formulating the next part of my plan out loud. 'And the quickest way to George's heart isn't clothes or wine or jealousy… it's *music*.'

'You're finally joining the choir?'

'I made him a mixtape for our nine-month anniversary,' I ignore Marie's latest comment, pacing from side to side outside the station, buoyed by my new idea. 'Every song will remind him of us. I could play it to him tomorrow. What do you think?'

'Apart from the fact that my last husband forgot our *actual* anniversary and you and George were the kind to celebrate them monthly…' Marie says, and the way she's envying our relationship, the way that almost all our friends do, reminds me why I'm standing out here freezing my tits off on a Sunday night in the first place. God knows my relationships weren't enviable before. 'I'd say it's the kind of blast from the past that could just secure your future.'

Chapter Six

Monday, 29 November

Nine-track mixtape

I press my ear to the bedroom wall and wait for the familiar click of George closing the door to our apartment behind him as he heads out for his morning workout. If you'd have told me just a week ago that I would have gone on a date with a random stranger, I wouldn't have believed you. If you'd have told me I would be up and dressed before eight after four drinks on said date, I'd have believed you even less. George was fast asleep when I came in last night – so much for making him jealous. But then, Marie's plan was never going to cut it because she doesn't know George like I do. But this tape idea is perfect.

Pushing the door ajar, I grab my keys and stalk George's shadow out into the frosty winter air. Except this time, I'm not stalking. Not even subconsciously. This time, I am heading out to get all the ingredients I need to accompany this morning's rendition of our Remember How Great Our Relationship Is? nine-track mixtape. In the months since I was made redundant, George may have encouraged me to have a bit more get-up-and-go. Well, if being up, dressed (throwing on dungarees) and bound for all the ingredients of a home-cooked breakfast isn't get up and go, then I'm not sure what is. If only he could see me now.

'Poppy?'

I bump into a strong cold chest.

'Are you okay, gorge—' George's familiar voice stops short of calling me by his usual endearment. 'Are you following me again?' He asks this sensitively, but *still...*

'I wasn't following you *before*,' I take a step back to mutter up at him. Does he really need to be so handsome? It's only then that I notice that he's not in his usual running kit; that he's dressed in something like leisurewear and holding a duffle bag. I didn't even know George owned leisurewear. Never mind a duffle bag.

'Then, what are you up to?' He smiles awkwardly, looking from left to right like he's looking for an emergency exit. What is he trying to hide? My heart hammers at the thought. I can't lose George now. I haven't been myself these past few months, the same months that George hasn't felt sure about us. He just needs to know that I'm still the old *me*.

'I'm going for a run.'

Well, that's new.

'A run?' George looks confused. I'm not sure whether it's the unlikeliness of me going for a morning run or the unlikeliness of *anyone* running in dungarees.

'Yes, so...' I begin, now looking for my own emergency exit even though everything in me wants to follow him and work out where the hell he's going, whether it's further to or away from me.

But no, I need to stick to the plan. This breakfast, this mixtape, this run. Oh crap, I'm really going to have to run. 'See you back at the apartment, yeah?'

I don't look back to see George's expression as I set off at an ungainly jog. I don't need to. It'll be the same as those of the other four people I'm passing, so slowly that I can see every inch of their faces morph from confusion to concern. I'm red-faced in blue denim and look to all the world like I'm running away from something when really, I hope I'm running one step closer to being *us* again.

I dash around the supermarket and back to the apartment in record time, a rush of relief running through me as I realise that George may still be out, but he's left his laptop behind. Wherever he's going, whatever he's got in that duffle bag, I know he's got to come home. And he's going to come home to the perfect, pre-redundancy Poppy.

Dusting off the retro mixtape and the old-school tape player I bought just for our nine-month anniversary, I pray that the tape is actually going to work – in more ways than one. I remember George's face when I first gave it to him. He was confused, then concerned that he hadn't bought me anything before I pointed out that I hadn't technically bought him anything either. Then that beautiful smile had spread over his face, wider and wider with each track that played before he held me in his arms and whispered, 'I guess it only takes nine months for something special to be born,' and I teased him relentlessly for this cringe-worthy line.

Ignoring the lump in my throat, I tell myself this is going to work. This *has* to work. Holding my breath, I click 'play' and before I know it, the plinky-plonky notes of 'Tarantella Napoletana' fill our kitchen and I'm transported back to our first dinner date, over five years ago. As I take the ingredients out of my shopping bag and line them up on the countertop I remember swiping right on George's profile and the dopamine hit when the app told me that he liked me too. I reach for the grater, as my mind fills with all the cheesy lines he sent my way in those early days, when I couldn't believe a guy like him would fall for a girl like me. Chopping up the sausages, I remember how we had shared a large pepperoni pizza and how our conversations flowed as easily as the drinks, how he didn't seem to mind that I skirted every story about my past and was just content to be with me in the present.

I begin to fry the eggs as I remember him grabbing my hand and pulling me onto the table as the waiters started to sing. I fry the mince as I remember how he offered to walk me home, but I decided to go back to his and even though all we did was talk, the way he listened to me, the way he looked at me like I was worthy of every last drop of his attention, felt like the most intimate thing of all. Throwing everything into the oven, I look around the apartment as track nine finishes and I restart the soundtrack to our relationship all over again.

'Poppy?' I hear George come back from his workout, not sweaty but with his hair a little wet. I purposefully busy myself in the kitchen, the last place he'd expect me to be. Gone are my running dungarees and in their place is the very same outfit I wore on our first date, a thankfully floaty sage top covering my now unbuttoned skinny jeans. 'What's that smell?'

'Breakfast.' I don't look up but hear George walk further into the room, trying to work out at what part of a relationship you begin to recognise the other person's every move. I turn the music up and reach to pull the steaming dish out of the oven.

'What is it?' George says, crinkling his nose suspiciously as I hand him a plate. For a moment, I stall as I feel the sting of his words from before: *a bit... needy.* And here I am waiting on him hand and foot. But then, he hears the music in the background and I see the flicker of a smile on his face, encouraging me on. 'Is this...'

'What?' I say, feigning nonchalance. 'Oh, the music? Yeah, I found it lying around.'

'I love this song,' George smiles, before looking back down at the so-called breakfast before him, the juice from the mince pooling around the plate, threatening to overflow.

'It's breakfast lasagne.'

I *know*, but you try and come up with something Italian and breakfast-appropriate.

'Poppy, I'm not sure...' George begins, taking a cautious bite. It's totally a thing. I saw it on this cooking show we watched together one time. 'I don't think it's meant to have mince in it...' But it's a lasagne. 'It's just supposed to be the bacon and the sausage and...' George must see my face fall because he takes another bite. Then song two begins.

'I guess I should be thankful it's not mincemeat,' George grumbles.

'I'm not *that* bad a cook.'

George just looks up at me, eyebrows raised, biting back a smile and for a moment I can read his mind: *well, you're not good.* For a moment, things feel normal between us.

Coming to sit beside him, I take a bite of my breakfast. Oh crap, this is disgusting. But he's still eating it, still grinning back at me generously. That has to mean something.

'Can you remember when we first heard this song?' I ask, trying to prompt some sort of nostalgia in him. I've already missed my opportunity to start dancing on tables. Track two's thrash metal fills the room, the perfect reminder that I used to rarely stay in my comfort zone. Out of the corner of my eye I can see that my top has ridden up, my undone buttons exposed. I casually balance my knife and fork on my plate, subtly reaching down to my top.

'Was it when we went to that axe-throwing place?'

My knife crashes to the floor. *Shit.* I look back up to George, hoping he'll see the funny side of this coincidence, of me knife-throwing even now, hoping that he too is remembering how he held me from behind, guiding my throw, teaching me how to stand. But he's just looking at the stain on the floor, worried by the imperfection.

Track three begins as George stands to put his barely eaten lasagne on the countertop. It's an acoustic number that he wrote especially for *me*.

'Ninety-one days, forever to go…' The sound of a twenty-two-year-old George fills the room. Twenty-seven-year-old George is walking back towards me, a little smile on his face.

'I remember this one,' he grins as I abandon my plate to stand before him. His body moves closer to mine automatically, as if there's a magnetic force field between us, his hands hovering by his sides like he's longing to hold me.

'Every moment, every move, with you ever more,' I sing his promises back to him. George takes another step closer, until we are standing inches apart in the very spot where we had stood in that damn couples' jumper before everything fell apart. He looks down at me, listening to me sing as he parts his lips, and I wait for him to put us back together. He exhales deeply and I swear I feel his breath on my cheek, heavy and warm.

'Leave it to the professionals, Pops,' he jokes warmly, giving my shoulder a little squeeze. I study his face, savouring his pet name, the warmth of his hand on my shoulder but still feel stung by the words. This wasn't what was supposed to happen. None of it. 'Thanks for the breakfast, that's really kind of you,' he adds as he walks towards the kitchen and reaches for the tape player, pressing 'stop' even though the best is yet to come.

George barely looks up as I leave for Church Street an hour later, the sloppy lasagne breakfast still pushed to one side. Closing the door behind me, I try not to cry. How am I supposed to use these last days of living together, of him working from home, being around the apartment, if I'm not even there? I pull my puffer closer around me as I walk away from our place. How am I going to make sure these aren't our last days of living together at all? As I turn onto Church Street, the ghost of George in the churchyard taunting me, staring back at me, I look up at the stained-glass angel. Praying for answers, for ways to fix this. But this, being here, being *away* from George is the very thing that's going to make him see that he doesn't want to be away from me for good.

Walking closer to the entrance of the church, I come to a stand-still just outside it. In quick succession I see my heeled boots and skinny jeans in the reflection of the glass doors, wondering why I didn't wear something more suitable this time until I realise it's the same reason I didn't wear something more suitable *last* time, the same reason I'm doing any of this: *George.* Next, I notice the people inside, as colourful and haphazard as the first time I peered into the church hall. *I don't belong here, I don't belong here, I don't belong here*, my reflection echoes back at me. Then I see Theo, standing in the centre of the hall, smiling broadly and ushering me inside and for a brief moment, I feel like I could.

'Well, this is a nice surprise…' Theo tries to smile, it's more of a grimace. His eyes linger on my heels in a way that make me pretty sure that everyone in the room is doing the same. 'Hello, cupcake.' *Cupcake?* Now, I'm surprised too. Then I realise that the words are coming not from Theo, but from a weathered-looking man behind him.

'Roger, this is Poppy.' Theo takes two cautious steps closer towards him.

'Cupcake,' Roger repeats, as if that's exactly what Theo has just said.

'Roger, you've only just met…' Theo says softly, placing a hand on Roger's back and beginning to steer him towards a nearby sofa. I can't help but notice Theo's hands again, those strong, scarred hands. 'Best hold off on the pet names for now.'

Roger sits obediently, his eyes threatening to close as soon as he does, and I roll George's pet name round and round my mind: *Pops*, he's still calling me Pops.

'Sorry about that,' Theo says quietly as he returns. 'We have a little saying here that people should feel welcome to "come as they are but not stay as they are" but sometimes the coming as you are bit looks a little messy.' Theo glances down at my fish-out-of-water fashion again like I have no idea what 'mess' even means. But who can blame him, seeing as I've spent the last five years or so pretending that I don't?

'Why not stay as you are?'

'Huh?' Theo looks put out; I'm learning that he usually does around me.

'I get the "come as you are" bit,' I go on. There's a thousand sounds and smells and activities going on around us, but Theo's intensity makes me feel like I'm the only one in the room. 'But why can't people "stay as they are?"'

'People rarely come to Church Street because they're doing well,' Theo says slowly, his eyes still searching me like he's trying to work out what *my* reason for being here is. 'And we want to make sure that people will leave here just a bit better off than they came…'

'By helping them get work and stuff?' I say, my stomach sinking. *Man, I need a job.*

'Yeah, but not just financially.' His eyes flick to my boots again, the ones his sister likes, and I feel like he's silently judging me. But Theo doesn't know anything about me. 'Better off emotionally, spiritually, better off in themselves… anyway, how did we get onto this?' He laughs, pushing a hand through his hair as I remember how lovely his smile is. Perhaps it's the rarity of it, given that he seems so serious most of the time.

'What was I even saying?'

'That you were surprised to see me?'

'Oh yeah,' Theo nods; we both know he didn't expect me to turn up. 'I think I said I was *nicely* surprised though.'

'So, what should I…?' I begin, trying my best to brush past any awkwardness. I'm here to win George back, to show him just how full my life is, even without him in it. But I may as well be useful whilst I'm here. It's just, I'm not sure how to be. 'I could help serve food…' I suggest cautiously, looking towards the volunteers buttering bread and slicing sausages, but the memory of my messed-up lasagne glues me to the spot.

I look to another handful of people, all wearing name badges, delivering cups of coffee from a small makeshift café in one corner of the room to the collection of visitors gathered around tables. Other volunteers are just chilling with the visitors, chatting and playing games. Roger is still sitting alone, heavy eyes narrowed in suspicion, one arm extended along the sofa, shaking slightly as he searches the room for an escape. 'I could go and sit with Roger?'

'I'm not sure I…' Theo looks from Roger's broad body and mud-marred coat and back to my squeaky-clean appearance. I know he thinks I'm not cut out for this. Right now, I don't feel it either. 'I think maybe we'll start you off with someone… something more…'

'Poppy!' Avery has appeared by my side, as sunny and keen as the first time I met her. 'Come and join us on the breakfast team!'

The Breakfast Club, I think, and it takes all my strength not to correct her. I know from their identity crisis of a noticeboard that this place isn't on brand, *any* brand. And if it *was* a breakfast club, this morning proved I don't deserve to be a part of it.

'Poppy's going to start on something more…' Theo says as Avery rolls her eyes.

'I know how to make conversation,' I say, not meaning to sound like a child. Theo's raised eyebrows seem to say: *you could have fooled me.* Is that what this is about? He's scared I won't be able to hold my own with someone like Roger, someone *not like me.*

'Do you know how to make food parcels?' Theo asks, ignoring my assurances completely. I force a tired smile.

'I'll show you!' Avery says, grabbing my arm and steering me away from Roger and Theo and over to a door leading out of the main hall and into a windowless larder hosting shelves and shelves of fresh fruit and packaged goods. A big stack of unassembled cardboard boxes lies in the centre of the dusty stone floor. Evidently the end of Theo's half-uttered objection was 'something more… *back office.*'

Three hours, fifty food parcels, one rodent-chewed cereal box and a Rice Krispie crisis later, and I'm finally getting into the swing of things. So what if Theo thinks I'm not front-of-house material? I don't even *want* to be front-of-house material. Plus, Theo's not the reason I'm here. George is. And I know leaving him alone with his thoughts, prompting him to wonder when I might be coming home, is exactly the kind of thing that will remind him how much better his life is with me in it. And, after almost a week of driving myself crazy with questions, something about the monotony of the one-person production line I've developed feels somewhat meditative.

Avery may have visited me three times in the first twenty minutes but since she left for school, I've kicked my boots off and am quietly singing along to my phone in the seemingly soundproof pantry. Reaching for the last packet of custard creams, I reach the high note of Mariah's 'All I Want for Christmas Is You'. Then, I hear the door swing open just in time to tell the inquisitive grin on Theo's face that all I want for Christmas is *him.*

'I was erm…' He looks down at me on my hands and knees, singing into my custard-cream microphone. 'I just wanted to check that you're okay, but clearly you're…' His eyes move to the boxes now assembled and towering around me. I stand as 'Fairy Tale of New York' begins. We both look down to my muck-covered knees and dust-bunnied socks. If this was a fairy tale, I would be Cinderella. Pre-transformation. 'You're okay, right?'

'I am, actually,' I say, looking at the boxes around me, feeling a hint of accomplishment even though I know it's misplaced. All I've done is put some food into boxes but they may actually help someone. And being here is helping me win back George.

'Good,' Theo says, taking a tentative step towards me. He seems even taller now that I've lost three inches of heel. 'You have a lovely voice, by the way.'

'You heard that?' I ask, shame filling my stomach. George was always the singer in our relationship; his voice has the power to woo anyone, but he chose to woo me.

'I think the whole of Church Street heard *that*,' Theo laughs and if it wasn't so dark in here, he would see me blushing. 'I forgot to give you this.' He looks down at the ream of stickers and big black marker in his hands. I watch as he scribbles on a sticker and then presses it to my chest. Neither of us know what to do with the contact. Theo looks horrified as my eyes journey down to his hand momentarily on my breast. I try not to laugh. But as soon as he walks out and I look down at the name badge, I do; he's written, 'Popstar'.

Chapter Seven

Friday, 3 December

Eight a.m. Workout

How you doing, cupcake? I look down at Marie's message, instantly thinking of Roger, back at Church Street. It's the last place I expected to find myself. It's also the last time I felt useful. The three days since then have come and gone with little to show for them. George has been out at the office, or rushing home to eat, or rushing out to band practice; rushing anywhere away from me. And I have stopped myself from drifting after him, forcing myself to sit in front of my laptop, sending out speculative work emails and watching only tumbleweed come in. Going freelance was meant to give me the space I needed to find out what I really want to do. Instead, it's turned me into a nobody and made me lose the one thing I know I have always wanted: true love, a family, *him.*

Rough few days, I type. *Nine-track mixtape was a mistake.* Not to mention the breakfast lasagne. *But I've had another idea that I think will bring us closer.* And thank God, because somewhere in these last indiscriminate days we've drifted into December. My favourite month. The one that had finally started to feel as special as it should, because of George.

How you holding up, friend? I read Aran's latest message to me, too. He remembers what it's like to go through a break-up better than anyone right now, but it sounds like his is for the best, for the greater good. But I know there's nothing good that could come from me not being with George and the only family I've ever known.

Placing my phone into my armband, I make my way into the living room to find George folding the sofa bed away. It still breaks my heart to see him sleeping out there. It's so unnecessary, this whole break-up is unnecessary. I watch as he reaches into his back pocket, pulling out his phone and typing away. I wonder who he is texting. It's only then that I realise that Dee hasn't called me all week. She must know about our break-up by now. That means she's either giving me space too or showing me she's taken sides, and not mine. But soon sides won't be necessary. Soon George will see that I've changed. Or rather, *haven't* changed. That I'm still his purposeful, hopeful, happy-go-lucky girlfriend. And thank God, because us getting back together is the only thing that can make me happy about doing *this* at eight o'clock in the morning.

'Poppy, are you going for a run?' George stops still on seeing me dressed in head-to-toe Lycra. As far as he is concerned, he didn't think I *owned* Lycra. He looks impressed for a moment and then I see his cheeks dimple as he grins mischievously. 'No dungarees?'

'I thought I'd join you,' I beam back at him. George has been asking me to join his eight a.m. workout for the past two years we've lived together. I've not once said yes. But over a week has passed since jumper-gate and it's time to pull out all the stops. To try something *new*.

'Oh, really?' George looks surprised. 'I thought you'd want some space.' He looks unsure for a second. 'Is this so we can spend some time together or—'

'Oh, *please*,' I speak over him quickly. 'I just fancy the exercise.'

'Okay,' he says slowly. 'But you're wearing the wrong…'

'Yes, I know. Dungarees,' I say, rolling my eyes playfully.

'No, Poppy,' he goes on, that faint smile on his face again. 'I'm not going running this morning. I'm going swimming, you'll need a…'

Swimming? Since when has George gone swimming? Before I can stop it, my mind is flooded with all the times we've been in water before. None of them very exercise-based. Well, apart from that time on holiday when we were almost caught red-handed in the heat of the moment. I feel my cheeks beginning to blush. George is looking back at me, still mumbling something about towels and equipment that he no doubt hopes will put me off. But no, if George's new thing is swimming, I guess I can make it my new thing too.

'I'd like to come with you.' Neither one of us is convinced. George tilts his head, a curious look on his face, before brushing a hand through his hair. As he does so, I remember that he had wet hair when he came home from his workout on the morning of my ill-fated Italian breakfast and it makes sense now.

'Okay, but you'll need—'

'Don't worry, I won't distract you…' I interrupt before I can hear any more of George's excuses. But, as I rush to our bedroom and fish out the tiniest bikini, the one I wore on that holiday – all the while cursing myself for the lack of feminism in my desperate thoughts – I know distracting him is precisely what I have in mind.

As we sit on the bus, side by side, I don't give George time to make small talk. Instead, I plug in my headphones and make a point of watching the world speed past, a world that doesn't revolve around him. Outside of the window, I see the increasingly festive city flash by. It would be enough to make me miserable if I couldn't see his reflection upon it, trying to work out how to interrupt me from my music. *People also want what they can't have.* I remind myself of Marie's words, back when she first made me believe I could fix this. Right now, it feels like George wants to talk to me, to tell me something. I'm going to keep it that way.

'Poppy, I…' I hear George say behind me as we reach the pool building and I stride purposely towards the changing room. I'm not turning back now. I can see he's trying to do this break-up well, to say and do all the things you're meant to. But he needs to see we were never meant to break up in the first place, that every couple has their blips. Walking past one or two women getting ready in the communal space, I pull on my bikini and check myself in the mirror, trying to convince my reflection I can do this. The bikini still fits, the strawberry print popping against the white fabric. It's absolutely *freezing* in here but soon I'll be in the lovely warm water and one step closer to restoring my lovely warm life with George. Pushing open the weathered-looking door brandishing a wave icon, I square my shoulders as I march towards the pool.

The bitter cold hits my face as soon as I'm outside. Oh crap, I'm actually *outside*. I look to the space where the ceiling should be, but a blanket of sky stretches as far as the eye can see. I look across the Olympic-sized pool to see George laughing and joking with some fellow swimmers and see that he's wearing a wetsuit. They're all wearing wetsuits. And I'm wearing a strawberry print bikini. Outside. In December. Shit. Shit. *Shit.*

George gives me a sheepish wave across the space between us. And now I have two choices: run back to the changing room, retreat into my comfort zone. Or I can stride across this pool to the man I love and show him just what kind of woman I am.

'I tried to tell you…' he whispers hurriedly as soon as I'm within earshot. I look down at his wetsuit. I didn't even know he *owned* a wetsuit. Where does he even *keep* a wetsuit? I already know the answer is the back of the wardrobe where we never ever venture or the walk-in cupboard we stashed everything we don't need but can't get rid of. A sinking feeling makes me question whether I'm not now one of the things that George can't shake.

'Tell me what?' I force myself to grin back at him, like I have no idea what he's talking about. One or two people dive into the pool, trying not to smirk in my direction. I'm sure my cheeks would blush if I wasn't ice-cold.

'You don't have to do this, Poppy,' George says, his eyes drifting to my bikini top.

Good. I don't want to do this. No part of me wants to do this.

'You've got nothing to prove,' he adds softly, that same sympathetic look in his eyes. But no, I won't wait to see it. I'm not a charity case, I never have been. Not even in the days before him, not really. Before I can think better of it, I throw myself in the pool, not nearly as gracefully as I would like. Oh *crap*, that's cold. The water hits me like daggers, death by a thousand cuts. Then I see a splash from above and George is in the water beside me, his body dangerously close, my body dangerously *cold*. My teeth chatter together as I hold onto the railing at the side.

'Are you sure you're okay?' George says, a genuine look of affection on his face. It makes me want to hold him. Can't he see how far I'd go for him, for *us*?

'Never wetter,' I say.

'Is that a swimming pun?'

'It's not *not* a swimming pun.' I would smile if my lips weren't blue. For a moment, things feel normal between us, like the ice has finally thawed. Ironic, really. He moves closer still, our bodies shivering and wet. His eyes drift to my neck, my clavicle; we both know that we'd be warmer together if he held me close and I wrapped my legs around him and…

'The far left lane is for club swimmers,' George forces the words through a heavy breath, looking away as if trying to put some distance between us. 'Then the lanes reduce in speed the further they get to the right, so maybe if you start…' His hand waves in the direction of the far right lane, not telling me which one to go in, but gesturing in the general vicinity. But I didn't come this far to play it safe. I don't have time to play it safe.

I duck under the ropes separating one lane from the other until I'm safely in the middle and begin to swim, pretty hard given that I can't feel my legs. Or my arms. I swim the length of the pool and no less than three swimmers pass me as I do.

I duck under the next lane and do another length, flailing my lifeless arms in what I hope looks like swimming. The pace is still too fast. And even though one of the swimmers who passes me is moving speedily, I can still hear an audible tut that I am holding him up.

Oh *crap*, this is so cold. Freezing. Definitely not strawberry-bikini season.

I move to the next right lane and this one feels better, almost manageable, until a woman who must be older than me and Dee combined speeds on past me, her swimming cap reading: *if you can't handle the cold, get out of the lido.*

I move to the right, again, then again, until I'm getting overtaken in the slow lane by people who are seeming to move so leisurely (for *them*) that they are smiling, swimming *and* smiling *at the same time* when I can't handle one simple task; and there's nowhere else to go.

Damn it. I come to a stop at the shallow lane of the pool, feeling like a failure, like I can't go the extra mile, not even for my one true love. It's like I've been trying so hard and for so long that my body is telling me to *just stop.* I scan the wetsuits for George. His head is ducking in and out of the water as his body slices through it with ease, entirely in the zone, thriving without me. I shiver at the thought, my body convulsing in the cold. I would cry if my eyes weren't frozen because I can see the situation so clearly. To me, we're George and Poppy, meant to be together, built to each other's mould. To everyone else, we're a popstar – a *real* one – and a popsicle – and a frigging strawberry one at that.

*

'Do you fancy a coffee?' I ask as I emerge from the women's changing room to find him waiting on the pavement outside.

'Oh, I would, Pops, but I've got to get back now…' George begins. Then why did he wait for me? 'I just wanted to check you hadn't died of hypothermia.' *Oh, yeah. There's that.*

'Go on, just one coffee,' I say, trying to sound more playful than I feel. This morning was about getting sweaty with George. Then getting half-naked with George. Clearly only one of us got the memo.

'I can't,' he says, more serious now. 'I've got work and…' *Some of us have jobs.*

'Yeah, and I'm heading to Church Street…'

'To volunteer?' George begins to walk towards the bus stop. I nod. It doesn't feel like enough. We're heading in the same direction but right now, he still feels miles away. And very soon, we'll be heading in literally different directions as he heads back home.

The closer I get to Church Street, the further I feel from George. This was meant to be about showing him who I was, proving that I was the same woman he fell in love with. But right now, I don't know who I am. I don't know who I am without him. It's probably the reason I've found it so hard going freelance; without someone directing me I just gravitate to him. A lump rises in my throat, tears gather in my eyes. And then I see that noticeboard. The damn mess of a noticeboard. And it's enough to make me break down completely.

I stand in the churchyard, shoulders heaving, holding my hands to my eyes, half-expecting someone to save me. But who? George is at home, expecting me to drift back there. Theo is inside, expecting me to bail. There's only one way to prove them both wrong.

'Popstar!' One of the other volunteers says as soon as I've stepped foot inside the hall. I hope it doesn't look like I've been crying. Something about this place makes me want to fall apart and I won't let it. I refuse. Then I notice Theo arriving beside her.

'You did this,' I narrow my eyes at him, before looking to the name sticker I've just made for myself. It clearly says 'Poppy'.

'I had no idea it would stick,' Theo smirks.

'Is that a sticker pun?'

'Nope,' he says. *It's not* not *a sticker pun*, I mentally correct him, but of course, he doesn't know his lines. He's not George. Plus, everything feels off-script at Church Street.

'Popstar!' someone else shouts in the background, I suspect Stanley with the cards.

'Cupcake!' Well, I know *that's* Roger. I watch as Theo gives him a five-minute sign. A part of me wants to go and sit with him, not to say anything, but just to be there. Another part wants to run into the back room, not to be anywhere near the supposedly *needy* when I'm trying to do everything to convince myself that I'm not one of them. That I never have been.

'Need a job, Popstar?' Theo teases again, as I narrow my eyes even further.

'Yes.' I've never needed anything more. 'I'll just go in the back, shall I?' I say, forcing my mind back into the hall, willing his gaze not to follow mine back to Roger. I don't belong here. Don't have anything to offer these people, not really. I'm only doing this for George. And yet, the niggle in my neck and the pull and push I feel both to and from Roger tell me that memories I've hidden deep beneath my surface are threatening to break out.

'Great.' Theo nods, perhaps keen to keep me at a distance from the visitors too. 'And perhaps later, when Avery turns up after school—'

'Avery's coming here this evening?' I interrupt him before I can stop myself.

'Why wouldn't she be?' Theo looks confused, more confused than he normally does when he looks at me – which is saying something.

'Because it's Friday,' I go on, as Theo's raised eyebrows seem to say *yes, and?* 'Shouldn't she be out with her friends or something?'

Avery is seventeen. If I could do seventeen again, I would have all the fun I could; it's not like I got the chance to be carefree back then. I will my eyes to remain on Theo, not the increasingly familiar feel of the hard times and messy lives of the people around the hall.

'These *are* our friends.' Theo sounds his usual serious self again, his guard back up.

'Of course, of course,' I put my hands up in defence. 'I just mean, her friends outside of Church Street… you *do* have friends outside of Church Street?'

'Some people actually *like* being here, Poppy.' No more *popstars* today, then.

'Theo, where do you want me today, buddy?' Another volunteer asks him, saving me from the tension that is clearly straining between the two of us.

'If you could be on chat team, Brian,' Theo says, feathers unruffled now that he's talking to someone else, someone who is clearly 'front of house' material. 'That'll be great.'

'Chat team?' I ask as soon as Brian has disappeared into the hubbub again.

'Just hanging out with the visitors,' Theo says plainly. 'Did you know loneliness is a much bigger issue in London than hunger is?'

I swallow, trying to push down those damn memories of when the lonely one was me.

'People just want connection.'

'Then why don't you just call it hanging out?' I ask, thinking out loud, conflicting emotions scrambling in my mind. 'Chat team makes the people here sound like a project.'

'That's not what—' Theo begins, clearly disgruntled.

'And *visitors* sound pretty temporary…'

'Well, like I said, we also consider them *friends*,' he objects. There, I've said the wrong thing again. Which is evidentially why Theo keeps finding jobs for me in the back room. But right now, looking around at these people that I have nothing in common with, anymore, that's precisely where I want to be.

Heading into the pantry, I feel the tears starting to fall once more. How on earth have I found myself in a place like this when not even a fortnight ago I was seeing in the start of my weekend with Dee on some rooftop bar in Shoreditch? Why hasn't she called? As soon as I close the door, I drop to my knees and try to remember that there are people out there more needy than me. Then a memory flashes across my mind, an image of a young girl starting yet another school and thinking that she's finally making friends, only to be laughed at for walking into class wearing trainers so worn that it was clear to everyone that they had had several more owners before. A girl that I've not thought about in a really, really long time.

*

'Ready to head home?'

I look up to see Theo standing at the entrance to the storeroom, pushed slightly ajar. I had no idea so much time had passed. Something about sitting here, knowing my mess of a life is benefitting *someone* is the momentary release I need. Now I have to head home and try to show George what he's missing when clearly the one who is missing something is me.

'Yeah,' I force the word, intending to sound more excited than I feel. Theo raises his eyebrows as he offers his hand out to pull me up from the ground. As I emerge into the main room, light is no longer forcing its way through the windows and most of the community centre visitors have gone home. That's if they have homes to go to. My stomach sinks.

'Coming, then?' Avery appears by my side.

'Coming where?' I say as she eyes her brother suspiciously.

'You haven't asked her?'

'Asked me *what*?'

'I tried to… earlier.' Theo turns to me. 'We're heading off to do some research tonight, pricing up what we'll need if we are allowed to open on Christmas Day. And we wondered whether you'd like to join us,' he mutters under his breath, not the warmest invitation.

'And by research, he means *shopping*,' Avery adds, like she's speaking my language.

'Where?' I ask, not sure from Theo's expression whether he *wants* me to say yes.

'Our favourite place in the city,' Avery buzzes. 'Southbank Christmas market.'

Their favourite place? Avery takes my hand and steers me in the direction of the door, Theo lingering behind to turn out the lights. I know I should head back home, that I need to show George that everything can go back to normal, but is normal what he wants? And right now, after this morning's strawberry-bikini debacle, I'm not in any rush to return.

'Okay then,' I say. Avery is already way in front. I slow down for Theo.

'No plans on a Friday night, then?' Theo asks teasingly. 'You *do* have friends outside of Church Street?' He mocks my words from before, but as I look to my phone to see that not one of my so-called friends has messaged me all day, right now I'm not so sure. From Dee and Charlie to Frankie and Jesse to Andy and Becca, all our friends are partnered up. I try not to draw conclusions from their silence. We'll be 'Poppy and George' again soon enough.

Avery slaloms through the crowds as we make our way further into the winter markets and I try to forget the last time I was here. The smiling faces and background music pumping out from every makeshift stall remind me that Christmas is coming soon, that even *not-until-December* George can't grinch his way out of that fact now.

'I just can't wait,' Avery hums with excitement. Unlike her brother.

'But you can?' I ask him, feeling his body brush against mine in the bustle of people.

'We've just got a lot to sort out at the centre before then.'

He thinks *he's* got a lot to sort out? I need to sort out my whole bloody life.

'Your eleven volunteers?' I shout. Christmas is literally all around us – and it's *loud*.

'Yeah,' Theo shouts back, concern written on every inch of his face. 'I know it might not seem like a big deal to you, but some of our visitors will have nowhere else to go.'

I gulp, remembering my first Christmas alone and remind myself that it won't come to that again. That in a couple of weeks I'll be looking forward to spending Christmas Day with George and the rest of his family. A Christmas like we shared together last year, where we all played Secret Santa and George's dad laughed when I gave him his gift before he called me the daughter he never had. For a man who has three sons it might have meant nothing to him, but to me it meant the world.

'He's still making me feel bad about not being there.' Avery turns to face us, breaking the thought and bringing me back into the moment, here in the Christmas market.

'No, I'm not,' Theo shakes his head. 'I know you want to be with your dad.'

So, they're half-siblings, then. I don't know why I'm surprised when I know full well that families don't come in one size.

'I usually spend the day with Theo,' Avery goes on. 'Our mum works abroad and can't afford to come back to the UK very often. And my dad is, well… sporadic, but this year he got in touch *ages* ago to make plans for Christmas.' She's so excited, she's fit to burst.

'What about you?' Theo asks, the intensity of his stare on mine silencing the rest of my questions. Avery slows before a stall overflowing with pick-and-mix, proceeding to take photos of the prices on display, working out what gifts they can afford to buy the people down at Church Street without blowing their budget completely.

'I'm heading to the Cotswolds with some friends.'

I do have them, by the way, I want to add, but then it hits me that I'm not even sure if the trip is going to happen anymore. But it has to. I'm the one who paid the deposit. The deposit that I will need to afford to rent a room somewhere if these twelve days to fix things come and go without a trace, without a *change*.

'For the whole of Christmas?' Theo asks, his green eyes piercing my own.

'Until Christmas Day morning.' And then George and I will go to his parents for the rest of the week and we'll have forgotten all about our mid-winter wobble.

'Stop trying to recruit her.' Avery shakes her head, giving him a playful push.

'I'm making *conversation*.'

'That makes a change.' Avery rolls her eyes, no edge to her voice. At least I know Theo's sullen strong-and-silent-type vibe isn't for my benefit only.

'It's still a bit up in the air,' I say. But not for long, everything is going to land exactly where it's supposed to be. 'But to be honest, I've never really understood the fuss about Christmas Day.'

Theo and Avery look back at me like I've just said I hate kittens.

'The food?' Avery says immediately. 'The presents? The family.'

'Celebrating the birth of a saviour?' Theo mutters under his breath. But he can't believe that, can he? Otherwise, how can he explain all the pain and crap and brokenness he must see every damn day? I push the sight of Roger and all he reminds me of away.

'Yeah,' I say, shrugging my shoulders. 'It's always been about Christmas Eve for me. The anticipation, the feeling that anything could happen...' At least it always *was* about Christmas Eve. Spending Christmas Day with George these past few years has almost convinced me that the main event can be as good as everyone else seems to think it is. Before I can stop them, my mind is flooded with memories of sitting in George's large family home, three drinks down and arguing over whether his stick figure looked like a duck in the big game of family Pictionary. It doesn't take long to feel those damn tears forming. *No, no, no!* I won't break down again, not here in the happiest place in the city. At least this time the happiest song in the world isn't playing too.

'On the ninth day of Christmas...'

For goodness' sake. Theo's eyes search mine, with that hint of recognition again, like he knows exactly what kind of girl I am. As we follow Avery around the next corner, the Cider Lodge and the twelve-piece choir come into view, running down their twelve days of Christmas at speed. There I see Marie and Aran and the other performers gathered together, bobbing up and down. Marie waves in my direction, surprised to see me. I look at Aran, clearly disgruntled to be bobbing again.

'Speaking of the Cotswolds...' I hear Theo's voice in my ear, his body close behind me. He is pointing to the left of the choir, to a large sign advertising their upcoming performance in none other than Broadway, the village we're heading to on our trip.

'You should join.' Theo goes on. I can't tell if he's joking or not.

'I don't sing.' He knows I'm lying. 'Outside of pantries.'

'You scared?' He raises his eyebrows, his words posing a challenge.

'No,' I reply quickly, even though I know I am. I've spent so long building a comfort zone, my comfortable life with George, that I've not wanted to risk doing anything that could shake our finely tuned routine, always looking to him to set our beat.

'Join! Join!' Avery's chants fill the space that the disbanded choir have just left.

'I've been telling her that all week.'

I turn to see Marie behind me and fling my arms around her. She holds me tightly and it feels ridiculous that we met in this very spot mere days ago, like our own festive miracle. Ridiculous that after years of trying to fit in, I kind of just slot into place with her and Aran.

'Tell me this is George,' Marie hisses into my hair, holding me hostage in the hug.

'It's not,' I whisper back, eyes darting to Theo, who is now shaking hands with Aran, both of them exchanging words before glancing in my direction.

'Then is he *single*?' Marie pulls away, giving me the briefest of winks before turning to Theo, a man no less than twenty-five years her junior.

'Poppy, you didn't tell me you were going to be in Broadway for Christmas!' Now it's Aran's turn to chime in, drawing me in for a quick embrace. Damn Theo for telling him.

'I didn't know you were, either,' I mutter back, not sure how I'm going to get out of this now. I've gone from feeling completely alone to feeling like it's four against one.

'You going to join us?' Marie asks, grinning like someone about to get their own way.

'You don't even know whether I can sing.'

'She can,' Theo confirms plainly. Damn him again.

'It doesn't even matter if you can't,' Marie says. 'It's just a bit of fun, a chance to meet some new people, try something *new…*' The way she accentuates the words makes it obvious that she thinks this is another chance to prove George wrong, to make him see that us being together is the right thing. And right now, with four sets of beady eyes staring back at me, encouraging me on, I think I might just have to be that 'yes' person again.

Chapter Eight

Sunday, 5 December

Seven Minutes in Heaven

The low winter sun coaxes me out of sleep sooner than necessary, much sooner. I reach for my phone, forcing myself to ignore the fact that George still isn't here, sleeping beside me.

Hey babeeeeeee, how's it going? I assume it is from Marie but as I read, through half-open eyes, I realise that it is not really her style. I have only known her for ten days but already I know she calls me 'honey' or 'cupcake' – which reminds me of Roger. I can't help the visitors, or 'friends', at Church Street from forcing their way into my mind but volunteering there was always going to be temporary, only ever about one thing.

I swipe open the message. Then, I notice the name of the sender. It's *Dee*. This makes more sense of the seven-e 'babe'. Well, it makes sense until you consider that George broke up with me twelve days ago and she hasn't been in touch once.

I look at the last message between us. *Did George like the jumper?* I never replied. Maybe she was just giving me space after all? Forcing myself to sit up in our too-big bed, I begin to reply. *Things are terrible, I don't know what's got into him. What does Charlie think? This is just a blip, right?* I delete the letters one by one. In our five years of friendship, it's not like Dee and I have ever really gone that deep. Plus, the more I can keep this from becoming a big deal, the more we'll all be able to gloss over it when things are back to normal again. *All good, just been busy.* I hit 'send' on my reply. It's technically not a lie. I've been busier than I have in months.

I watch the three dots on my screen as Dee begins to type, then I panic; I don't want her sympathy, don't want to acknowledge anything is wrong. I send her a question before she can question me: *How have you been? How's things with Charlie?*

Okay. He's been busy with the band and stuff; you know how it is, but all good x

Well, I did. It used to be fun, an exciting pastime for the boys, another way to blow off steam other than them spending time with us. Lately, it's grown from hobby to side hustle to a hungry time-eating beast. One that could even see us have to leave our city to follow them on tour or maybe even to relocate to New York or LA. But I can't; I grew up in this city. And though I don't want to remember my childhood, I also don't want to leave the place it happened. But Dee wouldn't mind; she loves it all. And being girlfriend groupies is a huge part of our friendship. Well, again, it *used* to be.

It's day five of my twelve days of George being here, at ours, whilst it's still *ours*. And I have nothing planned. Nada. After the ten-minute date, the nine-track mixtape and the eight o'clock workout disasters, it's hard to keep picking myself up. Especially when George has shown little sign of regretting his decision. But I've bounced back from worse. I shake the thought away. I have spent years building a life with him. I won't let it crumble now.

Walking into the living room, I expect to see him reassembling the sofa or on his laptop or just on his way to workout. Instead, I see the back of his body, deep inside our walk-in store cupboard, the kind that is unlocked so rarely that you almost forget it exists until someone fishes out a rickety windshield or dusty ladder or rogue wetsuit.

'What are you—?' I start to say as I creep closer towards him. I look down to see newly assembled cardboard boxes surrounding my feet. *What the…?*

Is he making food parcels too? But no. Why would he be making food parcels? George and his life, *our* life, is so far removed from the visitors at Church Street that he probably thinks food parcels are something you get on Deliveroo.

I glance down into the boxes and see a bunch of his old things. Books, jumpers, an old wetsuit. Has my recent performance turned him off swimming for life?

I watch as he reaches to the top shelf of the store cupboard. The one where we purposefully put everything we deemed important enough to move into the flat but unimportant enough that we knew we'd never actually need it. Not until we moved out, anyway. Oh no, he's preparing to move out.

It's only fifteen days until we're supposedly off to the Cotswolds, twenty-six days left on our lease. I filter though the figures in the way that I know George's mind has. Too damn logical to feel, not think. *Seven* more days stuck in the apartment with me. Except that he's not been stuck, has he? He's been walking away from my mixtape, swimming lengths away from me and my bikini. And Marie and I thought I'd have a captive audience. Before I can think better of it, I grab the key from the store cupboard and stash it in my pocket.

'Poppy, what are you doing?' George asks as he turns around to find me standing in the cupboard, just inches in front of him. There's not a lot of room for me to give him space. But George has four days a week for space. And forever, if I don't fix this before Christmas. *Ever more.* This is crazy. I can't lock my ex-boyfriend in a cupboard. He'll lock *me* up. *Every moment, every move, with you ever more…* I think of his lyrics, his promises, his gorgeous face looking back at me in confusion. It's all I need for the last shred of my logic to fall away.

'Shit!' I shout as I knock the door shut behind us. 'I was just coming to get that old recipe book…' In the low light of a single bulb hanging from the ceiling, I see George shake his head as if to say: *you couldn't have found it before you made that breakfast lasagne?*

'Sure,' he shrugs. 'I should really be starting work soon…' But it's a Sunday. He must mean band admin. Sunday always used to be our day. 'So, if you could just…' George moves past me and I feel the heat of his torso as his body brushes against mine. He presses against the door handle but the door itself doesn't move. 'You've got to be kidding me.'

He turns back to me, shaking his head again. I can feel the heat from his body.

'Please tell me you've got the key,' George looks down, still inches from me. Yes, I have the key. But if I let us out, if I let you go, then I'm scared we'll run out of time.

I just need to buy us a bit of time.

I shake my head slowly. I'll 'find' it in a bit. But right now, I need a captive audience. To show him why he can't give up on us, that our new dynamic isn't a forever thing. That he can be in his band and I can find work and we can still find time for it all.

'Bloody hell!' George curses under his breath and he's so close that I can feel it on my neck. He reaches for his phone only to realise that he's left it outside.

'It's okay, don't panic,' I say, forcing a smile to spread across my face. This is bonkers, desperate. But nothing else is working and I'm desperate for him to see that *we* do. 'I'll message John now...'

'Who is John?' George brushes a hand through his hair, his elbow nudging me as he does. I watch the crinkle in his brow grow deeper and deeper.

'Our neighbour?'

'When did you meet our neighbours?'

'When we first moved in. I went round to introduce myself, give them a spare key.'

'Why would you give a stranger a spare key?'

'In case of an emergency.'

I look at George, now red in the face. This is an emergency. Us breaking up is an emergency. And though I'm not going to message John, I'm going to tell George that I have so that he calms down and we have just a few minutes to finally talk, really talk, about us.

'Fine,' he says, sitting down on one of the boxes he's already filled with books.

'What were you doing in here, anyway?' I say softly, wanting to use the brief time we have together wisely. It's what I've been trying to do for the last ten days.

'I was starting to pack,' he says and for the briefest moment he looks gutted.

'For Christmas?' I say, ashamedly hopeful. George shakes his head and it takes all my strength not to beg him to stay. Begging being the very thing he doesn't want me to do. 'Looking forward to it?' I ask, neutrally, not knowing if I mean being home with his family or his future without me.

'Sure,' he says, a lack of certainty in his voice. 'Look, Poppy, I'm not meaning to make this worse, but I really need to get to work on our scheduling.' Sundays used to be for sleeping in and sleeping together and George getting wound up and me winding him down. I used to think he liked our balance before his getting so obsessed about the band stuff and my supposedly getting obsessed about him threw us off-kilter. 'It's been so stressful lately, trying to fit everything in, what with the band and…' George begins to open up and I want to unwrap him further. I knew this was the cause. Some kind of stress-related, quarter-life crisis. 'And then there's the "us" thing.' It's not a *thing*. I bite my lip, willing him to share more.

'Yeah, it's a lot,' I sigh.

'You seem to be handling it well though,' he says, a sad smile darting across his face.

What part of standing in a strawberry bikini in sub-zero temperatures suggests that?

'I mean, you're out and about more…'

I was out and about before the break-up. He means more *independently*. I shrug, pretending like it's no big deal. Like this whole thing isn't the biggest bloody deal.

'No point sitting around moping,' I say, shrugging the seismic weight on my shoulders. George must like my response though as he scoots to one side of the box and gestures for me to sit down next to him. I perch beside him, the side of his body slotting into mine. I pray he doesn't feel the key in my pocket.

'This is a good look on you,' he says, turning his face towards mine, closer than he has been in weeks. My heart throbs in my chest. He's noticed. The new things. The old me. Well, the old me he used to know. Not the broken mess I was before I met him.

'So was that bikini,' he adds, the corners of his mouth turning up at the thought. I look up to see his face now inches away from mine. 'Do you know what this reminds me of?' he says, looking around the storeroom. It reminds me of that larder at Church Street. No, no. I'm here, now. With George.

'What?' I ask, forcing my mind back into the cupboard.

'Seven minutes in heaven.' George's laugh echoes around the small space. For most people, being locked down with an ex would be more like hell. But then, we're not most people. We're special. I know it. He knows it. And now, he's starting to remember it again.

'You do remember that game, right?'

'What game?'

'Seven minutes in heaven,' he repeats, taking my blank expression as permission to go on. 'It's a game we used to play at school, back when I was boarding,' George says this as if it's as old hat as the box of junk we're sitting on, not the massive privilege that only a select few are fortunate enough to afford. 'Two people are forced into a closet or cupboard or something.' His eyes search the dim space around us. *Check.* 'And they're allowed to do whatever they like for seven minutes…' I feel the sexual charge between us and wonder if the way George is smiling at me means he feels it too.

'Oh,' I say, feeling George move even closer towards me. 'I never played that.' Some of us didn't go to boarding school. Some of us didn't stay at the same school long enough to make the kind of friends who get forced into closets together.

'Well, maybe, for old times' sake…' George looks at me with a quizzical expression, like he wants to explore the very depths of me. Like old times, before he learnt to predict my every monotonous move. He leans in closer, his breath heavy but lightly touching my skin.

Then, my phone rings.

'Is that the John guy?' George jumps up. Doubtful, seeing as I didn't message him. I reach for my phone, pulling it from my pocket as the key falls to the ground with a clatter.

'It's your mum,' I say, looking down at her name lighting up my screen.

'It's the *key*!' George bends down to pick it up, ignoring my sentence completely.

'George, why would your mum be calling me?'

'Why wouldn't you think to check your pockets?' he sighs as he turns the key in the door and the light from the living room breaks us from the seven-minute spell.

'Answer it,' I thrust the phone towards him. George shakes his head, moving to sit on the sofa and open his laptop whilst muttering something about now not being a good time.

'Sandra?' I pick up the call, looking over to George, who is now busy typing on his laptop. 'Is everything okay? Were you trying to get through to George?'

'I've been trying for weeks!' Sandra exclaims down the line. 'You know what he's like,' she laughs quickly. *Well, I thought I did.* 'I've been meaning to call you too...'

Oh, here goes. I've been waiting for this. The sympathetic: *we heard about the break-up, but you'll always have a place in our hearts* pity call. I'm not sure I can stomach it.

'You're both coming to ours for Christmas Day, for Christmas lunch, yes?'

I'm not sure I can answer that, not until George and I are officially back together. I look at him now, busying himself with band stuff, and try to work out the likeliness of that. Three minutes ago, I'd have said it was very likely, but now, he feels so distant again.

'Has George not said?' I say slowly; he's still looking busy, if not a little sheepish.

'He's not told me anything,' Sandra says, exasperation cutting through her usually warm tone. 'Between you and me, darling, every time I ask, he's been pretty noncommittal about it...' So, George is being noncommittal across the board? I knew his knee-jerk reactions and rogue decisions are a whole lot bigger than me. 'I thought that maybe...' Sandra stops herself short. *Maybe what?* 'That he had something planned for Christmas that he wanted to keep a surprise...'

'A surprise?'

'Let's just say,' Sandra begins, her usually cheery tone recovered now that our speculations are back onto familiar ground, *heartbreakingly* familiar ground. 'I thought he may have a prior *engagement* in mind…'

'Oh, I don't think…' I begin, heart hammering in my chest, George still avoiding my eye contact. 'I'm not sure that's on the cards this year.'

'Of course it is,' Sandra says, her confidence in George and me bolstering my bruised heart even further. 'You two being together is always on the cards. You're George and Poppy, for goodness' sake. Maybe he's just throwing you off the scent?'

It would be typical George to grab hold of an idea and take it too far. A little like me.

'Anyway, would you ask him to let me know what's happening and whether that involves his Royal Highness descending on Devon? We'd miss you too much if you don't.'

'I will.' I can't help but laugh at Sandra mocking her only son with such vigour. Part of me wants to stay on the line with her forever, to soak up every inch of her maternal tone, her maternal instinct that George and I belong together. Another part of me wants to cut our conversation short, pre-empting the pain of having to pull away from her for good.

'In fact, you can ask him your—' I walk closer to George but he looks up with pleading eyes, shaking his head. Why doesn't he want to talk to his own mother? I feel a rage surge through my body. If I had a mother who *wanted* to talk to me, I'd never miss her calls. 'I'll get him to call you back as soon as I can…'

'Thanks, Poppy.' I can almost hear Sandra smiling down the line. 'I'm not sure what we'd do without you.'

'I'm sure you'd cope,' I mutter, lump caught in my throat.

'What? And have to organise things with my son directly? No thank you.'

We laugh again and despite my momentary annoyance at George, it feels so normal.

'Love you, Pops.'

'Love you too, Sandra... okay... bye now, goodbye...'

'What?' George looks up at me as soon as I've hung up the call. 'I'm really busy. And I'll call her soon, I just...' His sentence fades as he folds his arms, morphing from man to man-child right before my eyes. In all my pining I had forgotten how much I hate those two words, *I'm busy*. How George always wears them like a badge, showing me just how important his time is. And it *is* important, it's just so are the people in his life, those who make his busyness easier.

'She's not heard from you in weeks...'

'When was the last time you talked to your mum?'

For a second I feel stung by the words until I remember that George technically doesn't know how far the rift between me and my family goes. Because I've never *technically* told him. Before I met George, my messed-up family life used to stick to me like a shadow. Meeting him was a fresh start, a fresh chance to become the kind of woman I'd always wanted to be. The kind of woman a guy like him fell for in the first place.

'I haven't told her about the break-up, if that's what you're asking,' I say quietly, struggling to look him in the eye.

'I haven't told my mum either.' George softens too, coming to stand before me, the same tension brimming between us that I thought we'd just left in the closet.

'Why?' I ask, as my voice breaks. George takes another step closer towards me.

'I guess…' He begins, a sad smile turning up the corners of his tired mouth. 'After being together for so long, I just want a bit of time to get my head around not being together, you know, before everyone else starts adding their two cents into the mix…'

I watch George's mouth form the words but the fact that his hand is now on my arm, that his eyes are lingering on my lips again, makes me sure my suspicions are right; that he's getting his head around whether us not being together is something he even *wants*. That he's had his head so full of the band and his work and my lack of it that something had to give. And now that it has, he's wondering whether he's giving away the right thing.

'But you should still call her back,' I say, not wanting to scare his honesty away, not meaning a smile to spread across my face. I feel the warmth of George's hand on my arm, the way he's leaning a little bit more of his weight onto me, and know that he's struggling too. That his stressed-out mind may have flagged me as needy, but he needs me to lean on too. 'She wants to know what you're doing for Christmas Day.' Well, what *we're* doing. And about another 'engagement' that until recently, I know we've both been counting on.

'Sure,' George sighs. 'But not right now. I will soon, but this morning, I'm busy…'

Those two damn words again. But then I remember the moment that we've just shared, and what he said about admiring me for being out and about more, and I turn to leave him behind. This time, I'm a bit more confident that I'm leaving him wanting more.

Chapter Nine

It doesn't take me long to realise I'm walking to Church Street. Unlike George, juggling work and band stuff and friends and family phone calls, it's not like I have anywhere else to go right now. The thought of him shrugging his own mother off like that niggles around my neck, tensing up my shoulders. But then I remember how much he loves her, that he *is* busy and, most importantly, how he looked at me just before she rang, that he's keeping our break-up to himself, like even he knows the split won't stick.

I scribble my name onto the sticker and place it on my chest.

'Popstar!' Avery sings as soon as I've stepped foot into the church hall. Turns out the label is pretty pointless once people have already decided who you are. She throws her arms around me and I feel the warmth of her embrace.

'What are you doing here? On a Sunday?' I can't tell her I had nothing better to do.

'I had some time,' I shrug. 'Thought I'd come and hang out. Where's Theo?' I look around for his strawberry-blond mop and sultry expression.

'It's his day off,' Avery explains, following my gaze around the room. I have no idea why I'm disappointed. 'I bet he'll pop in later though…' And now I have no idea why I'm relieved. 'He can barely keep away from this place.'

'You're one to talk,' I tease back, before I see her smile drop. 'In a good way.'

'Cupcake!' Roger slurs from the same position he was slumped in at the beginning of the week, completely alone. The thought of anyone being alone at this time of year breaks my heart. I give him a little wave from across the room. He grunts back.

'I assume there are more food parcels in the back…' I begin, unable to take my eyes off him. Why isn't he joining in with the others, chatting and playing cards around the room?

'If you don't mind, yeah, we can hardly keep up with the demand,' Avery says, but I can see she's following my gaze back to Roger.

'Is he okay?' I ask, before I can stop myself.

'Roger has a drinking problem,' Avery begins sadly. 'He's getting help, going to AA and everything, but lately he's been struggling…' She goes on, sounding wiser than her years as the size of his struggles shrink mine down to size. 'We just want him to know that he can always come and sit in here with us, that this is a safe place…'

'Come as you are, but don't stay as you are,' I repeat Theo's words from before. I wish I'd had people like him and Avery to help me. I had to help myself. Still do. But it's working. Soon, I won't have to be hiding out here at all.

'Yeah, it's just the "don't stay as you are" bit is taking a bit longer with Rog.'

'I see, well…' I say, shaking my head, trying to stop my mind from drifting back to my past. 'I'll just be in the…' I force my legs towards the larder, back into my safe place. But then I see Roger again, so broken and alone, and I feel my legs redirecting, gravitating towards him.

'Oh, I'm not sure…' I hear Avery say behind me, gluing me to the spot. 'Roger doesn't like to mix with the others here and, well, he can be a bit aggressive, and Theo is really protective…' Is that why he's been keeping me in the back? He thinks I'm too fragile?

'Cupcake!' Roger grunts as I approach him and despite my defiance, up close, he does look quite scary. He's still wearing his mud-covered coat and his thinning hair looks like it hasn't been washed in weeks. As I approach the old sofa, I can see that his heavily lined face is tattooed with teardrops. I rack my mind for what this symbolises. That he's spent time in prison? That he's killed somebody? That someone he loved has died?

'Hi Roger,' I say slowly. 'I'm Poppy,' I put a hand up to my chest and can feel my heart throbbing beneath my chunky knit, one of the new jumpers I bought for our Cotswolds trip. I never expected to be wearing it somewhere like here. 'How are you?'

Roger just looks at me, eyes narrowed, brow crinkled, as if he doesn't know where I've come from and is busy working out how to make me go away. Sitting beside him, I can smell the stale alcohol on his breath, the body odour escaping through his outerwear. But I don't move. I just sit there, remembering how it felt to be the outsider, before I met George and he made me feel like I was finally invited inside.

'I'm having a bit of a hard time myself at the moment,' I say, instantly wishing I'd gone with a different opener. He's looking back at me like I couldn't possibly know a hard time if it hit me round the face.

'Family problems,' I say, because that's the only term broad and vague enough to encapsulate what George means to me. 'Trying to work out what they want…'

'Cupcake?' Roger grunts again. Well, at least it's something.

'Maybe,' I laugh, taking this so-called pet name as permission to go on. 'It certainly wasn't breakfast lasagne…' I look to Roger, who's still not cracking a smile.

'You bring cupcakes,' Roger slurs again. Part of me wants to recoil but another wants to hold him, to show him that his addiction isn't everything he is.

'Here? To Church Street?' I laugh, the fact that I've got three words out of him feeling like a win. I haven't talked to anyone like Roger in years. Only designer-donned Insta influencers primed to perfection. On the outside, at least.

'Theo,' Roger says, and I look up to see that he's materialised across the hall. This place is clearly an addiction of sorts for him, too. 'Theo's girlfriend bring cupcakes,' Roger slurs again and I sense he's getting agitated, like he's trying to tell me something. Does he think I'm Theo's girlfriend? I look up to see Theo has moved closer towards us.

'Does she come here too?' I lower my voice to ask the question. 'Theo's girlfriend?'

'She used to.'

I sit with Roger in silence until it's time for the community centre to close up and the visitors to go home. I don't want to ask how many of them haven't got homes to go to. I know I should be getting back too, that after this morning there's a good chance that George is at home wondering where I am, marvelling at my renewed motivation. But for some reason, I'm not in a rush to leave this place. Perhaps now that he is showing signs of remorse, I'm actually starting to believe my hours volunteering here are numbered.

I watch as Theo holds Roger's arm to guide him across the hall and over to the door, offering him a bottle of water as he does. Part of me wants to run after him, to tell him that he can come and sleep on our sofa; that he doesn't need to do this alone. But then I remember that right now, George is sleeping on our sofa and I need to fix that or risk being alone too.

'Nice chat?' Theo says as he retraces his steps back to me.

'Yes, actually,' I say, not knowing why I still feel I have something to prove to him. Maybe because I'm not a benevolent cupcake-baker like his seemingly perfect girlfriend? 'Look, I know you want me to keep out of the way, that you don't think I'm serious about volunteering and that you need to protect me or something...'

'Who said anything about protecting you?' Theo asks, towering in front of me, his grubby cable knit-covered arms crossed before him.

'Avery said,' I begin, realising that she said he was protective but didn't say of whom.

'I'm protective of our visitors,' Theo says slowly. 'So many of them are really vulnerable and vulnerable people get attached quickly. They can make someone their whole world,' he goes on and it's like he's talking from experience, 'and then they get a new job or decide to volunteer someplace else and like that, they're gone.'

'And they're not strong enough to deal with that?'

Theo should give them some credit. I can't help anger from bubbling up inside me.

'And all Roger seems attached to is alcohol…' I go on, wishing I can take it back. I know it's never that simple. 'And cupcakes.'

'My ex-girlfriend's cupcakes.' Theo nods, a weary expression washing over his face. *Theo's girlfriend bring cupcakes. She used to.* 'I overheard some of what he was saying to you.'

'Because you were trying to,' I argue back, but unlike George, Theo doesn't bite.

'I think he was getting confused, that he thought you were her, that you were Lucy.'

'Oh,' I say, a thousand questions filling my mind at once. 'Do I look like her?'

'A bit,' Theo says, before adding quickly, 'but don't worry, you're nothing like her.'

No, I bet she was smart and composed and naturally caring because the world didn't teach her not to be. I look to Theo and have no idea why I'm even bothered. I am only here for George. To show him that I'm still me. Just not the version of me I was before him.

You still on for tonight? The message rumbles through my vibrating phone and I look down to see that it's from Marie. It's a good job it does, as I totally forgot what tonight is.

'Everything okay?' Theo asks, seeing my whole body stiffen as I study the words.

'Not really,' I reply slowly, his face dropping with concern. 'I have to go and sing in a choir now,' I go on, his eyes still searching my expression. 'And it's all your fault.'

'How is it my fault?' Theo puts a large hand to his chest, his face incredulous.

'I was resisting their advances just fine before you told them about my trip!'

'What can I say, Poppy?' Theo's seriousness fades to be replaced by a cheeky-looking smirk, the rarity of it sending ripples through my torso. 'You're born for Broadway.'

Theo's words warm me as I walk through the cold winter air to my first choir practice. I guess my being here isn't *all* his fault. Right now, George will be at home, wrapping up his work and looking for someone to offload to, and after this morning I'm pretty convinced he wants that person to be me. I allow the thought of his eyes on mine, hidden together in our own secret cupboard-heaven, to fill the spaces of my mind that threaten to fill with fear: fear of the future, of what might happen if my plan to fix things doesn't work. Fear of how the hell I'm going to be able to afford an apartment or even a room in a house-share if I don't make George see that we belong together before it's too late. At least being at Church Street *looks* like a job, creates some absence for his heart to grow fonder. He *seemed* fonder this morning. Oh, and fear of singing for the first time with a bunch of people I don't know.

I drift on the thought as I walk the two short miles to the location Marie has sent me but as I arrive at the venue for the practice, my legs refuse to step inside. This is the second church hall I've visited in two weeks. The last time I visited one before that, I wasn't trying to prove I wasn't needy. It was obvious I was. Simply, unescapably. I had arrived there looking for something, or someone, to help me make sense of why I was there seeking help in a church hall like this in the first place.

I gaze up at the intimidating red-brick building, an amber light glowing from inside. *Just leave it to the professionals, babe.* George's joke reverberates around my mind, fixing me to the spot. Other than that brief moment with Theo, I haven't used my voice in years.

'Hey, stranger.'

I turn around to see Aran standing there, as tall, dark and handsome as the first time I spotted him in the choir, back before I became unlucky member number thirteen. He flings his arms wide and as I snuggle into his side, I don't feel like we're strangers at all. I feel like after years of searching, Aran and Marie are the kind of people I've always needed to meet.

Theo isn't half bad, either.

'You coming in, then?' Aran's lips curl into a smile. And reluctantly, I nod.

This church hall looks nothing like Church Street, not heaving and hectic but neat and orderly, each person looking like they've just walked in from a day at work or a moment of family life – neither of which I had, before George.

In quick succession Aran introduces me to a pretty young woman in her twenties called Rosie, who tells me that she comes here to help with her mental health; a rosy-cheeked man in his sixties called Toto, a retired music teacher with three grandchildren who love to see him sing at their shows; and Kimmy, a woman in her forties, who joined the choir as a way to make friends when she first arrived in London from her home in Japan, so far away.

'It must be really hard, being so far away from home,' I respond to Kimmy's story. She just smiles, glancing in quick succession to the other choir members around the room.

'It was at first, but I guess I've learnt you can make family anywhere,' she grins.

I wish I knew what that was like, although between Marie and Aran part of me feels like I'm beginning to. My head spins with the speed at which new people are darting into my life, all so different and with a thousand different reasons for being here. I'm only here for one.

'Poppy!' Marie flurries across the room, arms wide open. 'I'm so glad you're here.'

Within minutes, I'm forced into position, hanging on the edge of the group. Then we're handed song sheets and I look down at the notes.

'"Do They Know It's Christmas?"?' I turn to Marie, hissing under my voice.

'I didn't say it wasn't cheesy,' she laughs over her shoulder. But that's not what I am worried about. This song, the one that makes everyone feel so Christmassy, just reminds me of all of the years that didn't feel like Christmas at all. And, though I know better than to think that when Bono and co were asking whether 'they' know it's Christmastime they were thinking of a young girl spending Christmas Day in an unfamiliar bedroom, it still makes me think of her; the song still makes me think of the person I used to be.

'How are things going with George?' Marie whispers, as the choir's conductor, a petite brunette with her hair tied high on top of her head, gets into position.

'Okay, I think,' I hiss back, remembering again the way he had looked at me today.

'So, the plan is working?' My Ghost of Christmas Future beams back at me.

Before I can answer, the conductor raises her hands and the choir begins to sing as one. I force myself to sing along. And yet, ten minutes in, it doesn't feel like forcing it at all. It feels like flying. It feels like everything inside me that has been bottled up, trying to be perfect, to never make a bum note or a wrong choice, is hurtling out from inside of me.

As we reach the final bars of 'A Spaceman Came Travelling' it takes all my strength not to break down completely, not to become the mess I was when Marie first found me. But singing here is reminding me I'm not a mess. I'm the one who got it together, who got my whole damn life together before George. And now I'm days away from doing it again.

'Wow, I…' I turn to Marie as the song finally comes to a close.

'I *told* you you'd enjoy it.' Her eyes shine with joy and after the past fifteen minutes or so I understand why. 'And you never told me your answer. The plan? Is it working?'

'Yes,' I say, my confidence reaching a crescendo. 'Yes, it's going to work.'

Chapter Ten

Monday, 6 December

I look up to the bathroom ceiling, letting the hard pressure of the shower wash away my fitful sleep. I haven't got my full eight hours for almost two weeks now, ever since that fateful, festive jumper-wearing afternoon. Memories of mould-scattered ceilings flash across my mind before I reach for a flannel and wipe them away. It's the kind of memory that I've locked away and has somehow shaken loose ever since I stepped foot in the community centre. But they don't belong here. Not in this apartment, this life, with George.

It's only as I step out of the shower that I realise I've left all of the clean towels in the washing basket by the machine in the kitchen. And there's not a dirty one in sight. *Oh, crap.*

I look back at my naked reflection, which looks more toned than it has in weeks. I know better than to think it's because of my one workout with George. It's walking to and from Church Street. Or the natural appetite-suppressor that a break-up can be.

I wonder how Theo fared after his? I bet he accepted it like a grown-up and moved on without looking back. But then, if he's so well adjusted, why does he keep people at arm's length? Well, *some* people. Why am I thinking about *Theo*? Especially when naked.

I'm *naked.* The thought cements in my mind. If the strawberry bikini was enough to rouse some break-up remorse in George, then wearing less should muster even more. The way he looked at me when we were stuck in the cupboard together, I know he was about to kiss me. Was just teetering on the edge. Maybe this is all he needs to push him over to 'our' side?

Walking into the living room, I hold my shoulders back, my head high. I never used to be confident naked, never used to be confident full stop. But George changed that. George changed a lot of things. I come to stand in the middle of the room, right where I slumped like a melted snowman only a fortnight ago. But George is nowhere to be seen. The sofa bed is reassembled, his laptop gone. Well, that's morning six of our twelve gone to waste. As I walk across the room, preparing to hide the towels from the apartment completely, I notice that there are a couple of new additions to our mantelpiece: two chocolate advent calendars, one with my name on and one with his. Our first Christmas card stands between them and I open it to read: *Just a little something to tide you over until family time, Mum x* As I read the three letters of her title, I don't know whether to laugh or cry; Sandra still thinks everything is as it should be. I study the closed squares of the calendar, six of which should be open by now. For the first time in five years, I'm willing the doors to stay closed rather than race down to Christmas Day. But as I read the card from Sandra again, remembering her phone call, that George hasn't told her yet, that she still thinks George proposing is a possibility, I feel that same confidence coursing through me, the confidence that George injected into me in the first place. Then, I see there is another note on the mantelpiece, one scribbled from George to me.

Pops.

I was going to give this to you last night, but you must have been out – you used to love it when you forgot a day and realised you had two chocolates to eat at once. Now you have six – kind of hope I'm around to see the sugar high.

Maybe see you at the gig later?
G x

I take the note in my hand, still naked. George used to leave me little letters like this all the time, before he got busy, and I became a house-bound freelancer. I guess now that I've been out more, he has reason to write them. And after whatever spark reignited during our seven minutes together in the cupboard, he actually wants to write them again. And he wants me at his gig?

Moving closer to our bedroom to get dressed, I notice that the boxes that George was packing yesterday are now empty. And, as I walk past the kitchen area, I see that the cookbook I said I was looking for in the cupboard is now propped up on the countertop. George has put it there for me. I'm not naïve enough to think that Sandra is right, that an engagement will happen this year, but I'm now hopeful enough that one day it might.

Dee: You coming tonight? My phone buzzes on the bedroom table as soon as I'm safely back in our room. *The gig?* I study Dee's messages, still not sure why she's not mentioning the break-up. Maybe our friends don't know either? Maybe that's why no one has asked about our plans for the Cotswolds and whether they could have changed?

No, sorry. I type, knowing that being busy is beginning to work. *I've got other plans.*

Walking the familiar way to Church Street, I savour the memory of George's advent calendar next to mine. A promise of better things to come. Switching on some music, I find Spotify is still on Christmas classics. As I listen to Mariah hit her high notes, the thought of Theo catching me singing the lyrics back to him forces a smile. Not even that damn noticeboard can stem my festive feeling now; the feeling that everything is going to be okay.

Stepping into the entrance to the church, I even write 'Popstar' on my name badge. I'll be back together with a real one before long, so why not make the most of being centre stage? It's only as I walk into the main hall that I realise it's a little quieter than normal in here, not quite as chaotic. Then, I realise the time. It's the first time I've been here before eight, the first time I've not hung around back home to see when George may be coming back from his workout or lingering to watch him fire up his laptop. Looking around the room, I see a handful of familiar faces. They all smile back at me. Roger is here, slumped in his usual spot on the sofa. Theo is nowhere to be seen.

I walk over to Roger slowly, wondering just how similar I am to Theo's ex-girlfriend, how much of his rant about the visitors getting too connected was prompted by her. *They get a new job or decide to volunteer someplace else…*

'Cupcake!' Roger says, true to form, as I move closer to his sofa.

'Morning, Roger,' I say softly, noticing the same scent of stale alcohol on his breath. I wonder how he spent his night but remember that it's more important that he's decided to come here today. 'I wanted to properly introduce myself,' I say, too formally, like I've forgotten how to speak to people. I told him my name yesterday, but sadly, he probably won't remember that. Clearly, the memory of Lucy and her cupcakes is lodged in his oversaturated mind.

'I'm actually not the one with the cupcakes,' I begin, hating again how being in this place brings back those old familiar feelings of rootlessness, of feeling 'without'. 'I'm Poppy, I'm the one with the…' I smile, Roger isn't bothered but he does seem to be listening. 'I'm the one who is… not Theo's ex-girlfriend… I'm just… me.'

'Poppy,' Roger says my name slowly, a slight smile lighting up his face for a moment before I realise that I shouldn't be doing this. That Theo is right. I shouldn't be getting the visitors to trust me, to care for me, if I'm just going to abandon them too as soon as I am back together with George and have my old life back.

'I'm just going to…' I begin, not sure what I'm going to do. Just that I have the sudden urge to put some distance between us.

As I walk to the back of the hall, I can't quite believe it's only been two and a half weeks since Theo first showed me around here. *Vulnerable people get attached quickly…*

I lean against the back wall and fish out my phone, distracting myself from the memory of Theo's words. I'm not vulnerable. I swipe to re-read my last message to Dee. In fact, I feel stronger than I have in weeks.

From underneath the angel, I can see the room beginning to fill with colour, both from the light flooding through the stained-glass windows themselves and the smorgasbord of visitors and volunteers now milling around it. But I still can't see Theo or Avery.

Flicking open Instagram, I swipe through the colourful squares, clocking no less than five photos of recently engaged couples boasting *'he did it!'* and *'I will!'* and *'the easiest yes I've ever said'*. 'Tis the season, I guess.

I haven't been on here much since the break-up and now I remember why. These comparison-rife squares are enough to steal anybody's Christmas cheer. Still, I can't help but notice my already healthy following has gone up by a few hundred. How can I have thousands of followers and still feel like George is my only friend? Well, until I met Marie and Aran and Theo, and they started to feel like friends too.

Something juts into my back and I turn to see that I've started to lean on one of the many framed photographs hanging from the wall. I study it more closely. It's a group of forty or so service users, with Theo and a couple of the other volunteers on each side. From the tinsel wrapped around some of their necks, it's clear this was taken at Christmastime.

I look into the shiny, happy faces – so many of them weathered and warm. Theo's face is beaming back at me too, his arm slung around someone. People who have fallen on hard times that he's managed to help back on their feet. It must be a pretty nice feeling. Until they leave. I replay his words about Lucy again. Could this be the real reason Theo doesn't want people getting attached? Not to protect the visitors but to protect the volunteers from getting too invested themselves? I imagine it must hurt to love and lose that many times. The lump in my throat and pain in my heart tells me I don't need to imagine it. I try and fail to conjure an image of my mum in my mind's eye; it was all so long ago now.

My eyes scan though the photographs, from face to shining face until one in particular draws my attention. It's a picture of a guy in his late forties or early fifties, with deep laughter lines drawing patterns from his eyes down to the bottom of his cheeks. He's standing tall, broad shoulders setting him almost twice as wide as the person he's standing alongside.

Do I *know* him from somewhere?

The pain in my heart drops to my stomach, as my breath shortens, and the room starts to spin around me. I steady myself, reaching a hand to the photo-scattered wall. No. No, I can't. I turn and reach for my phone again in time to see Theo walking into the room.

'Hey T! Any news yet?' one of the visitors shouts as he walks further inside.

'Not yet,' Theo replies quickly. 'Please just be patient, mate.' He forces a smile. Even from here, I can see it looks tired. 'We're doing everything we can.'

'Good!' another says, loud enough to hear from the other side of the hall. 'Because I've got nowhere else to go.'

'Me neither,' yet another chimes in, this time a short and sweet-looking elderly woman in her seventies or eighties. 'And I can't cook for shit.'

'Language,' Theo says, but I can tell the unexpectedness of said language has tickled him. I can't help but laugh too.

'I'd come if we had sandwiches, as long as it means we're together.' This latest sentence, said by one of the younger guys, makes Theo's face fall again. There's quite the group gathering around him and I can sense the pressure on him from here. Then he sees me.

His eyes fix on mine and it's like he's as surprised to see me as the first time I showed up here. I smile back at him and he grins, moving to bridge the gap between us.

'I see you've finally owned your true persona.' He grins down at me, his hair as messy as ever, the bags under his eyes telling me he's slept even less than me. What? He's looking down at my chest. My cheeks blush. Oh, *Popstar*. I remember what I wrote on my sticker.

'It appears I can fight it no longer…' I can't help but beam back at him. 'Trust me, I tried. Speaking of fighting…' I look at the rabble of people he's left behind him, all congregating and chattering in circles. 'What was all that about?'

'Whether we'll be able to open on Christmas Day or not,' Theo says, his trademark seriousness settling on his features. 'I'm trying my best, but people just don't want to commit to volunteer when they've got their own families and friends to be with. It's only a couple of hours of their day and yet it would mean so much to these guys and…' Theo stops himself short. He knows I'm planning to be in the Cotswolds this Christmas. That his own sister is going to be spending it with her dad, but what about Theo?

'What will you do if—'

'Anything good on there?' Now it's my turn to be cut short. Clearly, Theo doesn't want to talk about his family. And I get it. I don't want to talk about my family either.

I look down at the phone in my hands, still open on Instagram, my digital distraction. It sounds like we both need a distraction right now.

'Oh, just a thousand people getting engaged.'

'It's the time of year for it, I guess,' Theo says plainly, coming to stand by my side to see an image of someone I knew from one of the schools I went to pressing her hand into her new fiancé's chest, her large diamond engagement ring sparkling through the screen.

'Yeah, I wonder how many couples get engaged during the week between Christmas and New Year?' I muse, swiping to the next, a notification flashing up to tell me that ten new faux friends are now following me as I do.

'Not as many as the disappointed partners who *think* they're opening an engagement ring to find they've got a new pair of earrings in an unfortunately ring-shaped box.'

'I can't imagine how awkward that must be for the gift-giver,' I laugh.

'I don't need to.'

'Oh no,' I say, putting a hand up to my mouth, trying to stifle my giggles. 'Sorry.'

'Don't be,' Theo shakes his head. 'It was a long time ago. And the break-up was for the best,' he adds with confidence; the same confidence I have that mine *isn't* for the best.

He holds my eye contact and I want to tell him that everything will be okay. That he'll find the volunteers he needs to open on Christmas Day. That everything will work out exactly as it needs to. Just like Marie told me. Except, she didn't say that, did she? She said that given the time pressures, I probably shouldn't leave it to chance. That I should take my fate into my own hands and make sure it happens for good.

'Question…'

'Answer…' Theo says, as my eyes scan across the busy room once more.

'Does Church Street have a social media presence?'

'Define presence?'

'Like, if people wanted to search for you, where would they go?'

'The not—'

'And please don't say the noticeboard.'

'Wasn't going to,' Theo says quickly, trying to hide his tired smile. 'We have an Instagram,' he admits. 'Avery started it, but then she's got school and it's distracting and well… we have about thirty followers.'

'And how many of them are in this room?' I ask as Theo follows my gaze.

'A solid fifty per cent.'

'I see,' I say, an idea percolating in my mind, one that's telling me that I may be able to fix this too. 'How would you feel if I gave it a go?' I say, flicking to my own profile. 'I work in PR…' At least, I did, I'm trying to. 'And I've got a fair few followers…'

'I've already seen.'

He's already seen? I didn't think old-before-his-time Theo would know how to use social media, never mind look me up on it. *Why* has he been looking me up on it?

'So yeah, I could populate the page a bit more, share it from my own socials,' I go on, sounding a bit like every pitch I've sent off over the past few months, except this time I'm starting to care about the end result. 'I'm sure that we can get you your eleven volunteers.'

'I don't know…' Theo says slowly, shaking his head, seriousness resumed. 'I don't think people should really have to be manipulated to want to help out.'

'That's not what this is,' I say, shaking my head.

'This place has been here for longer than social media was a thing…'

'Yes, but not enough people *know* that,' I object, feeling surer than this will work.

'They would if they cared enough.'

'Not when there's a thousand other causes being bombarded at them.'

Theo still looks far from convinced.

'Trust me, this is what I do for a living.' At least, it's what I used to do. It's what I should be doing. But at least this will look like a job – a real job – one that George so desperately wants me to find. 'And it *works*.'

'I can't pay you,' Theo says, slowly, like this might put me off. I know from my brief chats with Avery and her weighing up the price of pick-and-mix that Theo's budget isn't big.

'That's okay, consider it a gift.' I smile. It might even make it into my portfolio.

'Well, actually…' Theo says, looking over to the makeshift coffee shop and brushing a hand over his stubbled chin. 'You said you're in between work?'

I nod, very much in the in-between bit.

'We're looking for an extra pair of hands in the coffee shop. We pay minimum wage for that but any time you're not serving people I guess you could be on social media.' Theo reluctantly gives me permission to do something most employees have been doing for years. 'Could that work? And then that way, if the social media thing doesn't work, you'll still…'

'So, I'd be getting paid for the coffee shop part and not the social media part?'

'Sadly,' Theo says as I mentally promote my position to Communications Manager, at least for George and my future CV's sake. 'But don't feel you have to say yes.'

'That could work,' I say, a smile spreading wide across my face. Secure Theo's volunteers whilst securing my future with George? This could *actually* work.

The rest of the afternoon goes by in a blur, chatting to the visitors, adjudicating a game of snap, eating lunch alongside Roger, snapping photographs of it all. Well, not Roger. He did *not* give his permission to be included in any posts. But everyone else was happy to.

Avery was beside herself when I told her about my social media mission. *Ohmigod, you're totally going to save Christmas,* she had squealed, somehow making me feel like her version of Marie, as if one stranger's generosity was sparking some kind of chain reaction. Now, I'm heading home and ready to fan any recent flirtation with George into flames.

I turn the key in the door and walk into the living room. The advent calendars are still on the mantelpiece. The boxes are still empty and pushed to one side. My never-used recipe book is still there, propped up by George like a sign he thinks things haven't toppled over completely. But he's nowhere to be seen. My heart falls at the missed opportunity. Right now, I wouldn't have to pretend to have purpose, get-up-and-go. I feel it.

'George?' I shout into the apartment. He's not here. But I'm full of energy, feeling more sociable, thanks to being on social media all day. And not just mindlessly scrolling through it but framing the friendly faces of the community centre, no filters required. I pull out my phone. I'm going to message Dee. To finally face whatever she has to tell me about the gossip in our group about me and George. But then I see her last message about the gig. That's where she'll be right now; that's where George will be too. I do have a message from Aran though: *Just checking in, doing okay?* And Marie: *Looking forward to catching up at practice. Remember that regardless of what happens, this heartbreak-hotel living situation is temporary.* I smile, savouring their support; right now, I don't feel that heartbroken at all. Looking around the empty apartment, I finally give myself permission to relax. Knowing George is out singing songs he once wrote about me, *wanting* me to be there, makes being here alone feel okay for the first time since before our break-up.

I swipe to Church Street's Instagram and smile at the new logo I managed to cobble together at some point this afternoon. I select a photo of Theo and Avery, standing in the middle of a rabble of service users all looping their arms around one another, just like the photographs hanging at the back of the hall.

I force the memory of the face I thought I recognised out of my mind and look down at the ones staring back at me from my screen. In the silence of our apartment and with Theo and Avery's eyes staring back at me from the frame, I post it. Then, I watch the 'likes' coming in, praying that Theo's eleven volunteers and George's admiration will follow.

Chapter Eleven

Tuesday, 7 December

I don't know where to begin. Literally. Do I upload more content? Do I target influencers? Tap into homeless shelter hashtags? Not that that's what Church Street is. How do I encapsulate all of their activities into one pithy bio?

I ponder the question as I drag myself out of bed, scrolling through my feed as I make my way into the shower. I posted about the community centre from my own social media account late last night, actually enjoying an evening lounging in the living room alone.

The gig must have run late or something as it was gone midnight by the time I heard George stumble in from the safety of our bedroom. Still, unlike the many nights he's been out since our 'break-up', the minutes didn't pass like hours, some of them even felt like seconds as I watched account after account begin to follow the story of the community centre.

Now, how to convert them into volunteers?

It's the only thing I can think of as I get into the shower, as I wash my hair, as I get back out again, wrapping an all-too-small towel around my body, not even bothering to dry myself before picking up my phone again: *666 followers*. Yes. That's great. Well, apart from the fact it's a pretty ominous number. And not very Christmassy. But still, it's a lot better than the thirty-two we started with yesterday. I watch as another person follows the account: 667. I smile down at my phone as I head into the living room. I can't wait to tell Theo.

'Poppy?'

I look up from my screen to see George still lying on the sofa bed, the winter morning sunlight flooding into the room. How had I not noticed him on my way into the bathroom? I look down at the phone clutched tightly in my hand, the one that hasn't left my hand since Theo gave me the go-ahead to put yet another plan into action. Oh yeah, that's how.

'You look…' George's gruff voice tells me these are his first words of the morning. He's brushing the sleep out of his eyes and looking me up and down like I'm a mirage. Then, I realise I'm in a towel. A tiny hand towel at that. One that conceals even less than my bikini. I watch a coy smile spread across his face. It's what I was hoping for yesterday. Am still hoping for. But I'm also dangerously close to being late for my first shift. And I want to squeeze in an extra half hour of taking photos before the coffee shop opens up.

'Morning,' I say, hurriedly, holding the towel closer around my middle. 'Did I wake you? Sorry. I didn't think you'd be…' I go on, cursing myself for apologising. This is still my home too. Then, I remember that it's a Tuesday, not one of 'our' days; that he should probably be in the office by now before heading straight to the band. 'You're not at work?'

'Oh, crap!' George looks back at me. 'What time is it?' He reaches for his watch. 'Oh, thank God! I thought that it was later than…' He looks at me standing there before him, used to me surfacing and showering around midday lately. Not anymore. 'I must have forgotten to set my alarm last night…' He looks a little green.

'Yeah, well, I've got an early start,' I smile, making my way towards the bedroom.

'Poppy, wait…' George smiles again, searching the short hem of my towel-dress with his eyes. His hair is messy, his eyes puffy, like he's still a little drunk. 'Do you want to…'

'I'm really sorry.' Damn it, Poppy. Stop apologising. And stop *objecting*.

Time with George is precisely what I want. But I've only just got a job, and this account, and Theo didn't even *want* me to start it because he thinks it'll attract flaky people who don't really care; so, I need to show him that I do. 'I've really got to go.'

I rush to the bedroom and throw on some clothes and make-up, watching my phone light up with new followers as I do: *678. 680. 684.* I remember when I first got social media, soon after meeting George. That initial buzz. Before posting and scrolling became about showing off. But now, now I feel like it's got purpose to it. Like *I've* got a purpose.

'Poppy, have you got a second to chat?' George says as soon as I walk past him, still half cocooned by the covers, his broad body taking up most of the sofa bed made for two. One of his legs is pushed free of his covers, muscular, naked and leading my eye upwards.

'I've really got to…' I begin, looking from George to the door. I want to chat to him, I do. I just wasn't expecting him to be in this morning. It wasn't one of our days. And I have a job to do. And for the first time in a long time, I feel like it matters. 'Is it important?'

'No, no,' George begins quickly, his voice low. 'I just thought we could catch up.'

'Oh, okay,' I say, looking from a sleepy George to my buzzing phone: *689*. 'I've actually really got to go, though. Can we chat later?' It's not even a make-him-jealous or a show-him-something lie this time. 'Theo will kill me if I'm late for my first shift.'

'Who's Theo?' George asks, pushing himself to sit up. Damn you, torso. I don't need to see those toned abs right now. He lets the sheet fall further down. 'First shift where?'

'I've picked up some more work, social media management type thing,' I say at speed, not knowing why working in a community centre coffee shop wouldn't be enough.

'You've got another job?' he asks, genuinely interested, his eyes searching me again.

Another job? I thought my freelance work or lack thereof didn't count before.

'Yeah, and look, I'll tell you more about it later, but Theo…' I reach for the door handle and let the rest of my sentence finish itself, smiling as I leave him behind.

Approaching the church, my mind is still running on overdrive, trying to work out how on earth I'm going to secure the eleven followers we need to open the centre on Christmas Day. Well, *Theo* needs. I need to focus. I've grown account followings before. I've worked on their engagement. But I don't even know where to start with *recruitment*.

Maybe I should start with that noticeboard?

It's the first thing I see as I arrive in the churchyard. Walking closer to it, I remember the first time I saw it. The day after the break-up when I wondered momentarily whether I'd ever be able to fix this. Fixing things with George now feels a whole lot easier than fixing the nightmare of a noticeboard in front of me.

One by one, I begin to take down the papers for events that are now months out of date, some of them by *years*. Maybe one of the forthcoming events might be a good thing to hook the recruitment drive to? I'm sure some members of the Nimble Nineties club could help out, but we could also really do with some more youthful muscle when it comes to the heavy lifting needed to set the community centre up for Christmas dinner. And if Instagram can help us with anything, it's attracting a younger, perhaps more energetic, crowd. I rip down a number of A4 pages advertising things like van hires and running clubs that have nothing to do with this place. I don't know when people started using this as public property. Another advertisement catches my eye, this time for 'Hot Horny Babes' promising me a good time. No wonder the right people struggle to find Church Street. I reach for the page, pulling it from the noticeboard, covering the poor model's modesty as I do.

'If you want a good time, Popstar, I'm sure there's people I can set you up with.'

Damn it! I turn around to see Theo standing there, a silly smirk on his face.

'I'm not… it's not… I'm doing this for you.'

'I didn't ask you to sort the noticeboard out.'

'No, but it's drowning…'

'Bit dramatic,' he mumbles.

'And the damn thing is *begging* for me to save it…'

'Well,' Theo grins back at me and it makes me feel kind of fuzzy inside, 'we all really appreciate it…' He didn't seem convinced yesterday but maybe my commitment is convincing him. 'And I know the guys in the coffee shop appreciate you helping out.'

The way Theo says 'helping out' even though I'm meant to be getting paid for the coffee-shop job reminds me of just how minimal minimum wage is. But then, this has never been about the money. The things I've wanted in life have never been about money.

Following Theo's tall frame into the community centre, I'm greeted by a barrage of smiles and welcomes and 'Popstars!' called from across the room. This makes me feel fuzzy too. Theo introduces me to Ruth, working in the coffee-shop corner, and she welcomes me with a massive great hug that makes me want to hold onto her for just a moment longer. She smells of cinnamon and hope and it's exactly how I'd imagine a grandma smelling.

'Popstar!' she says as soon as Theo has left our side. 'You're gorgeous!'

'Am I?' I laugh, taken aback by her effortless forwardness.

'Are you kidding me?' Ruth puts her hands on her hips. She's a little thing. All bones. But it makes her smile seem even bigger. 'Now, don't tell me there's been a man – or a woman – who has made you feel anything but?' She corrects herself quickly, like she knows that in the twenty-first century you can't assume being straight is the norm.

'No,' I reply. 'Well, not really. No.'

Ruth cocks an eyebrow.

'My long-term boyfriend and I are going through a bit of a thing but it's more to do with him, really. He's having a bit of a... he's been stressed out,' I correct myself. 'But we're going to be okay.'

'Oh, thank God.' Ruth puts a hand to her heart. 'It's not good for man to be alone,' she says, and I feel like she's quoting something. 'My Derek was no exception.'

'Was?' I say, and instantly regret it.

'He died, dear,' Ruth sighs. 'Over six years ago now. Marriage may look like a destination to you little ones,' she says it in a way that makes me feel like I'm young even though every time I go on social media, I feel anything but, like time is running away. Well, until yesterday when I started posting as Church Street. 'But it's really just the beginning.'

And this is really just the beginning of Ruth teaching me a thing or two. Not only how to make a flat white, but how to make each customer feel like they've just walked into The Ritz even though they've literally rocked up to the corner of a community centre. And before I know it, over four hours have passed and I have no idea where they went. Theo was right when he said that the coffee corner was in need of some help.

'You guys need a break?' He appears at our stall, less solemn all of a sudden. I almost let myself think I've had something to do with this.

'No, no...'

'Definitely,' my words cut across Ruth's objection. I instantly feel guilty for them. Maybe she's got that stiff upper lip stoicism of the older generation that I never really knew.

'Great,' Theo says, ushering us to sit down at a nearby table whilst another volunteer comes to take over our coffee-shop responsibilities. 'We're playing Articulate.'

'Articulwhat?' I ask, looking around the smattering of people sat around the table.

'You've never played Articulate?' Theo looks stunned, his square jaw dropping. Seven minutes in heaven. Articulate. Happy families. There's a lot I haven't played. I shake my head. 'Okay, well, it's easy. You just have to describe what's on the card without saying the word on it.' I nod, the slumped figure of Roger distracting me from the sidelines.

Before I know it, service users are fighting and laughing across one another.

'It's an erotic bird!' Linda is shouting, flapping her make-believe wings.

'A playboy? A stripper?' Stanley shouts back at her with urgency.

'An *erotic* bird!' she says again, face sterner still.

'I don't think we can guess it,' Theo says, shaking his head diplomatically, casting a sly look to me to show me he has no idea what's going on. I try my best not to laugh.

'A flamingo!' Linda throws her arms in the air in exasperation.

'Do you mean *exotic* bird?' Theo asks her kindly. I can't look at him just in case he gives me *that* look again, sure I'll crumble into a fit of giggles immediately. This is too much.

'That's the badger!'

'No,' Roger says, he's arrived by my side. 'It's a flamingo.'

And with his last words, I can't hold back the laughter anymore. Before I know it, I'm laughing so hard that my shoulders are heaving and tears are falling from my eyes with all the intensity of when I was breaking down in front of the twelve-piece choir only weeks ago.

I pull across a nearby chair and Roger sits down beside me. I smile. He doesn't say much; in fact, he doesn't say much for the rest of the game. But he's here. And he doesn't have to say anything to belong here, to be a part of this. And, when I arrive at Church Street the next morning, I pin the sign that I spent yesterday evening making onto the noticeboard, the one with the message I was inspired to write after sitting in companionable silence with Roger: *You May Only Be Visiting But You Already Belong Here.*

Chapter Twelve

Friday, 10 December

Six Band Members

The next few days come and go in a blur of early mornings and coffee making and increasingly competitive games of Articulate until I'm actually getting pretty good at it. I'm feeling pretty good too. I've left George at home, yet again asking to chat, impressed by my busyness. I'm the woman I was before the break-up. The woman he fell in love with again.

I eat the Number Ten of my advent calendar chocolate before heading out in the evening, recalling George's note to me over again. It's day seven of our twelve that George is *meant* to be around the apartment but he's out at another gig. Dee will be there too. We're meant to be meeting for coffee later this weekend, but I still don't know what she knows about the break-up; she still hasn't mentioned it, or our trip to the Cotswolds, once.

When I arrive at choir practice, I stride confidently into the room, Rosie racing over to me as soon as I do. As she throws her arms around me, I marvel at how easy it has been to feel a part of something here. I know Rosie and I are a similar age and that the fact she's singing to help her mental health shows me she's lived through or is *living* through some struggles too, but I still can't believe the speed at which I'm being embraced – literally *and* metaphorically. Not when for years I felt like I was on the outside of everything, always looking in. Until I met George and his friendship group became my own.

'How's it going, living with your ex?' Rosie crinkles her nose at the idea of it.

'How do you…?' I begin, releasing our embrace; I've never technically told her that.

'Oh, babe,' Rosie throws a hand to her hip. 'Nothing stays secret here for very long, but don't worry, what happens in the choir stays in the choir.' And if her words don't already make me feel like I've unintentionally joined the world's quaintest Fight Club she lowers her voice to add, 'You're one of us now.' Her laughter feels warm as it echoes around the hall.

'So, I guess Marie's told you that it's not really over between me and him too?'

'Oh yes,' Rosie's grin fills my stomach with hope. 'She says it's only just beginning.'

As we take to the stage at the back of the hall and Marie jostles in beside me, I actually feel excited to sing. And sure enough, the same euphoria I felt the first time fills me from the tip of my head to my toes. Despite everything that has happened these past weeks, losing myself in a sea of voices like this is enough to make me find my festive spirit. The past week has made me sure that our break-up is just a blip, that things with George are at a tipping point, that just one more push will convince him entirely. That it's *only just beginning* for George and me all over again.

'What's the latest with George?' Marie reads my mind as soon as the practice is over. Saying that, it's hardly difficult to guess who is occupying my thoughts at the best of times, never mind when we've just been singing 'I'll Be Home for Christmas'. The others around the room walk off purposefully into their evenings, a small number lingering behind to chat in twos and threes. Out of the corner of my eye, I see Aran grab his bag, moving towards Marie and me, making our little trio feel complete.

'All going to plan,' I say with all the energy and purpose I've felt this week.

'Great, so George has said he's made a mistake? Asked for you back?'

'Not yet,' I begin slowly, feeling my heartbeat quicken at the sight of her face falling. 'But we're getting there. He's not packing anything, not preparing to move out. He's lingering around the apartment, saying he wants to catch up. But I have actually been so busy,' I beam back at her. 'Theo is driving me hard.'

Marie raises an eyebrow, and I know she'd let Theo drive her anywhere.

'Not like that. You know I only have eyes for George.'

'And he only has eyes for you?'

'Yes!' I say, feeling less confident the more she questions.

'But he's still sleeping on the sofa?'

It's only been two weeks or so since we first broke up. Marie said I had my twelve days with George. So why is she looking at me like I've somehow failed because he hasn't vocalised his relationship one-eighty yet?

'Not yet,' I object, looking from her to Aran. 'But very almost. Things around the apartment have felt exotic...' I say, laughing to myself. 'I mean, erotic... like, the sexual tension is so clearly there between us.' The thought of Theo's face, trying to hold back his amusement when playing Articulate with the visitors is almost enough to push me over the edge into giggles. That's all I have to do with George. Just one last push to being 'us' again.

'He's definitely noticed a change in me though, I think he just needs to *see* it now...'

'What do you mean *see it*?' Aran asks, somewhere between confusion and concern. 'Everyone here can see how wonderful you are, Poppy,' he smiles softly, holding his hands out to indicate the other choir members milling around the hall. From across the room Toto waves in my direction, grabbing his bag and preparing to go home for a night of looking after his grandchildren so his daughter finally has time to go late-night shopping for their Christmas gifts. *If only Santa was real*, I think before remembering how young I was when I realised he wasn't; I was only five or six and I had wished for a Barbie but got given a hand-me-down doll instead, her golden-blonde hair already matted and marred.

'I mean,' I begin, forcing the thought away and my busy mind back to the task in hand. 'All this volunteering I've done at Church Street, the job I have there now, the work I'm doing on socials...' I go on, remembering that last part had a lot more to do with Theo and the visitors there. 'Right now, George can only imagine it. Maybe there's a small part of him that still thinks I'm just trying to win him back.'

'But you *are* trying to win him back,' Aran says, plainly.

'Well, yes... but he's my true love...' I say, looking at Marie, willing her to confirm.

'That's right, sweetie,' she says, but not with nearly as much force as a fortnight ago. 'I just didn't think he'd take this much convincing. You're a catch, Poppy...'

'This much convincing?' I shrug away her compliment; I've never known how to take them. 'It's just... it's not him... it's the plan. Sure, I needed to be out all the time to show him that I am trying new things; that my life doesn't revolve around him...' I go on, feeling adrenaline and hope rush through my veins. 'But he needs a reason to come into the community centre and see the activities I'm involved in there, all the things I'm busy with. He needs to see that I'm not the kind of woman he wants to push away.'

'He does,' Marie nods. 'He needs to see that you're a catch.'

'Without being manipulated into seeing it,' Aran adds, and Marie nods. But she's the one who told me I shouldn't leave things to chance in the first place.

'I'm not *manipulating* him into seeing it,' I say slowly. These two were Team True Love until tonight, until I started throwing myself into life on Church Street. So, why the change? 'But this whole plan was about showing George I am the same woman he fell in love with, that I'm not needy, dependent... and I know you said that being *out* was drawing him in, but...' I go on. I don't need Marie and Aran's assurance: George's face, the note, the way he's asking to spend time with me now; it's all the evidence I need that he knows we belong together. 'I'm doing amazing things at Church Street and—'

'Yes, you are,' Marie says kindly. 'You're clearly loving it there.'

'I am and perhaps it's time he saw it first-hand.'

'You're going to ask George to volunteer with you?' Aran asks, slowly, unconvinced.

'Oh no, not that, he's too busy with work and the band already and…'

'He sounds a little obsessed,' Aran adds. No, George is *passionate*. I'm passionate too. And for the past five years we've been passionate about our life together.

'It's just a priority for him,' I begin, my mind cranking through the gears, formulating the next part of my plan out loud. I need to get him into Church Street and I know the one thing he'd never refuse. A gig, a crowd – a crowd that might just attract one or two volunteers to Theo's Christmas cause in the process. 'We need a gig.'

'We've got one,' Aran objects quickly, looking around the disbanded choir.

'In Broadway, in the Cotswolds,' Marie adds, encouraging grin resumed.

'A real gig,' I say, before I realise how harsh that sounds. They both know I love it here, that they are quickly becoming true friends. But I also have other friends to consider, too – or so I hope – friends that I'm about to have a whole week of fun with provided I can pull this next part of my plan off. No one has pulled out because no one thinks this break-up is going to stick. Least of all George. He *knows* we're going to spend Christmas together. And the tiny bit of him that thinks I may be getting in the way of his band dreams? Well, that's about to be history. And inviting him to headline our Christmas Church Street fundraiser? That's the thing that's going to secure our future.

Chapter Thirteen

Sunday, 12 December

Five Teen Mean Girls

I can see Dee sitting at the window table as soon as the café comes into view. Her long blonde hair is pulled to one side as she suspends her phone in the air to take a bird's eye view of her recently purchased flat white. I can already see that there's a coffee waiting for me. Is this Dee's attempt at empathy? Better late than never, I suppose. She's either choosing to ignore our break-up or she really doesn't know. It's one thing for George not to tell his mum, but not to tell his best friends? It makes me even surer that our break-up is just a bump, one that this gig is going to speed us over soon enough.

I press my hands to the door into the café, closed to keep the heat in, and notice that there is dirt under my nails, that I haven't had them done in weeks. It's not something I noticed down at Church Street but with every step I take towards a pristine-looking Dee, I begin to see my imperfections in high definition. She looks up and smiles as I hide my hands.

'Babe!' she squeals, phone still suspended in mid-air.

'Babe!' I echo back to her and I almost sound like myself again. Just five more days of my twelve days of Christmas and I will be. With this gig, I might not need all twelve.

'I've not seen you in forever.' She looks across at me, as I try to see beneath my bestie's flawless surface. She knows, right? She must. Her boyfriend and my boyfriend are best friends. Best friends tell each other everything. 'What's new?'

'Not much.' Okay, so best friends don't tell each other *everything*. 'Well, actually…'

'Omigod, darling, I wasn't even thinking…' She reaches across the table to place a hand on mine. Here it is. The empathy, or sympathy, or *something* I was waiting for. But it's misplaced. Everything is going to be okay. Everything is going to plan. 'Tell me everything.'

'Well, it happened two weeks ago last Wednesday—'

'Oh, Charlie said it happened last weekend,' Dee says, her hand still in mine. Why would Charlie think that? 'Typical Charlie. Is it as good as everyone says it is?'

Being single? Being jilted in a Christmas jumper just days before Christmas?

'The new espresso machine?' she presses on.

'Pardon?'

'Charlie said George bought you guys one of those expensive brass ones,' she grins wider still. 'Or is he spreading rumours again?'

I watch her face morph into momentary annoyance, trying to stop my own from displaying my confusion.

'I don't know,' I reply slowly, never meaning words more. I don't know about George buying us a new coffee maker. I don't know why Dee is asking about this.

'Omigod, I hope it's not a Christmas present,' she throws a perfectly manicured hand up to cover her painted lips. 'Do you know what you're getting?'

My boyfriend back? I didn't see him in the apartment this morning but I'm not even sure that matters. Not after the unpacking and the sexual tension and the advent calendars and other hints that we're still counting down to spending Christmas together. And now this. The fact that not a single soul other than George and me – and Aran and Marie – seem to know we've ever been planning to do any different. The two of them may have been oddly cautious about the gig idea but I know it's the perfect final push. I'm sure Dee will think so too.

'I'm hoping I get a little velvet box,' Dee says. Well, I'm sure she'll think it's a good idea when I've managed to get a word in edgeways.

'Earrings?' I say, trying to hide my smile as Theo forces his way into my thoughts.

'A *ring*,' Dee goes on, missing my joke completely. The thought of him rolling his eyes at my friend's optimism makes me annoyed and amused in equal measure.

'That's if Charlie can actually take a hint. You know what he's like. And lately, he's being shady about something. I'm not quite sure what's going on with him…'

'Oh really?' I ask, my intrigue piqued. Gossiping with Dee used to be a favourite pastime. It still is. Even though the time that has passed between the break-up and now has stretched on for days, *weeks*. I really thought she was avoiding me.

'Yeah, but you know how the boys are about their band news.' Dee forces another smile. 'There's always something hush-hush that's bubbling up, the next big thing.' She's right. There is always something bubbling, always another dream for them to work towards. No wonder George worried my lack of direction or dreams felt at odds with his lifestyle. For a brief time, I dreamed of working out why things with my family played out the way they did, but then my life with George got busy and full and it didn't seem to matter anymore. 'We missed you at the last gig,' Dee goes on, as I try to concentrate on what she's saying. 'Where were you? You seem a bit... distracted?'

'You know Church Street near our place?' Now it's Dee's turn to look intrigued.

'Sure, the one George's office is on?'

'Well, yes, but not on Church Street, *at* Church Street – Church Street Community Centre,' I go on, unable to hold back a giggle as I remember mine and Theo's first run-in. Dee just looks at me like I'm deranged. 'I've been volunteering there...' Dee crinkles her nose and something twists inside me. 'Well, working there, doing their social media...'

'What happened to working with luxury brands?'

'You haven't seen Theo's fleece,' I quip, forgetting who my audience is.

'Who's Theo?'

'It doesn't matter,' I say, shaking my head and thrusting my phone in her direction, open on Church Street's Instagram page. She scrolls through the account as I study her pinched expression. For some reason, it makes me want to swipe my phone back. Roger and Linda and the rest of the crew might not be as polished as the brands I used to work with – well, they're not a brand at all – but they are real people, really good people.

'You've got more followers than this.' Dee focuses on the metrics that matter.

'Yes, but when I started working on it, we only had thirty odd – now we have three thousand,' I say, not knowing why I need to prove myself to her too, prove myself to our whole damn group. 'I'm planning an event for them too… a gig.'

'For the boys?'

Well, they're grown men. Allegedly. I force my feistiness back down. I don't know why it's here right now. I'm back with Dee, talking about the band. Being normal again.

'Yes,' I say. 'It'll be great for their brand, playing for a good cause,' I go on as Dee's fingers scroll further down the feed. 'Especially at this time of year.' Convincing Dee feels like a trial run for pitching this idea to Theo; I fear he's going to be an even tougher crowd.

'I'm not sure…' Dee says slowly. 'They're pretty busy…' Her fingers stop on one photo and I can see from the way she's pinching the screen that she's zooming in. I bet it's on Theo. Or, you know, Roger's tear tattoos.

'Oh, shit.' Dee's jaw drops. *What?* I don't *think* it means he's killed anyone. Especially now I know that underneath his unapproachable exterior, he's really a big softy. 'Molly Mathers just messaged you.'

Her eyes widen and for a moment I can't place the name. Then I remember she's an Instagram influencer I crossed paths with back when I was at the PR firm. She's got a huge following and can get your brand or product in front of tens of thousands. For the right price.

'She's messaged Church Street?' I say, knowing that Dee is already tapping through to the message, that despite our secrets this kind of privacy has never existed between us.

'No, she messaged *your* account,' Dee smiles as I reach across the table to rescue my phone before she can see it. 'Omigod, if she offers you some work you won't need to—'

'I already have work,' I say, not meaning to sound so short. It's just, why does my income need to be of a certain size or at a certain place to make it count?

Still, as I swipe to Molly's message, my heart is throbbing, my mind racing with all the things she could have said. I've emailed her about projects and collaborations countless times since leaving the firm, but she's never replied. What if she is offering work? Does that mean I won't have time for the gig? A wave of disappointment washes over me before I can stop it. *@mmmmathers: Hey Babe! Long time, no speak.*

I read her opening line and instantly imagine Theo's disdain. I push it away. Yes, she sounds like a faux friend who wants something but it's a tone I know. It's a tone I've used.

Saw your new project. The community centre one. Giving back is so in right now.

My mind jolts to that stupid magazine article, the one that seemed to paint needy causes as the hottest new trend, the one I was reading before George decided I was 'needy' too.

I look up from her message to see Dee's imploring expression looking back at me. Ignoring the stone in my stomach, I read on. This is a *good* thing. Isn't it?

Volunteering is so chic. Let me know how I can help. MM x

'What did she say?'

'Oh, she just…' I begin, looking across the table to see Dee's mascara-laced lashes blinking back at me. Molly Mathers is offering to help me help others. This is amazing. This is exactly what we need. But then why does it make me feel so needy again? Like the people on Church Street need the higher echelons of society to swoop in and save them?

'I emailed her about some work and she says she might have something for me,' I lie, not knowing why I feel the need to, why I can't stomach seeing Dee's opinion of Church Street swing from indifference to endearment because of one influencer.

'Oh, that's amazing,' Dee hums. 'Now you can get stuck into some real work!'

'Yeah,' I say, not knowing why this real work suddenly feels so fake.

As I hug Dee goodbye and make my way to Church Street, I try to let go of her words. *Real work.* If she really knew the truth about the people here, if she knew the truth about me, she wouldn't have said them. She hardly knows the full story. She doesn't even know the truth about me and George.

As the church comes into view, I remember the reason I was here in the first place. The reason I'm still here. George. It just so happens that I get to help out this place in the process. That I get to fix their Christmas whilst fixing my own.

'Theo, we need to talk,' I say to his back as he reaches up to grab a rogue volleyball that has somehow got wedged on top of one of the hall's many storage units.

'Are you breaking up with me?' He spins around to look down at me as I realise I'm now just inches from his chest, the ball he's holding between us touching both our bodies.

'Would I sound so happy about it if I was?' I ask, remembering again how I had forced George into festive frivolity just moments before he said he wanted to break up. But actions speak louder than words. And his actions lately have told me that breaking up, being without me, is the last thing he wants. Seeing me here will make him sure of it.

'I don't know,' Theo says, throwing the volleyball into a scramble of people gathered at the far end of the hall. I look to the other side and see that another crowd of people, mostly children and teenagers, are gathered there too, enjoying having a place to escape to on the weekends. 'Have I worked you too hard?'

'It's gone midday and I haven't even started my shift.'

'It's a Sunday,' Theo says, with a tired smile. 'Day of rest and all that?'

But who is making sure that Theo rests? Does he ever take a day off? Go out and see friends, have fun, date? Is that why things with Lucy ended? I wasn't working hard enough for *a few months* and I get ditched. Theo is working too hard and he gets the same? Who knew that love is such a fragile thing?

Well, I did. Once. But I thought that was behind me now. But lately, the memories seem to be coming thick and fast when until recently, I hardly thought of my past at all.

'I've got a plan!' I remind myself and Theo at the same time.

'A plan?'

'To get you your volunteers.' And get me my life back. 'Before Christmas.'

'The social media account?' Theo says, brushing a hand through his beard again, bushier with each day we get closer to the centre's Christmas closure. I can tell he has more faith in my coffee making than the social accounts to bring in a crowd.

'No, an event,' I say, hoping the sheer width of my smile will have him convinced. More convinced than Aran and Marie combined. 'A gig, actually. I just thought, it's all very well and good showing what we do on the socials, but isn't it better to get people to actually step foot inside here, to meet some of the people they'll be helping?'

'A gig?' Theo repeats, still trying to get his head around the word. 'Here?'

'Where else?' I say, as we both look at the makeshift volleyball net and the makeshift coffee shop area and the makeshift, well, everything. 'Okay, so we may need to move some things around, but the band will bring all of their equipment and well, maybe we can just spruce the place up a bit...'

'Spruce?' Theo can only handle monosyllabic words right now.

'Yeah, like hang some Christmas decorations or something,' I say, only then noticing that this must be the only place that isn't green and red and glittery all over by mid-December. 'Hey, why don't...'

'Decorations are expensive, Poppy.' Theo's tone is short, his words clipped. 'Plus, it's not looking like we can open on Christmas Day anyway...' He lowers his voice to say this.

'Yes, I know but that's what this gig is about.' Mostly. 'Your eleven volunteers…' And the fact that these six band members might just save my five-year relationship.

'When?' Theo asks. Still monosyllabic. But better. More pragmatic. A question I probably should have thought about earlier. A weekend? It'll have to be to attract a crowd. Friday would be best. Before most young Londoners head out of town for Christmas. Like our friends are planning to do the following Monday. Are still planning to do, as far as I am aware. George hasn't cancelled. And no one else knows we've broken up. Not even momentarily. Which means that our moment for this gig is really only…

'Friday.'

'Which Friday?' Theo looks alarmed.

'Next Friday.' I feel a bit startled too.

'Isn't that a bit soon?' Theo asks the question we're both thinking. 'To book the band, to advertise it, to sell tickets, to *spruce*?' His upward inflection makes me sure he's never *spruced* in his life. I look into his eyes and will myself to look more confident than I feel. Yes, Theo, it *is* soon. But soon my twelve days to fix everything will be over. Christmas is so close. And I am so very close to spending this one and those to come with George and his picture-perfect family, the one that feels like a mould made for me.

'We can call it a pop-up?'

'What if we don't sell enough tickets?'

'What if we do?' I smile, praying it's wide enough to cover all the gaping holes in my plan. But I'm sure this will work. I have faith. I just need Theo to have a bit of faith in me, too.

'What if no volunteers sign up and it's all for nothing?'

I look from Theo's worry-crinkled forehead, following his gaze around the room, looking from Linda and Stanley squabbling over their cards to the volleyball game recently resumed and finally to Roger, still on his sofa but with another one of the volunteers now sitting beside him, chatting to him gently as he grunts back in return. I try to object but feel the words catching in my throat before they're fully formed. The people here deserve some Christmas cheer, to know that their presence, their very existence, isn't so temporary that they don't deserve decorations; that they don't deserve being invested in.

'Do you really think that giving this group a proper Christmas party would be "all for nothing?"' I say and I know from Theo's widening eyes fixed upon me that he is softening to the idea. 'Plus, I'm sure we'll be able to actually *sell* tickets to non-visitors too, raise some money for the centre... the social media account is thriving,' I say, reaching for my phone and turning it around to face him, pointing to the ever-growing 'followed by' figure in case thirty-going-on-seventy Theo doesn't know where to look.

'Poppy, that's amazing!' Avery appears behind Theo, making him jump. He smiles at his sister, shaking his head; he knows that she's probably been listening to us talk about the gig already, that she'll be Team Poppy all the way. But I need to make him see that though we may want different things, *we're* both on the same side. 'Three thousand followers!'

'It's great, really.' Theo says softly. 'But following an account doesn't actually mean anything,' he goes on, that righteousness in his voice again. 'Ever heard of virtue signalling?'

'Shit!' Avery whispers, dipping behind her brother as quickly as she appeared.

'Yes, it is shit,' Theo says, vindicated somehow.

'What are *they* doing here?' I follow Avery's eye-line towards a small gang of skinny girls gathered by the entrance into the hall. From their outfits, all rolled-up skirts and low-cut tops – and *thankfully* big puffer jackets so they don't die of hypothermia – I would have guessed they were in their mid-twenties. From the way that Avery is hiding behind Theo, I can tell that they must be girls from her school. But why doesn't she want to see them here?

'I'm not sure, I...' Theo begins, eyes darting from his sister to the strangers, every bit as unwelcoming as he was when I first stepped foot inside here.

'They're from my school. They're here to make fun of me,' Avery whispers under her breath to no one in particular. *They wouldn't dare.* But then I remember how mean girls can be. I watch as Avery morphs from confident seventeen-year-old to quivering twelve-year-old right before my eyes and realise that same little girl is still inside me.

'Wait here,' I turn to her, squaring my shoulders and holding my head high, becoming the big sister I wish had been around to defend me.

Striding with purpose, I walk over to the giggling gaggle ready to tell them to get the hell out if they've got nothing nice to say.

'Can I help you?' I say, hand on my hip as I register Theo's broad body next to me, the big brother to my big sister. Except, not related. That would be weird. But why? It's not like there's anything going on between us.

I look up to him now, his arms folded and game face on. I see one girl's mouth fall open whilst another two nudge each another in the side. Okay, so I guess he does look handsome in a sort of rugged, retro-wear way.

'Yes,' the leader of the pack removes her coat as she takes a step forward, a flash of red underwear just visible above her low-riding skirt. And here I thought the visible thong trend was left in the noughties.

'We're here to…' Bully Avery? Make fun of the clients? '… volunteer.'

They're what? Theo looks at me aghast and I can't help but smile.

'Yeah, like,' another chimes up, this time her rosy cheeks and crimped hair make her look her age. 'We saw your Instagram and we've got a bit of time now that exams are over and wondered whether we can, like, help out?'

'Oh, well…' Theo begins, his shock evident. 'It's not really a pop-in, pop-out…' I look at him accusingly. The last time he took a chance, he was landed with me. 'Sure,' he concedes.

Soon Theo is welcoming the five young girls further into the hall and one by one, he finds them little jobs to do, places to help out. I watch as he beckons Avery across and introduces her, arm slung around her as he did when she was first introduced to me. It shouldn't matter but I know that having a good-looking big brother will buy Avery some cool points with the girls. But as I see her helping the others get to grip with their roles, introducing them to specific visitors – pure and enthusiastic persona resumed and unapologetically herself once more – I realise she's already cool without him.

'You're going soft,' Theo arrives by my side. No, I'm not. I'm as strong and determined as I've ever been. 'Apparently they're the "meat girls" from her school.'

'You mean "mean girls"?' I turn to face him. 'Theo, did you grow up under a rock?'

'Not much better than that,' he says, not lingering on the thought long. But for some reason I want him to. And I want to be honest with him. To let somebody in.

'I know how you feel,' I begin, preparing to tell Theo about the first Christmas I spent completely alone, the one I was excited to share with my social worker, who actually really cared for me, before a family emergency meant she had to cancel. A family emergency that reminded me that, kind as she was, she was never going to be family to *me*.

'You've got twenty-four hours.' Theo's words cut across my sentence, and for a second, I'm not sure whether he didn't hear me or just doesn't want to talk about our pasts anymore, that he wants to focus on our future. Twenty-four hours? I finally register what he's saying. *What?* I had twelve days. I look back at Theo, from his eyes to his smile. 'You've got until tomorrow to sort out the gig or it's not happening.'

'Thank you, thank you, thank you!' I say, throwing my hands together, feeling more and more like Avery. It doesn't feel bad. And as she walks across the room with a massive smile on her face, it feels even better. This gig is going to be good for everyone.

'It's happening?' Avery squeals.

'If Poppy can pull it off,' Theo nods and for a brief moment my eyes linger on his. But I need to focus. If I thought twelve days to fix things with George was too little, then twenty-four hours to pull off a gig feels even less. But I need to do this. For us. Theo and Avery are both staring back at me, smiles so wide that I have to remind myself that by 'us' I mean 'me and George' not 'me and them'.

'We need to celebrate!' Avery says.

'Yes!' I agree, buoyed by her enthusiasm and an almost impossible task. But it's not impossible. I *am* going to make this happen.

'I thought you had a gig to plan?' Theo eyes me with feigned suspicion.

'It's all sorted,' I say, or at least it will be once I ask George. 'I just need to share about it on the social media…'

'Woah! Not until we've got all the logistics in place.' Theo puts his hands in the air.

'I can't do that until later tonight,' I begin, not until George and I are back in the apartment together. 'So, I guess I have time for one drink?' Avery lets out another excited squeal, something fast becoming her trademark. 'Up for it?'

'Need I remind you you're seventeen?' Theo asks her.

'Lighten up, T.' I nudge him playfully. He stiffens, but a small smile escapes.

'You guys go,' Theo says quickly, looking around the hall. 'I'll hold the fort.' A small part of me feels disappointed. I know how it feels to have to be the strong one. 'But remember, you've only got twenty-four hours to sort the gig.'

'Yes, and only one drink,' I turn to Avery, who is grinning back at me.

One drink. Then it'll be time to offer George the one thing he can't refuse.

Chapter Fourteen

Four 'One Last' Drinks

'I've always wanted to come here,' Avery says, her hungry eyes searching the light-scattered roof terrace, the only place in this area that I knew wouldn't ID her at the door. It isn't cheap, but the view is worth it. And I never used to notice the prices when I came here with George. She takes a sip of the mocktail I've just bought her. 'Do you come here a lot?'

'I used to,' I say honestly, reminding myself that my days of coming here with George are far from over, especially when I ask him what I'm planning to ask him when I get home. I take a sip of my salt-scattered margarita as a wave of nostalgia washes over me. I don't miss George paying for the drinks, not really, not even on my now-minimum wage. It's more the feeling of knowing that if I did forget my money, or forget myself for a moment, there was always someone to cover me, always someone to help me find my way back.

'With your boyfriend?' Avery probes and I realise that I've not told her any of this; that despite spending so much of the last two weeks together, I don't really know her at all, other than the fact that she's Theo's little sister and for some reason that makes me not want to answer her question. What would they think if they knew I was only here for George? And why would she be asking if I had a boyfriend? For Theo? Then again, she is a seventeen-year-old girl and from what I remember, they love gossiping about love lives. I was obsessed with my first crush. I'm *still* fighting for my first love.

'What was up with those girls today?' I say, shamefully steering the conversation onto safer ground. Avery's usually shiny face drops, the same way it had when they first arrived.

'Oh,' she stalls on the sudden change of conversation. 'They're from school.'

'Friends?' I already know this next answer too. Avery shakes her head slowly.

'One of them used to be. Lily,' she says her name quietly. 'The tall one.'

'What happened?' I'm not just trying to change the conversation now, I actually care.

'She made friends with the other girls who came in today and then we had nothing in common anymore,' Avery goes on. 'Well, *they* decided we had nothing in common anymore, I guess. I don't really have that many friends at school.'

'But you're wonderful,' I say, reaching my arm across the table to hold her hand in mine like Dee did when she was preparing to ask me about a flipping brass espresso machine. This feels more important than that. But then, I haven't ever seen this coffee maker.

'I mean it,' I go on as Avery's eyes brim with tears. She needs to be told this. 'You're smart and kind and thoughtful,' I go on, and I feel tears starting to form in my own eyes. Not because my motivational speech is giving Michelle Obama a run for her money but because they're almost the exact same words that George once said to me. After years of being shunted from family to family and school to school, never ever being able to settle, it meant the world that he invited me to settle down with him.

'And you're so beautiful,' I tell Avery, meaning the words but remembering how George had once told me all the things my heart needed to hear. 'Inside and out.'

'Thanks, Poppy,' Avery says, wiping a tear from my eye. 'That means a lot coming from someone like you.'

'Someone like me?'

'You know, like, pretty and funny and fashionable and... well, one of the cool girls.'

'You think I'm one of the cool girls?'

'Look at you! You swanned into Church Street in exactly the same way those girls did today, like you just came in on a whim. Not like me, who feels more connected to a seventy-year-old poker champ than the girls my own age.'

'Stanley or Linda?'

'Linda, obvs.' We both laugh, a warm sound that goes straight to my chest. Avery may be ten years younger than me, but she makes me feel like I can be myself – despite the fact that she clearly thinks I'm somebody else.

'Avery, you're smart,' I say, shaking my head as I do. 'But if you think I'm one of the cool girls, you ain't *that* smart.' I laugh again, sounding more like Marie did when we first met than I mean to. But I don't hate it. Somehow it feels better than *babeeeeeee*. 'You want another drink?' I look down at her empty mocktail glass.

'I thought you're meant to be planning this gig?' Her raised eyebrow makes her look like her brother. I *am* supposed to be planning the gig, but George has been coming home later and later. Another hour won't hurt. Plus, I don't really want to leave yet. 'One last drink? But this time do you think we can get away with…'

'No, you're getting another mocktail,' I say, before grinning and adding in a whisper, 'but obviously if we happen to get mixed up and you have a few sips of mine…'

'You're like the big sister I never had.'

I laugh, heading to the bar, all the while wondering whether had I had a sibling – or any family members – to encourage me, support me, George would have still become the only anchor holding me at bay.

'So, you weren't one of the Plastics?' Avery laughs over her second mock-margarita, making yet another *Mean Girls* reference that would be totally lost on Theo.

'Absolutely not.' I shake my head. 'I even had braces when I was eighteen.'

'But you're so confident, I bet you've never had to change yourself to fit in.'

I take a long sip of my drink, letting the alcohol warm me from the inside out. Changing yourself to fit in assumes that you had a fixed identity to begin with. I was floating, shapeless, before I met George and he gave me something solid to build upon.

Oh crap, I really need to get back to the apartment, to make the most of one of my twelve days. But for some reason, being here with Avery feels important too. Of all the influencers I have crossed paths with, and all the influencing I have supposedly done whilst working in PR, I don't think anyone has ever hung on my words as much as this. This kind of influence feels tangible, real, and it makes me really not want to balls it up.

'You shouldn't ever change yourself for anyone,' I say, suddenly aware of the margarita churning in my stomach at the hypocrisy of my words. But this is not what I'm doing with George, I remind myself again. These last few months have changed me and I'm just changing back, is all. I shrug away the thought. 'Did you know Theo thinks the movie is called *Meat* Girls?' I grin at the memory.

'Nothing that boy says or does surprises me,' she shakes her head. 'Did you know we both went to this spa thing one Christmas—'

'Theo going to a *spa* surprises me,' I say, loving an insight into the seemingly serious Theo, a man I've clearly just scratched the surface of.

'It was a Groupon,' Avery says as if this explains everything. 'Well, we got facials and they gave us a little card afterwards, you know, the ones telling you all the expensive products you need to buy to look fabulous?' She rolls her eyes. 'Well, Theo looks down at his skin type and says – as serious as anything – "I'm normal Larry. It actually said he was "normal/dry".' She laughs again at the memory. 'The woman's writing just made it look like an "L" and an "A". But ever since, he's been Normal Larry to me.' She glows and for some reason I feel the same glow deep inside me too.

'I would have loved a sibling. What you guys have is anything but normal.'

'We're all each other has,' Avery shrugs, before correcting herself quickly. 'Well, not *everything*, we have our parents and stuff but that's all pretty messy so, it's like… you know.' Avery looks like she's said too much, not for herself but for Theo. I get what it's like to not want everyone to know your background, to not want your past to define your future.

'One more drink?' I say, looking down at our empty glasses. Avery nods and before too long, I'm heading to the bar and returning with another cocktail and mocktail and picking up our conversation precisely where we left off. With Theo surprising me all over again.

'I can't imagine Theo in a spa,' I say, shaking my head again, smiling. I don't want to probe into their personal matters, it's not the reason I'm here. Then again, it's kind of nice to know I'm not alone. And I'm not. I have George. And very soon he'll have me again. 'I can't actually imagine him anywhere other than Church Street.' I force the conversation forward.

'Yeah, he doesn't get out much,' Avery sighs. 'But he has his reasons.'

I can't help but be intrigued.

'His dad,' Avery goes on, her face falling, once again reminding me that they're technically half-siblings despite being fully devoted to one another. 'Mine can be unreliable but Theo's has got a drinking problem and has always been a bit of a mess. And his dad's dad had a drinking problem too.' My heart lurches for Theo, for both of them. 'I think he's so determined not to be like him, to break the family cycle, that he throws himself into helping others, doing good to stop him from being bad.'

'I don't think Theo has a bad bone in his body,' I say, as Avery's eyes widen a little at the size of my grin. I try to stash it, but it's too late.

'You two…' Avery begins, a glimmer of mischief in her eyes.

'We just have a lot more in common than I thought we did,' I say, trying to get my head around the thought. Being around George made me feel like I was the only one with family issues. His are so perfect and so kind and he was generous enough to share them with me. To the point where mine kind of just became irrelevant, something I used to think about before him. And he never really asked about them. So, I never really told him.

'Your family are bonkers, too?'

'I don't really know them,' I shrug. It's something I've not said out loud for years and now I'm saying it to a seventeen-year-old girl when I'm meant to be saving the only family, the only stability, I've ever known. 'It's way too complicated.' But then again, it's so simple. They weren't there. George was; he always has been. And tonight, I'm going to make sure he knows that I can always be there *for* him without always being there *with* him.

'Like me.' Avery looks down at her glass; she looks down in more ways than one.

'You're not way too complicated,' I shake my head.

'You know Theo's type?'

His type? What is his type? Girls who volunteer and make cupcakes and then disappear without a trace? Girls like me. Well, except the cupcake bit.

'Normal Larry?' Oh, his *skin* type. 'My skin type was "combination",' she laughs again. 'I think it sums us up perfectly. He's normal, stable, safe and I'm up and down and all over the shop. I'm complicated.'

'I think there's a difference between being complicated and a combination.' I'm a combination of all of the bits of me George told me were beautiful.

'So wise,' Avery grins again. I don't think wisdom was ever in my mix. But something about being here with Avery makes me feel like it could be. Maybe an opportunity to learn from my mistakes? A little like Theo with his father? I shake the thought away again. I need to get back to George. To ask him about this gig. 'One last drink?'

This will be our fourth last drink. But something about the way Avery is opening up is making me want to stay, beckoning me into the bond she and Theo share. George is my family, I know that. But being around theirs is making me feel like a part of something too.

As I finally walk up to our apartment, I realise how tipsy I am. Thank God we started early. All I need to do is stay awake long enough to see George when he gets in. To tell him about my gig idea. To tell him to get his tight arse into Church Street. Where he and Theo can meet properly for the first time. For some reason, imagining that makes me feel funny. But then, after four margaritas on an empty stomach, everything feels a little funny.

'Where have you been?' George looks up from his spot on the sofa as soon as I stumble into the room. *Oh, he's already home.*

'Just a quick drink,' I say, and the fact that I'm trying so hard not to slur my words makes me sure that George knows this isn't true. 'Okay, well, four.'

George laughs – he used to love Drunk Poppy – but then his smile fades.

'Who with?' His eyes search from my T-shirt, rolled up at the sleeves to my ripped jeans and black trainers. I haven't got changed since coffee with Dee this morning. This hardly passes the 'show him what he's missing' dress code but it'll have to do. Plus, I won't need any of Marie's silly games now that I'm steps away from a concrete plan.

'Just a friend.' I smile as I gracelessly remove one shoe and then the other, coming to sit tentatively on the sofa beside him. He scoots up to make room for me.

'Which friend?' George asks, smiling again; is he trying to sound nonchalant?

'Someone from Church Street.'

'You're spending a lot of time there.'

I swear he scoots a little closer on the sofa.

'Yeah, it kind of sucks you in; Theo's there all the time…' I say, laughing again at the thought of our conversations this morning. Laughing again at his Normal Larry mix-up. Life may have given him reasons to be serious, but it's good to know it's given him loads to laugh about too. And lots of those laughs have happened down at Church Street.

'Is that the guy I saw you with in the churchyard?' George asks, his cute features crinkling a little as he does, his fingers inching closer to my leg, as if wanting to touch it.

'When I was "following" you?' I can't help but laugh. Something about the alcohol and the inquisitive look on his face is making me feel braver. That and the knowledge that he's not told a single soul about our so-called break-up.

'Yeah, I genuinely thought for a second you were,' George says, forcing a little laugh as if the thought is now preposterous. Even so, it feels good for this apartment to ring with giggles again, the way it always used to. He reaches his arm out along the sofa towards me now. 'But I know that you were really there to work. That this *Theo* is working you hard.' The way he says 'this Theo' feels a bit loaded. Is he *jealous*? 'What is it you do there, anyway?'

'I'm in charge of their social media,' I say. It's not technically a lie.

'That's great, Poppy,' George says, eyes darting to my lips. 'I'm proud of you.'

'And events,' I add quickly. Well, *event*. He looks even more impressed, fixing his eyes back on mine. 'In fact, I think I may have booked a gig for you.'

'For me?'

'Yeah, we're planning this amazing fundraiser and we need a band and I thought that maybe…' I go on, knowing I'm speaking too fast, that I need to slow down. But I don't have time to slow down. I don't have time to see if George is coming round. I need to *know*. 'It'll be great for the band,' I say, mustering all the confidence I can. 'Another headline gig.'

'In a community centre?' George says, and for a moment it sounds a little unkind, like he thinks he's above this kind of venue when in reality, I've followed him around every beer-stained local pub in London. Then he smiles and my worries subside. 'When is it?'

'Friday.'

'This Friday?' George exclaims. 'We'd need to rehearse, make a set list…' Except every gig I've been to has always been the same. I know his band is going from strength to strength, that usually they get booked in advance, but George always used to say he'd push it all aside for me. And something about the alcohol and Avery's admissions are making his reluctance really annoying. But he's not usually annoying. He's usually kind and sweet and doting and there for me and I'm always there for him too.

'It'd mean a lot to the people there,' I say, choosing my words carefully. 'And it'd mean a lot to me.'

George's eyes linger on mine. He looks a little blurry, like I can't quite see the man I fell in love with, but I know he's there. That we need to get past this thing.

'I know, Poppy, and I want to do this for you…' George begins. I can feel a 'but' coming. 'And I guess it *could* work, but…' But I don't want to hear it. Not when we're so close to being what we used to be.

'Molly Mathers is going to be there,' I blurt before George has time to object.

'She is?'

I look back at George like a deer in the headlights. Is she? Well, not technically. Not yet. But she did say to let her know how she could help. If her coming along gets George's band there, then needs must. I see his posture change before me as he moves a little closer.

'This Friday?' he repeats. I nod, making a mental note to message Molly ASAP.

'Okay, well, yeah… sure, sign us up. Be good to see where you've been working…'

That's the plan, I think, trying to ignore how quickly he changed his tune at the utterance of an influencer – someone who can give him something in return. *Volunteering is so chic.* Her words reverberate around my mind, making me feel uneasy somehow. But that's not what George is doing here.

'It'll be good to meet this Theo guy you keep talking about, too.'

This Theo again. And I don't keep talking about him.

'Great.' I know the gig is the right thing, even though right now, something feels wrong. George begins to yawn, stretching his arm further along the sofa until it reaches mine.

'You ready for bed?' he says, leaning in closer to me. Oh, *this* is his bed.

'Yeah, I'll see you in the morning,' I say, staggering to my feet.

'Oh, okay then…' George says, coming to stand before me. His eyes fix on mine and for a moment, I think he's going to kiss me. Then, he leans in closer and my breath catches. His face is before me, and my lips know to part and I want him so much it hurts. Then he exhales, leaning in further, kissing me on the forehead, lingering to inhale the scent of my shampoo, the way he used to do. 'Sleep well, darling,' he whispers and it feels like a dream.

As I turn to walk towards our bedroom, I can hear Theo's voice lingering in my mind: *ever heard of virtue signalling?* But I don't have time for Theo's piousness, right now. I only have twelve hours to put on a gig to secure eleven volunteers. And I only have four days left where George and I will be in the apartment together to prove to him that we belong this way.

Chapter Fifteen

Monday, 13 December

Three Tickets in Minutes

I rush into the living room. The sofa bed is reassembled and George is nowhere to be seen. But I remember last night and know it's okay. He's been busy lately and so have I.

I stall at the mantelpiece to see our two advent calendars still standing side by side, three or four more cards now propped up beside them. In quick succession I check inside; each one is still addressed to 'George and Poppy'.

Moving to the kitchen, I open my phone and message Molly Mathers for the hundredth time since I went freelance. This time I'm messaging her back. *I know it's last minute but we're hosting a gig at the community centre later this week and it would mean the world to our visitors if you were there. Side Hustle will be performing too.*

I press 'send', praying that it will be enough. Molly must be one of the last influencers of her size that I know doesn't have an assistant, who is in control of her own diary. I just hope her pre-Christmas promotional plans have margin for something meaningful.

Or something that looks meaningful, Theo's voice niggles in my mind again. But if it helps Church Street, surely, he won't mind? And George will love it when he gets there. The thought of him turning his nose up at the venue is annoyingly present too, but then I don't know for sure that's what he was doing. And each time I remember that kiss on the forehead any hint of disdain disappears. He's always had a taste for the finer things in life, but then it's not his fault, it's all he knows. And Charlie and Dee. It's almost laughable how excited she was about some state-of-the-art coffee maker George has bought. One I still haven't seen.

Searching through the cupboards, I try to locate it but can't find it anywhere. I bend to look into the cupboards and hear the front door swing open.

'What are you looking for?' George says from somewhere above me. I move to stand, feeling caught in the act. But which act, I'm not quite sure.

'The coffee maker,' I say as plainly as I can, praying I'm not ruining a surprise.

'Isn't it in the dishwasher?' he asks, moving to stand before me. Our old cafetière is there. But what about this new, shiny thing? 'You won't be needing it today, though.'

Has he found out that I work in a coffee shop? That my social media manager role is a stretch?

'One skinny flat white for you, Poptart.' I narrow my eyes at his worst pet name for me but the fact that he is using it fills me with hope. As does the fact he's thrusting a takeaway cup into my hands.

'Oh, thanks,' I say, unable to hide my confusion. I was just going to make one at Church Street. Or better still, get Ruth to make one for me as there's clearly some hidden grandma-love ingredient she slips into them that makes them taste infinitely better.

'You know, because…' George takes a sip of his own coffee, his broad body seeming to shrink before me though I'm not sure why. Because of what? 'Our tradition.' Which one? We have so many. 'The second Monday of every month… you've…' George's eyes linger on mine, 'forgotten?' Oh crap, I really had. In all of my plotting and planning I've forgotten some of the basic things I used to do for him.

'Don't worry,' George says. He needs to tell that to his face. If I didn't know any better, I'd say he looks a little insecure, which is a look I've never really seen on George before. He's looking at me like I'm a stranger to him too: busy, distant, nonchalant. But I'm not nonchalant, I'm anything but – I just forgot.

'You've got me a coffee every second Monday of our whole relationship,' he smiles softly. He takes a step towards me, putting his free hand to my side. It makes me want to hold him. 'I guess it's my turn to be a bit more thoughtful.' Thoughtful? He called it *needy*.

A few months. I remind myself of that fact over and over again; he only had doubts for a few months. All the times before that, he liked how I doted on him, how thoughtful I was. I knew it. His work and his music and my lack of work and motivation, it's all just thrown us off-balance. But here he is, readdressing it. Remembering again.

'Oh, yeah…' I say slowly as my phone begins to ring. It's Aran. 'Thanks. I actually can't stay to drink it with you though…' I force my legs to move towards the door. The plan is really working. 'I've got loads to do.'

'With Theo?' George splutters. 'And the centre and the gig?' He adds quickly, as I glance down at the phone screen flashing with Aran's name.

'You're up for it, yes?' I ask, turning around just as I reach our front door to catch George looking me up and down. He blushes.

'For you, Poppy?' George smiles and he looks like the man I knew before. 'Anything. Plus, I've really missed having you there in the crowd, cheering me on.'

'Hey!' Aran says, as I pick up the call as soon as I've stepped a foot outside. 'How are you doing?'

I figure from the fact that he's calling me at this time that he must have a specific reason for doing so. But I also know enough about Aran and Marie by now to know that they always make time to genuinely ask how people are and be willing to really listen to their reply. Thankfully, today I don't feel like I need an agony aunt.

'I'm good, thanks!' I say, retracing my journey back to Church Street as I have countless times in the past couple of weeks. Today feels nothing like that first day I made the journey, when I was lost and alone. 'How about you? Everything okay?'

'Yeah, sweet,' Aran says and his natural coolness makes me grin. I've never met anyone like him and yet the easiness and simplicity of our friendship makes me feel like I don't need to act up to impress him at all. Perhaps Marie was right about setting us up on our friend-date, maybe she knew this was exactly what we needed. 'I've been roped into arranging some of the music for our performance in Broadway,' he goes on.

'That's what you get for being a successful musician,' I laugh down the line.

'Yeah, all the big gigs flock to me,' Aran jokes back, but his tone is so warm and light that he manages to say it in a way that doesn't put himself or the choir down one bit. 'Anyway, I wondered if you'd be up for singing a solo?'

A solo? No part of me has ever wanted to be *solo*. And I'm fully intending to be in Broadway, but with George. I wonder how he'll feel about watching *me* centre stage?

'I…' I begin, not sure if this is something I want to commit to. 'I'm flattered, but…' I've only ever wanted to commit to George. For some reason, the thought of him and our friends watching me belt out a tune makes me feel unsteady, unsure of myself. 'What about Marie?'

'Oh, Marie would do it in a heartbeat,' Aran laughs again. 'But I wanted to give you an opportunity to step in first, wanted you to know you've not been overlooked.'

'Thank you,' I say, a warm glow filling me from the inside out. 'But…'

'No thank you?' Aran guesses the end of my sentence before I have the chance to say it.

'Not this time,' I confirm.

'Rejected again,' Aran says, pretending to be offended as I argue that I didn't technically reject him the first time, but as we hang up the call I smile; not one part of me regrets taking my new friend's advice to go on that ten-minute date.

@mmmmathers Babeeee. I have a thousand things on, you know how it is…

I look down at Molly's reply, as I see the spire of Church Street coming into view. Three weeks ago, I wouldn't 'know how it is' at all. But now, between the coffee shop and the choir and planning a gig of my own, I'm beginning to.

@mmmmathers But I'm at another event around there that night. Never heard of the band but I'll try and make an appearance. One photo, free of charge. Good for the brand. And it's Christmas after all x

I reread the message, looking from my photo to the noticeboard and back again. Molly hasn't exactly confirmed that she'll be here, but then, people like that need to pull out all the time. It's not like George will ever need to know the truth. Not about that. …*You Already Belong Here.* I smile at the sign, at how perfectly it captures the heart of this place. *And I belong with George*, I remind myself, savouring the last sip of the coffee he bought for me.

'You're *obsessed* with that noticeboard.'

I swing around to see Theo standing there, in a denim shirt I've never seen him wear before, rolled up at the sleeves so that I can see the strong veins on his forearms. The fact he's not wearing a coat in this cold weather tells me he's probably been setting out coffee tables or doing some other sort of heavy lifting for the community centre inside. He's holding some kind of paper in his hands, but I'm distracted by his hair: has he had it cut? My eyes search his face, weathered but somehow warmer now that I've learnt more about him from Avery.

'No, I'm not…' I say, throwing my spare hand up in the air in objection, still clutching my gift from George in my other. 'I'm just trying to find a space for something.'

'Is that right?' Theo takes a step towards me. I can't believe we met in this precise space only two and a half weeks ago. It feels like I've known him forever and yet haven't got to know enough about him at all. There's so much I want to know. 'Oh, wait… The gig?'

'The band is secured and some good advertising too,' I say, proudly. 'I told you I'd be able to pull it off.'

For you, Poppy. Anything. I savour George's words with my final sip of his coffee. But then, he did take a bit of convincing and it was the message from Molly that seemed to sway it. I push the thought away, because it really doesn't matter what convinced him, it's just brilliant that he is on board, that he's finally starting to be convinced by me, too.

Theo brushes past me, moving over to my once-nemesis of a noticeboard, pressing the paper in his hands up to it and pinning it into the cork. He takes a step back to look at it. *The Gig That Keeps on Giving. Join us for fun and fundraising this Friday. Details to come.* But how did he even know it would be happening? I've only just told him about it.

'I didn't doubt you for a second.'

'I think that's the last of them,' Ruth smiles, as she hands me what must be my tenth coffee of the day. Between the busyness of the coffee shop and uploading our events page, I've needed them. The daylight hours have drifted into evening and now it's almost time to call it a night. But it's all set.

I've been messaging George back and forth about the logistics all day, each of his replies quicker and warmer than the last. It reminds me of the first time we started messaging, when the initial caution of dating a stranger wanes and only excitement and anticipation are left in their place. I feel that same anticipation today.

'Theodore,' Ruth looks up from scanning the Church Street Instagram page to see him standing on the other side of the makeshift service bar. Turns out she's already on social media too; she got it to keep in touch with her grandchildren.

'Ruth,' Theo nods back at her and I swear I see the seventy-nine-year-old swoon. 'Popstar,' he then smirks at me for the hundredth time today. We decided to keep the gig under wraps until it was time for the centre to close up, knowing that there'd be way too much excitement to keep the multifaceted temperaments of this place at bay all day.

'Larry,' I nod back to him and Theo narrows his eyes immediately.

'I knew I shouldn't let you two go out together,' he says, but with such a soft smile that I know he doesn't mean it. Avery has been raving about our drinks since she arrived here after school and I told her that the gig will be happening. She thinks Lily and the other girls will be right in the front row. The girls at her school have actually heard of Side Hustle. Unlike Molly Mathers. Not that I'm going to tell George that. 'Ready to tell everyone?'

'It's all set, so feel free,' I smile back at him, as Ruth looks at me mischievously. I told her about the gig earlier but made her swear to keep it a secret, a surprise for the rest of them.

'Off you go then,' Theo says, as I make my way to the other side of the counter.

'You tell them,' I say, shaking my head at speed.

'It's *your* fundraiser,' Theo smiles, like he is happy for me to take all the glory.

'It's *your* community centre,' I say back, but the words feel forced, like I'm trying to put some distance between us. This gig will help them raise some money and raise the profile of this place, secure some volunteers. But for me, it's about George. It's always been about George. After we speed over our bump in the road, I won't be able to look back. Not until after Christmas anyway. Maybe not even then. Not if George wants me cheering him on at every one of his gigs again. His interests have a habit of splurging into the space for mine.

'It's not *mine*.' Theo shakes his head quickly. Technically, he just works here, employed by the local council or the local church or something. But I know Theo isn't saying this, he's saying that it's *ours*, that community runs to the very core of this place.

'Let's tell them together.' He smiles again, putting a broad hand to my back; it makes me feel strong. 'Guys!' Theo addresses the room and all but a few faces, still stubbornly looking at their cards, look up at him. 'We've got an exciting announcement to make. Poppy?' Theo's hand pushes me forward, the clients now gathered in a circle.

'This place is amazing,' I begin, not knowing why I feel emotional. Maybe because after this gig, I know my days here will be numbered. 'And we want more people to get to experience it, both volunteers and visitors, and so we thought we'd throw a…'

'This 'bout the gig?' Stanley shouts from across the ring of people.

'The one happening on Friday?' Linda nods, next to him, encouraging him on.

'Where Side Hustle are playing?' Roger grunts. Now, I love George to pieces, I would follow him anywhere, but there is *no way* that Roger knows about his band.

'How do you all…?' I begin, shaking my head.

'Well, there's t' poster on t' board t' begin with…' Stanley says again.

'You actually *read* that?' Theo asks, incredulous. I look to him like *I told you so*.

'And Ruth told us everything!' Linda laughs. I whip around to look at her.

'What?' She looks at me sheepishly. 'I literally get *paid* to gossip,' she laughs.

'What happens at Church Street is known by the whole of Church Street,' Theo shrugs, apologetically. So much for the big reveal. 'Now, let's make sure it doesn't *stay* at Church Street,' he continues, but he says so cautiously. Like this safe place is about to be invaded by influencers, fancy band-boys and virtue signallers. But he trusts me. Oh crap, he really trusts me. So this had better work.

'Time to set the event page live!' Theo says, nodding down at my phone. I have another message from George, promising he'll be there, that everything will be okay. And despite a rocky couple of weeks, we've got half a decade of trust to build upon.

'And it's live!' I say, as a number of people cheer. Roger doesn't, he just grunts a little louder, but I can tell from the glimmer in his eye that he's excited. And I am too. Flicking through to Church Street's social media account, I share the link before one, two, *three* notifications vibrate through my phone. 'We've sold three tickets already.'

'Three tickets in minutes,' Theo says, smiling down at me. 'I'd love to see what you can do with the next three days.'

The next three days. I have one Friday, Sunday and Monday until George and I are meant to be heading off to the Cotswolds for our couples' getaway. But hopefully this Friday, this gig, will be all the time I need to make him admit his mistake.

'Fancy a drink to celebrate?' Theo asks as my phone vibrates in my hands.

'I've already had, like, ten coffees,' I laugh, which accounts for some of my shakes.

'I meant a *drink* drink,' he says slowly. 'Like, not at Church Street.' Like a date? But no, this isn't a date. This is just two friends celebrating a mutually beneficial success. 'I'll need to stay late to close up, prepare some stuff for tomorrow,' he goes on. 'But I'll be able to head out of here around ten?'

Ten? Theo really does work too hard. And probably *really* needs this drink. I wonder when he last let himself enjoy something outside of this place. But if I want to steal another moment with George before he's up and off to the office tomorrow morning, I need to head home way before then. That said, he has been coming home later and later. And I still saw him after the drinks last night.

'Fine,' I say as Theo's smile spreads across his face. 'You've got one hour for a drink, tops,' I tease, remembering again Avery's words about how Theo rarely drinks. Is this him pushing himself out of his comfort zone? Like I've been trying to do for George all this time?

'Hmmm,' Theo says, dimples deepening. 'Let's see if we can make that two.'

Chapter Sixteen

Two Hours with Theo

Theo pushes open the door into a local pub, gesturing for me to walk through it in front of him. It's an old-school gesture that is perfectly at place in this old-man pub. As we walk into the room, no fewer than seven sets of eyes stare back at me. We're both a good fifty years younger than everyone here. And now I make up fifty per cent of the females present. This place is a far cry from the rooftop bar I took Avery to yesterday, the chic (if not a little pretentious) places that George and our group call our locals. This pub is a real local. Literally a three-minute walk from Church Street. And the way two or three of the elderly gentlemen sat drinking here nod in Theo's direction tells me that they could be ex-clients. That even when Theo is 'off', he's never really off. That the place is a part of him.

'What can I get for you?' Theo leads us to the bar and leans one elbow against it. In the low light he has that movie-magic, bad-boy look about him, the rough-and-ready charm. 'A rosé for the lady?' Then I remember, there's nothing bad about him.

'I'll take a red,' I smile back at him. I never drink red wine on dates with George. My lips get stained and my tongue goes black within moments. But this isn't a date. At all.

'Great, find us a seat and I'll bring them over.'

I look around the dusty, dim pub, past the two men sitting at a comfortable distance away from each other by the bar and over to a round table in the back corner of the room. Three weeks ago, I would have taken one look at this place and walked right back out of it. But as I walk past the two guys, each of them turns to give me a warm smile and I feel at home.

Peeling off my puffer jacket, I let the open fire soothe me, reminding me of mine and George's fake fire at home and the cards written to a very real couple on top of the mantelpiece. Then I see Theo walking over to me, moving slowly but confidently across the room, his hair cut short but his unshaven chin still strong and stubbled.

'Thanks,' I grin back at him as he takes one of the misshapen armchairs beside me. I watch as he takes a sip of his half pint and note his self-control. Now I know why it's there.

'I love this place.' Theo smiles around the room, taking his own jacket off, his denim shirt riding up a little as he does. I force my eyes to stay on his face.

'I didn't think you got out much.'

'Yes, I get it. You think I live at Church Street…' Theo says, shaking his head at what he thinks is banter. I actually wasn't joking this time.

'No, it was just something Avery said last night,' I say, unsure as to how much I can repeat here, how much of our conversation was meant to be confidential.

'Oh yeah?' Theo crinkles his brow, fingers fiddling with his folded sleeve.

'Yeah, just something about your dad,' I say quietly. 'Mine was a class act too,' I add, rolling my eyes, before I can stop myself. I don't want to talk about my dad. I haven't got all that much to say, I didn't know him. But something about Theo's rawness and the fact I'm probing at it makes me want to tell him that my life isn't as perfect as I make out.

'He's a good guy,' Theo objects, so good himself that he's unable to speak badly of anyone. 'He's just got his issues.'

'Haven't we all?' I take a sip of my wine, watching Theo's eyes scan across my lips.

'Go on, then.' Theo swigs his beer, stretching an arm along the back of his chair, his fingers lingering on the edge of my own. 'What are my issues?'

'You can't ask me that.' I laugh across my glass. Trust Theo to be so blunt.

'I just did,' he says, his teasing tone making me feel warm. Or maybe it's the fire.

'You work too much,' I say. It feels like the obvious answer. I can't really tell him that I think he judges people too quickly when I evidently do the same. Or at least, I *did*.

'You sound like Lucy,' Theo grumbles, his standard seriousness resumed.

'Is that why you guys broke up?'

'One of the reasons,' he admits. 'But I'm just really passionate about what I do.'

I look at him, his arms folded but his shirtsleeves messy. He may look like he's got his guard high, but I can tell that for him, just being here shows a willingness to open up.

'That's great,' I say, moving a hand to rest on his before remembering he's not George. It's the kind of encouragement I've given to George every day since I met him, telling him that I don't just think he can make his band dreams become a reality but that I *know* it. 'It's great to be passionate about something,' I tell Theo, reminding myself too.

'I think Lucy wanted me to be a bit more passionate about her.'

'I bet if you were, she'd run a mile,' I say, not meaning to laugh. It's just, I know what it's like to be passionate about a person. At least Theo is passionate about helping them.

'What do you mean?'

'Sometimes people want what they can't have,' I say, as if this wisdom is my own and not just recycling what Marie said to me. Before she distanced herself from my 'show him what he's missing' plans. Theo's eyes search me again. I wish I knew what he was thinking. But unlike George, who I can read like a book, Theo seems more complex, deeper somehow. A combination. Despite his *Normal Larry* type.

'I think being passionate about what you do is a good thing,' I say again, reminding myself that this is one of the very many things I love about George.

'Even when it gets in the way of other things?'

'Even then,' I nod. 'The people you love should love what you're passionate about, shouldn't stand in the way…' But maybe that love and support should run both ways? I guess I never found out what made me tick, other than just George. It's what I was trying to work out just before he broke up with me. 'I wish I was passionate about something.'

'You're joking!' Theo looks at me like I've just said something crazy. Is this the part where he tells me that having a cause or a calling is akin to having an albatross around your neck, a heavy burden that only a select few can carry?

'Poppy, you have more passion in your little finger than anyone I've ever met.'

'Now *you're* joking.' My mouth hangs open. I close it quickly. The red wine stains.

'I'm not.' He shakes his head, still looking at me like I'm crazy – but in a kind of endearing way. 'I've never known someone throw themselves into things the way you do,' he goes on. 'You half-heartedly offer to volunteer,' he says and I wince, remembering again how I met him amid George's stalker allegations. 'Then before you know it, you're here every day.' *You're always here*: the words of our break-up burn like a scar. But Theo doesn't look unhappy about that. 'You turn your hand to social media and within moments, it's thriving. You decide to plan a gig and in twenty-four hours, it's all anyone can talk about,' He goes on, his face becoming more and more animated as he does.

I shrug. Being good at social media seems pretty small compared to heading up a community centre or making it in a band.

'But it's more than that,' Theo goes on. 'The way you speak to Roger, the way you open up even the most closed-off people. The way you gossip with Ruth and people who are nothing like you, like they could be your best friends. The way you've taken Avery under your wing and I've seen her confidence soar. You hum with passion, Poppy,' he grins again. 'You sing with it, too.' He laughs and I know he's thinking of my custard cream microphone.

'I guess I never thought of it like that,' I say, part of me wishing I could tell Theo the truth; that the only reason I threw myself into any of this is because I'm passionate about *George*. Another part of me, though, wants to stay silent so Theo will carry on looking at me like this.

'Do you want to know what your issue is?' Theo asks.

Not really. I'm already painfully aware of my issues. I've been trying to forget about them, shake them off and bury them in the past for years...

'You need to believe in yourself more,' Theo says, reaching for my hand and holding it in his for a moment. It's strange and it's awkward but I don't really want it to stop.

'Last orders!' A woman behind the bar rings a large bell. She needn't have, seeing as her shout was far louder than the chimes. I pull my hand away from Theo's in shock.

'What time is it?' I ask, trying to rally through the awkwardness. I wonder whether Theo feels it too.

'Just before midnight.'

'Oh crap, I was only going to stay for an hour!' I say, wondering where in all of our talking and teasing two hours have gone.

'Best get home before you turn into a pumpkin...'

'I'm not sure the princess turns into a pumpkin,' I say, gathering my coat and my thoughts, and getting to my feet. I need to head home to George. I look back to Theo.

'Who said you were the princess?' Theo mutters, following me to the door.

Nice to know that whatever magic has just brimmed between us has gone. I don't have time for it. I have to get home and make sure George and I get the fairy-tale ending we deserve.

Chapter Seventeen

Tuesday, 14 December

One 'Last Night' with George

I run up the stairs to our apartment, cursing this evening with every step I take. Sure, being with Theo was fun. Lovely, even. Especially after today. But I need to keep my focus. I hope this gig will help the community centre; I do. Still, I am so close to making things right with George, being able to pick up our relationship right where we left off. I can't get distracted now. This gig is my last opportunity to fix everything before Christmas.

As I come to our front door, I try to recall the next part of my plan. The plan that stopped me from completely breaking down after our break-up. The plan Marie prompted but that I've run with at a thousand miles per hour since then. But I don't have any more ideas. All I have is this gig. I push open the door into our apartment, praying that George is still up, that he isn't already curled up asleep on the sofa bed when, by now, he's meant to be back in our bed with me.

The living room is dark as I pace across the floor, but as I get closer to the sofa bed, I see that the spot where George has been sleeping for weeks now is empty. Is he still out? But where? Another gig? I don't know whether to be disappointed that he's not here or relieved that I haven't wasted another evening when he would have been here in the apartment with me before we're meant to be moving out. I decide to set my alarm for six in the morning and try to catch him before he leaves for the office, maybe even walk with him there.

Pushing open the door into our bedroom, stumbling out of my shoes, I strip down to my underwear. Even after ten coffees – eleven, if you count the one from George – I am too exhausted by today to waste time finding my pyjamas. Especially if I'm setting my alarm for six. Peeling back the duvet, I climb into bed, preparing myself for the feel of cold sheets against my naked skin. Instead, I feel heat and a breathing body and a warm hand reaching for me.

'Poppy, is that you?' I hear George whisper beside me, his breath heavy and hot. George is here. In my bed. Next to me. He's exactly where he belongs. It actually *worked*.

'Who else would it be?' He's still half asleep. I feel like I'm dreaming.

'I'm sorry, I didn't know if you were coming back tonight,' George says, and my heart skips a beat. So, he thought the whole bed was empty, not just the side meant for him?

'It's okay,' I say, trying to keep my voice measured. He probably won't even remember this tomorrow. 'I'll sleep on the sofa tonight.' But as I reach for my phone and move to get out of bed, George grabs my hand and it stops me in my tracks.

'It's okay,' he whispers, his hand still on mine when less than an hour ago, it was Theo's fingers touching me. But this, being here with George, is right. 'You can sleep here.'

I wait for him to roll out of bed, but he simply takes the phone out of my hand and puts it on the bedside table so that he's able to hold both of my hands in his. 'Stay with me.'

I lie back down, covering myself with the duvet again as I feel George by my side. This is the most natural thing of all. George's hand reaches for my skin, moving over my stomach, as his body shapes itself around mine. We're the perfect fit. Always have been; always will be.

Every moment, every move, with you ever more, the lyrics he wrote about me circle my mind as his breath falls heavy and he holds himself above me, leaning down to draw me into him. He kisses me harder, longer, until every inch of me opens up to him all over again.

Afterwards, he wraps himself around me, his breath falling heavier still. I can feel his chest rise and fall against my back as I force my breathing to match his, to rest into this moment, to trust that this is not a dream. My eyes grow heavy and my heart flutters lightly, as I finally fold back into being one half of George and Poppy. And it feels as easy as breathing.

The loud hum of my phone chattering against the bedside table shocks me awake. It's still dark outside. I reach for my phone but can't find it and stretch in the other direction only to find George still lying by my side. *He's still here, next to me. He asked me to stay with him.* Then, he opens his eyes, all soft and sleepy, and fixes them on me.

'Poppy?' he whispers. He looks surprised to see me, but pleasantly so.

'Don't worry, it's early,' I whisper back, as George tries and fails to fight his sleep. I reach across his naked body and grab my phone from his side of the bedside table.

'Just switching off my alarm,' I say, but his eyes are already closed again. I feel for my phone in the dark, the backlight blaring bright as I struggle to swipe the noise of my alarm away. Low vibrations continue to clatter on his bedside table but there's no alarm icon on the phone in my hands. Just a message.

Last night was fun, baby. Thanks for the espresso machine. It's the perfect gift…

I drop the phone from my hands like a piece of red-hot coal. I can see my own phone alarm still flashing bright from George's bedside table. Before he can wake up again, I silence the alarm, but nothing can stop the alarm bells going off in my mind.

It was George's phone I was holding. George's phone that I've just dropped. George's phone that just got a message from someone who calls him *baby*. Someone he knows well enough to buy a gift for and discuss with his best friend.

I look at his sleeping body, stirring beside me, and I don't know whether to hit him awake, scream at him, demand answers or simply cry. But I can't do anything. Can't move. Can't comprehend what this could mean.

I thought the plan was working. I thought it was working so well that I wouldn't even need the last three of my twelve precious days to win him back. That all it would take was one last push, one last gig. When in reality, I've just unknowingly spent one last night with my one true love.

Chapter Eighteen

Wednesday, 15 December

I wake up and instantly wish I hadn't. Everything hurts. Just like it has every time I've woken up and fallen back to sleep since it happened. After hearing George stir the morning after the night before, the sound of him grabbing his phone – no doubt reading *that message* – and then fumbling as he headed out into the living room, I have floated between restlessness and unconsciousness. I never thought George would cheat on me. Except he isn't cheating, is he? Because we're not together. Unless things were happening between them before? It's hardly a long time since we broke up. It's three weeks to the day. To the day that George changed my world forever. To the day when he said something so unfounded and unexpected that I thought it could never stick. So unfounded that I supercharged my whole routine to make him realise it was the wrong thing to do. So unexpected that I took every last scrap of affection he had for me as a sign.

The moment in the closet, hidden away. That his mum and our friends knew nothing about our break-up. The kiss on the forehead. The flat white he bought me on the second Monday of the month.

The body that wrapped around me just the night before last. All moments so personal, so private, so precious that I assumed they were a secret just for us, a promise of all the stolen moments to come. I didn't think he was hiding *me* from someone else. I turn over to see his empty side of the bed and instantly feel sick.

Pain courses through my body, from my toes to my chest. The place where he was lying, the sheets that are still crumpled are evidence that our last night together was real. That all those moments were real. That they once meant something. I've had twenty nights of sleeping in this bed without him. I didn't think I could stomach one. And yet, something about meeting Marie, formulating a plan, made me feel purposeful, *passionate*.

I remember Theo's words from our drink together, just before my night with George. If George isn't my true love, if he's not going to give me another chance before Christmas, I'm not sure I've got the strength to start again. It took everything I had the last time.

I reach for my phone, remembering again what I saw the last time I did: *Last night was fun, baby…* How could I have got it all wrong?

I haven't crossed paths with George since he was here in this bed. I mean, why would we? It isn't one of our twelve days together. Not that he knew that's what they were, that there was anything of note about them other than the fact that they were one step closer to his life without me. And I've not had the energy to leave the space where he left me. Being with him had given me my identity. Winning him back had given me purpose. And now?

Now I feel like I have neither.

Poppy, are you okay? We missed you at practice last night. I read Aran's message, and the memory of our date and the choir and all the lengths I've gone to for George – the literal lengths I've swum – flood through my mind, swimming in my stomach.

Ghost of Christmas Future, checking in. How's it going? I flick to Marie's words, not knowing whether to hold them to my chest or fling my phone across the room. If I hadn't bumped into her that day at the market, would I even be in this position right now? Well, yes. George had already dumped me. All her plan did was postpone my broken heart. That, and made me cook and join the choir and rock up to a community centre on Church Street.

Popstar, you coming in today?

Pops, where are you?

Poppy, are you okay?

Poppy, please call me back.

I scroll through Theo's messages, each one making me feel worse. No, I'm not okay. Not in the slightest. I might have fooled him for a second that I was passionate, that I'm good at my job, good with people, that I'm a good role model for his little sister. That I'm someone he can trust. I thought I had been fooling George too. When I was only fooling myself.

I pull the covers over me, hiding in the safety of the sheets. But nothing feels safe anymore. George was my safe place. That was, until his breaking up with me caught me by surprise. But is it really that shocking? Perhaps the biggest shock was that he put up with me for five years. It's longer than anyone else has managed, family included. George saved me for a moment. He was my partner, my team. He shared his family with me. Now I have to start over again, go it alone again. And I'm not quite sure I've got the energy to do it all again.

Poppy, I really need to know if you're okay. Is it things with the gig?

I read Theo's words, the ones that have just forced their way onto my screen, lighting up the darkness I've created in my cover-cocoon. Shit, the gig! There is no way I can face that now. No way I can accept George's last-ditch attempt at charity. I just never thought the charity case would be me. I may have followed him around the country, stood there swaying at too many gigs to number, but I draw the line at standing there, looking up at him and Charlie when I know they've been hiding *coffee girl* from me all this time.

Dee, I really need to see you. I send the message. She clearly had no idea that George was calling anyone other than me 'babe'. I watch as one tick turns to two. Then I wait a little longer for the three dots to appear underneath my message, telling me she's penning exactly what I need to hear. But they don't come. Does she know the truth by now? Has she finally taken sides? I know our friendship has always floated on the surface but she's the closest I've got to a best friend – other than George. The least she could do is tell me the truth to my face.

Oh crap, Theo is calling me now. I look down at the phone in my hand, my mind jolting to us sharing a drink together on Monday night. Back when we were celebrating selling three tickets to our gig. The least I can do is tell him that I won't be there to make it happen. Face to face. That's if George still wants to do *anything* for me, now that he and his coffee cutie are exchanging gifts. Maybe I should have known that George's passion would stretch to buying someone gifts after just a few short weeks? He's always been passionate. And he used to like that I was passionate too, supporting him in his work, at his gigs. Oh God, is coffee girl going to be at the gig as well? I can't do this. None of it. Not the gig. Not the trip. Not the pretending to be perfect for George when in reality, he doesn't give a shit.

And nor do I. I don't give a shit when I drag myself out of bed. I don't give one when I make my way out of the house without a scrap of make-up on or without showering for the first time since the start of the week. I don't give one as I storm past concerned-looking strangers on my walk to Church Street. I don't give any as I walk past the noticeboard to see the large poster about the gig layered over the centre of the sign so that it simply reads: *You Belong*. I don't belong here. The only place I've ever felt like I belonged is with George.

Before entering the building, I pull out my phone and swipe to Church Street's social media account to find we have one hundred and seventy new followers, at least twenty new messages. But for all the '*cool*' and '*love this*' messages, Theo still doesn't have the eleven volunteer sign-ups he needs to open on Christmas Day. How the hell are over three thousand people following this place and yet only one per cent of those people have bothered to step foot inside? Maybe Theo is right. It's all appearances, no substance.

A little like things with George. I swipe to my latest message from
Molly Mathers and start to type.

I might not be there on Friday. You'll still be able to pop in, right? It takes
all my strength not to cry at the memory of Theo's first warning to
me: it's not really a pop-in, pop-out situation. Soon, I'm going to
be the next in a line of people to let him down.

But that's life, isn't it? I've been let down enough too.

'Popstar!' Linda shouts as soon as I walk into the hall, Stanley
smiles beside her. I nod, biting my lip, trying to keep my emotion
at bay. Despite what Theo says, today *is* a pop-in, pop-out situation.
I just need to tell him that the gig can still happen, but I won't be
there. But something tells me this was just George's final attempt to
be there for me, to soften the blow of the break-up. That without a
link to this place, this will be just another venue to him. One he's
already turned his nose up at. Still, that's not my problem. All I
did was come up with the idea, anyone can do that.

'Cupcake,' Roger nods and all I want to do is sit alongside him
in silence, to shed a thousand tattooed teardrops beside someone
who understands. Who understands what it's like to lose family, to
lose themselves. But no, I'm here for one reason only.

'Poppy!' Avery bounds up to me and I feel the tears gathering in
my lashes. I force them back down. Avery doesn't need my negativ-
ity – or any of my so-called influence for that matter. 'Lily came,'
she beams back at me, and I look across the room to see Avery's
tall school friend waving to both of us from across the room. So,
that's one good thing that's come out of our social media. But the
rest, the rest is going to be a massive let down.

@mmmmathers Sorry, babe. Don't really want to risk going to a place like that without knowing there'll be someone like me there. Rain check?

What does she mean, *risk*? I look to Roger, his tattooed cheeks and weathered hands looking like they could cause some serious damage, but I know the only one he's damaged lately is himself. But he's trying, he's changing. Coming as he is, but not staying as he is. And what does she mean *someone like me*? That she and I are alike? Someone who eats fifty-pound breakfasts and drinks through the equivalent of Church Street's budget on a wild night out?

I feel tears of rage starting to prickle in my eyes. I've tried to be everything George and Dee and my friends, *his* friends, want me to be. For five years. And it's isn't enough. It's never been enough. I hate to think what they'd make of the people here at the community centre. Broken, messy, damaged. Damaged goods like me; passed around from house to house for as long as I can remember and never once feeling at home. And there was no way I could be 'returned to sender' seeing as my parents didn't *want* to be found.

'Poppy,' Theo says my name softly behind me and I turn to see him standing there. I've missed two of my shifts here, not been in touch since we last said goodbye and now, I'm here to say goodbye to him, this place, this gig. But he's just smiling, reaching an arm out to me softly. And it's enough. It's enough to make me break into a thousand pieces.

The tears fall, my shoulders shake, and I feel like I'm exactly where I was three weeks ago, standing in that Christmas market listening to the 'Twelve Days of Christmas' before Marie found me. Except this is worse. This time, I have no plans, no time. No time to force a different conclusion than the one I have to face.

'I've ruined everything,' I sob and before I know it, Theo's broad arms are around me and I'm nestled in his chest, crying into his fleece. And it's really flipping warm.

'Let us help you fix it.'

Let us help you fix it. Theo's words roll around my mind as he steers me to a safe place at the back of the hall, all the while held under his arm. He didn't say, *let me fix it.* He said, let me *help you* fix it. Which is probably what makes this place so special.

Coming to stand under the stained-glass angel, I see the haphazard photographs hanging from the wall and turn to see the tapestry of individuals held up, held together by this place. It's the kind of place that might have had the power to keep my family together.

'Poppy,' Theo says, again, holding me close. Only one or two heads are looking in our direction, the rest have resumed playing cards and eating hot meals and drinking hot drinks. They've all seen enough drama in their lives not to make a big deal of my breakdown now. 'What's this about? The gig? Is it too stressful?' He looks concerned, not letting me go.

'Kind of,' I sigh. 'It's everything. It's a long story…'

'I've got time,' Theo says, as we hear a massive crash from the back of the hall. Some of the kids are playing, pulling out a chair for each other at the exact moment they go to sit down, allowing the other to fall. They've either finished school or sacked it off but either way, Theo won't turn them away. Theo doesn't have time for me. He has tens of people depending on him. And only ten days until Christmas Day. But here he is, wasting his time with me.

'It's just…' I begin again and so do the tears. I'm not sure they've ever stopped. 'You know you said your plans for Christmas were uncertain?'

Theo nods, every part of him painfully aware of this fact.

'Well, mine were too. Still are. Ever since I met you.'

Theo looks at me with wide eyes, his arm still holding me protectively, and suddenly I feel embarrassed by the words. I didn't mean meeting *Theo* had an effect on my plans…

'Your trip to the Cotswolds?' he asks, holding me closer still.

'And the rest,' I say, not meaning to sound as dramatic as I feel. 'It felt like everything was up in the air, like confetti…' I say, smiling at the memory of all of the moments and nearlys and maybes I'd fabricated with George, before the heaviness in my legs reminds me that things weren't like confetti at all. 'Turns out it was something else.'

'No confetti?' Theo asks, brows twisted in concern, his face open like a window when only three weeks ago, it was so guarded and closed.

'More like shrapnel.'

'Well, how can we help?' he says, looking around the room as his hand on my back begins stroking back and forth.

'You've already done enough,' I whisper, forcing a smile. Theo may have thought this place was using me, paying me minimum wage, not paying me for handling the social media at all, when in fact, it is me who was using them all along.

'No, seriously, Poppy.' Theo gazes into my eyes earnestly, coming to stand in front of me, his back to the room. The intensity of his stare makes me inch back until that same damn photo frame is jutting into my back and then falling to the floor.

'Thanks to you, we actually have a chance of opening this place on Christmas Day,' Theo goes on.

I bend to pick up the photo frame, noticing the same figure that had caught my eye last week. The man. Early fifties. Laugher lines. Broad shoulders. The one I thought I recognised, *remembered*, from somewhere.

'This gig is going to make sure of it. I can feel it.'

With shaking hands, I take the photo and turn to hook it back onto the wall, in its rightful place. The wall of people who managed to get back onto their own two feet. When it's taking all my strength not to fall to the ground. Even if I do remember him, even if we do share a past, he's moved forward now and it's not like he ever came looking for me.

'Is it all set for Friday?' Theo goes on. 'Only you could pull something like this off in the space of a week.' I don't know if he means it or he's just saying it to be nice but it's making me feel so much worse. I've exploited my connections. Connections that I've spent years cultivating, maybe even manipulating. Connections that won't give a crap about this place if I'm not here to cheer them on at the end of the week.

Someone like me. Molly Mather's words jut into my side again, just like that damn photo. The only reason I could possibly recognise someone in that photograph is because I'm a lot less like Molly Mathers and a lot more like the people in this church hall.

I'm someone like *them*.

'Yeah, about the gig…' I begin, tears still making tracks down my face. 'I need to tell you something about…' I go on but notice that something has piqued Theo's attention from across the room. I follow his gaze to see he's looking at a tall, broad figure that has just walked into the room. Early fifties. Laugher lines. Broad shoulders. The man from the photo.

'Poppy,' Theo looks from the man back to me, confusion in his eyes. 'I just need to go and chat to…' His voice drifts off, a small smile turning up the corners of his mouth. 'Feel free to come with me or you know… I'll be back soon.'

I nod, lame and mute. I couldn't follow Theo over to the other side of the hall if I tried. I came here today for one reason: to tell Theo that I can't be there at the gig, that once George finds out the truth about Molly Mathers not being there, it might not even happen. But now, I can't think straight.

I watch as Theo greets the man from the photo, wrapping him in a big bear hug, like they are long-lost friends. But if he is who I think he is, Theo has no idea just how long-lost he's been. The hairs on my arms stand up on end and I know it has nothing to do with the weather outside. My heart races, my vision blurs. This can't be happening. *Can it?*

'Sorry about that,' Theo says, practically humming with happiness as he reappears before he sees the stray tears on my face and remembers I was just having a breakdown.

'Who was…?' I begin, the rest of my sentence escapes me.

'That guy's one of our old visitors here,' Theo says, with a grin. 'He's come back to volunteer.' He reaches a hand towards me, like it's a bit weird that we're not touching. I want to ask what his name is, but I can't bring myself to say the words. 'Because of you.'

'Because of me?' I croak, heart hammering in my chest. This is too much. Too much of my past. When, thanks to Monday night, my future feels completely out of reach.

'Yeah, he saw the Instagram page,' Theo says, dumbfounded, like, given that a fifty-year-old man is on social media that he ought to consider using it more regularly himself – and not just to find my profile. 'And guess what?'

I couldn't possibly. Not after today.

'He's going to volunteer on Christmas Day!' Theo is beaming now. 'That's eight volunteers now. Only three more to go.'

And only three more of my twelve days with George to go, too. Not that it matters now. Not that any of it matters now. I look to Theo, preparing to tell him the truth about the gig; that it was only about one thing and that it really doesn't matter now. Except, looking back at him, his head tilted, his eyes exploring my expression, trying to make sense of me like a puzzle he can't work out but may even be enjoying, I just can't. This place matters. The people inside and the ones that it's helped out now coming back to help others, they matter.

'Anyway, what did you want to tell me about the gig?' Theo asks.

He matters, too.

'Nothing, it's…' I begin. It has to happen. And George needs to be there. So, Molly Mathers needs to be there. Which means, I need to be there too. 'It's all good.'

'Great,' Theo says, looking from me to the man across the room again. I can't even hold his eye contact, fearful of who he is and what it might mean. 'And you know your Christmas plans, the Cotswolds trip?' he asks and the highs and lows of the past few days come rushing in at once. 'You're always welcome to spend Christmas here with us.'

'You trying to recruit me again?'

'No,' Theo says softly, taking another step towards me. 'Even if we don't get the volunteers we need to open, you can still spend Christmas with *me.*'

'Oh, I…' I begin, for some reason needing to catch my breath. Theo's kind eyes are looking back at me and then to the person he was just talking to across the room.

'I'm a big fan of yours,' Theo says and I take a step back, too overwhelmed by the last few days, by the man standing at the other end of the hall, to even comprehend what he's saying. This is too much. All of it. I just need everything to stop. To work out my next move. 'And so are a lot of other people, apparently,' Theo goes on and my heart stops still. 'Our latest volunteer wants to meet the smart woman behind the social media…'

Theo's smile spreads wide across his face and I know he's trying to make me feel better, but everything is so confusing right now. My life with George is over and my life before him seems to be hurtling back in and I just need everything to *stop*. No more Christmas countdowns. No more clocking the hours I have left with George, left of being *me.*

'I need more time,' I whisper, barely audible.

'More time?' Theo asks, confused by my words. 'For what?'

For me and George. To move out. To start again. To move on. To look back?

'To plan the gig,' I say quickly as Theo's face falls. 'No, no, it can still happen on Friday, I just… can I take a rain check on my shift today?' Like the last two days. Theo looks at me like he has no idea what's going on, but maybe me being busy planning the last-minute gig is a suitable reason for why I've been so MIA.

'The social media is taking up more of my time and I'm just finding it hard to juggle everything, so yeah… can I just concentrate on this between now and the gig?' I take a step back and the photo falls off the wall again. I don't need to linger over putting it back this time. Not when the man who had caught my attention is now standing in the same room.

Chapter Nineteen

The memory of Theo's new volunteer, catching my gaze for a millisecond as I shot out of Church Street, follows me all the way home. I'm not even sure if I remember him from somewhere or whether he just reminds me of someone I used to know. But right now, only one thought dominates: soon George is going to be someone I used to know too. And he's seemingly kept himself scarce since our one last night together.

As I turn my key into the front door to our apartment, I can't shake the memory of when we first arrived here, when we span around with our arms wide open in the empty space, marvelling about the fact it was *ours*. Walking into the empty apartment now, I know the thing I've been marvelling about all this time is that George was mine. That of all the Patronellas and Pandoras and Primaveras in the world, he picked me, just Poppy.

Gliding lifelessly to the kitchen area, I see our old cafetière standing there – nothing fancy but does the job – and I can't recall when that stopped being enough for George, when *I* stopped being enough? A few months ago, when I supposedly stopped trying? Or was it really that I let myself feel safe for a moment, that I forgot that I have been trying to be something I'm not for the entire last five years we've been together?

Before I can stop them, thoughts of Theo and Avery and the people down at Church Street fill my mind. I knew when I stepped foot in there that I was risking remembering who I was before George all over again. But I never expected that they would follow me *out*, that I would find myself caring about the people at Church Street when I was nowhere near that place – or that street – and that they'd somehow worm their way into my very core.

I look around the vacant apartment and know it's soon to be a lot emptier than this. Only for a moment. And then it will be full of someone else's things. My eyes catch on the discarded boxes that George began packing then unpacked again and a horrible realisation fills my mind: maybe he's not moving out at all, maybe she's moving in here with him? Suddenly, I can't breathe. What the hell am I going to do? The question reverberates around my mind, but I know the real question is: who the hell am I going to be now?

Before I can think any better of it, I begin to call Dee. If Charlie knows all about George and this coffee girl, surely, she must have some answers or suspicions? Plus, Dee has a way of grounding me, or reminding me who we are, what we should care about.

'Babeeeee,' she picks up quicker than I expect her to and for a moment, I'm relieved. Then I realise how jarring her greeting is, that what once felt familiar now feels foreign, forced. But that's just Theo. He's got into my mind. I push the thought away.

'Babe!' I say back to her, but I can't even pretend to be happy. It's meant to be the most joyful time of the year, the one I've actually allowed myself to make plans for now. I assumed things were so steady with George that I trusted they wouldn't shake. What a fool I've been. What a fool I *am*. I reach a fist to my mouth to muffle my tears.

'I've been meaning to call you,' Dee goes on as I cry harder still. A silence stretches between us and I hear her exhale, like she's about to say something important, but then she goes on, her normal cheery tone resumed. 'Charlie was wondering about the parking situation at the cottage. I know George is driving, but we'd like to as well and…'

'I'm not coming,' I say, sobbing the words. I've tried everything in my power to avoid having to say them, but I've got nothing left.

'What do you mean, you're not coming?' Dee snaps down the line.

'George broke up with me,' I say, shoulders heaving. I should have told her this as soon as it happened. Clearly, George told his best friend, I just assumed the news would make its way to her too. I hold my breath, waiting for the surge of sympathy to come next. 'He's seeing someone else. I saw a message on his phone from another girl, the girl he bought the stupid brass espresso machine for.' I hate how much I've thought about that machine.

'I *knew* Charlie was keeping something from me,' Dee says after some time. 'He's been shady for weeks and always whispering with George, I assumed… I *hoped*… that they were planning my engagement… I'm *so* embarrassed!'

She's embarrassed? When I've been throwing myself at a man who doesn't love me anymore, a man who has been seeing someone else? How has Dee managed to turn this around to being about herself in just a few short sentences? I feel waves of rage threatening to drown my sadness, but the force of the latter is too great.

'George was right,' I say, under my breath. Our worlds do revolve around them. I thought it was because of me, because of my past, because the ground was always moving beneath my feet before I met him and he gave me permission to feel stable.

'Right about what?' Dee barks. But what's her excuse? Dee is just like that. I was just like that too. *Someone like us.* Except, that was never the full story, was it?

'He said our relationship had become imbalanced,' I say slowly. Well, he said my world revolved around him, but I put a better spin on it; it's what I've always done.

'Your relationship is perfect,' Dee objects. *Was.* I had thought so too. 'This will just be a phase, you guys will get past this. And you'd better do it soon, because Christmas...'

'Yes, I know,' I cry. Of course I know that, it's all I've thought about lately. Turns out it's easy to make someone the centre of your universe when you've scrubbed out your history to the point where your story starts with them. But today, just hours ago, my history walked right into Church Street. Or at least, I think it did.

'I've been trying to make him see that we are, perfect, I mean,' I say quickly, not knowing why I feel the need to explain myself. Dee clearly doesn't want to hear it. 'I've been taking risks, trying new things. I was even volunteering down at Church Street for him, working in the coffee shop, making him breakfast, going swimming with him, *outside.* I made him a nine-track mixtape, for goodness' sake...' I go on, but right now, it's not the new things, but the old things, the things I thought I had left in the past that are occupying my mind. 'Look, Dee, something's come up, I have to go…'

'You can't just drop a bombshell like that and go,' she says. 'If you can't come to the Cotswolds, can you send me all the details so that I can…'

'I'll message them across,' I say, my voice cracking as I do, the last fragments of our friendship falling apart completely. I don't know what I was expecting Dee to say but I thought she'd be there, I thought she'd *listen* to me. I guess I could have predicted that George and Charlie were the only thing holding us together, as we orbit around their stars.

Heat prickles on my skin and my cries come in waves as my eyes search around our home for an emergency exit, some way to get out of the situation I've found myself in, a world that starts and ends with George. It's over now. Our home. Our relationship. Our future. This Christmas and all the Christmases to come. It was over three weeks ago. I was just too busy forcing George into a couples' jumper to see it, just trying to keep us connected.

I force my shaking legs to stand, to make my way back to the bedroom that I used to share with George. That I shared with him only a day ago. I ignore the bed, the crumpled covers from the day I spent in there before. I move over to the mirrored wardrobe, ignoring my red-faced reflection looking back at me. I can't stand to look at that girl right now. The one caught between a future that will never happen and a past that she's been pretending didn't. The one in no man's land. But I can't stay there anymore. I can't *pretend* anymore.

Sliding the wardrobe door open and dropping to my knees, I push past George's skiing gear, past the stacks of designer trainers he just *had to have* only to wear once or twice; past the discarded coats from winters before this one, winters where he was warmer – to me, at least – and then I find it, the box at the back of the space, unmarked, unopened since we moved in here.

Sitting in the centre of our bedroom floor, I prise it open and peer inside. Hands trembling, I push past my birth certificate, the one that has the name of a young girl on it, my mother, too much of a baby to take care of a baby herself. I push past a stack of Christmas cards from all of the families I stayed with for the holiday season, not one of them my own. And then I find it, the one thing I was looking for. A pile of old photographs so thin that they couldn't hope to fill an album. One by one, I flick through them, my tears falling onto the faces of people I feel like I've never met, holding me as a baby or as a very young girl. Before they passed me on to someone else, like the kind of present given one Christmas and re-gifted the next. Then I find it: the one group shot I have of the family I was born into. The one that looks nothing like the uniform smiles that fill George's family shots. One that looks every bit as hectic and eclectic, both too much and yet too little, as the people down at Church Street. The kind of people I've been trying to pretend aren't *people like me*.

I scan their faces, some happy, some uninterested, some pulling faces, some not getting the memo, until my eyes land on the one face I knew I'd seen somewhere. The face I recognised in one of the photos hanging under the stained-glass angel at Church Street because I'd seen the same face before in another photo, the photo I'm now holding in my shaking hands. Of course, he looks different in this photo to the one hanging at the community centre. It was taken almost twenty-five years ago. But there he is, younger, but recognisably him; the man who walked into Church Street earlier today. And in this photo, he's holding a baby in his arms and I know the baby is me.

I flip the photo over to see the pencil scribbles on the back, the kind that people used to write before social media captions made us feel like the moment would last forever. There it has the names of the people in the photo and the date on which it was taken. There, I find his name written next to mine. The man holding me is Bob. *Uncle Bob.*

Chapter Twenty

'So, let me get this straight,' Marie says, her eyes like saucers as she stares back at me from across the table. I should be at Church Street, but there's no way I can go back there now, not until I've worked out what I think about *this*. 'He's your uncle?'

'I think so,' I say slowly and she looks at me like every person I've ever spoken to about my family life before, like, *how could you not know?* It's the reason I decided to stop talking about my messed-up past in the first place, not wanting to see another person put me in that broken-home box. George never did. I never gave him a chance to. 'I didn't really know him, but I recognised him from this photograph.'

I pass the photo across the table, the one that until last night, I've not looked at in years. But the one that *since* last night, I've not stopped looking at, trying to work out why he walked into Church Street or how anyone could have given that baby, given *me*, away.

Marie stares back at me again, her own mind struggling to take this in. When she bought me that mulled wine in the Cider Lodge, she knew I was at rock bottom. I bet she never suspected that I'd found myself at rock bottom a thousand times before.

'Your parents don't keep in touch with him?' she asks, her face soft and kind. Ever since I found the photo last night, she was the only person I wanted to speak to about this. Well, her and Theo. But how can I possibly tell Theo everything without him feeling used? That he was just a pawn in mine and Marie's *Twelve Days to Save Christmas* plan?

'My parents don't keep in touch with *me*,' I say and though it feels like a confession, I don't feel any of the redemption or release that so many religions talk about.

'But…' Marie stutters the word, reaching to hold my hand across the table. 'Why?'

Why? It's a question I asked myself for years and years until the lack of answers made me want to give up trying to find out the truth. Then I met George and he looked at me like I wasn't carrying any baggage from the past. Like I was the kind of girl who was so light and breezy that he could pull me up to dance on top of tables with him. I loved the way he looked at me, the way he made me feel like I could be anyone I wanted to be.

'I don't know…' I begin, except I know parts, fragments of my past. 'All I know is that my mother was really young when she had me, like fifteen…' I look down at my empty coffee cup before me, the inside of it stained dark with grains. I'm sure I would cry if I hadn't spent the last few days doing just that. It's like I've run out of tears completely. 'And my dad just disappeared off the face of the earth. I guess, because my mum was fifteen and he was a bit older, it would have technically been…' My voice trails off into silence.

Is that why she wanted nothing to do with me, because my face reminded her of their biggest mistake?

'She tried to look after me for a bit but then when I was two, I was put into foster care.' The words feel strange to say, mostly because I haven't said them to anyone in years. I watch Marie's face for sympathy, to see the realisation in her eyes that I'm not the together-looking twenty-five-year-old she thinks I am. Or at least, imagined I was before the break-up. But someone stained with stigma, someone shifted from foster home to foster home because I was always too much or too little or just too hard to love.

'I'm so sorry, Poppy,' Marie says and I hate that I have to feel like this again, like I can't escape my rocky past, that I don't deserve a stable future. 'Did you try to find them?'

'Yes, for a long time,' I admit, another thing I failed at. 'As soon as I turned eighteen and could get out of the care system, I tried, but there was nothing – or, well, no reply – for at least two years. I even spent time visiting shelters and places similar to Church Street searching for leads – but there was nothing, no tracing her. I don't think she wanted to be found. Then I turned twenty, got my job at the PR firm and met George and well, I never looked back.' Oh, and there's the tears again. Just when I thought they'd run dry.

'Honestly, Marie,' I say, even though I'm already being more honest than I have in years. 'George became everything,' I sob. 'The family I never had.'

'Your true love,' Marie says softly, with a little smile.

'Except I ruined it,' I cry again. I couldn't keep my family, couldn't make them want me, and now I've pushed the man I love away too. So what if one rogue family member thinks he can swan back into my life right now? It doesn't change a thing. That the future I've carved out for myself with George is now just another thing I'll have to bury in the past.

'You didn't ruin it.'

'I couldn't *fix* it.' I shake my head, never imagining it would come to this. 'I've tried everything, Marie. It's been three weeks now and I've joined the twelve choir members, tried to source eleven volunteers. I've gone on a ten-minute date,' I go on, and see her smile faintly as I do, before I go on and see it fade.

'I've forced George to listen to a nine-track mixtape, I've done his eight o'clock bloody workout, I've trapped him in a grown-up game of seven minutes in heaven.'

I exhale, feeling the weight of the words and the fact that when George was using closets as a place to kiss girls at boarding school, for me they were just temporary storage for my belongings, waiting to be packed up and moved on to my next home.

'I've hired six band members, recruited five mean girls, shared four drinks with a maybe mentee, seen three tickets sell in minutes, shared two hours on a something-like-a-date with Theo,' I say, as Marie's jaw seems to drop open for a second before she forces it shut.

'And I've spent one last night with George.'

One last night. Never again. The pain in my heart is almost too much to bear. I've lost too much already to lose my family again. But this true love has nothing left to give.

'I'm done trying to win George back.'

'I just thought you'd go on a few dates…' Marie says slowly, recalling how it was her idea to try and show him what he was missing in the first place. She never knew I'd go this far. But then, she never knew how far I've come from who I used to be already.

'It didn't work, none of it. It wasn't enough.'

I wasn't enough.

'No, but you tried,' she says, squeezing my hand a little harder in her own. 'Do you know how brave it is to even stay and try to fix something? Most people just walk away, don't risk the heartache.' How could walking away hurt any less than this? 'So many people just put up walls, Poppy, protecting their hearts in hobbies and busyness...' I can't help but think of George, but then, not a day has gone by since I met him that I haven't been thinking of him. 'But you bring walls down. Don't ever beat yourself up for *trying*.'

'What's the point, though? If it doesn't change anything?'

'Maybe it's just not changing things in the way you expected?'

I look back at her, feeling more lost and yet more seen than I have in weeks. I wish she really was my Ghost of Christmas Future, that she could tell me for sure how everything is going to work out, whether it works out at all.

'All I know,' Marie says and I hold my breath. *Go on, fix this. Tell me things are going to be okay.* 'Is that true love shouldn't have to be this hard.'

'I thought you said it was worth the fight?'

'Yes, I did,' she says slowly now, she knows I've got nothing left to give too. 'But there comes a point where it takes two to fight. No one can do it alone, they shouldn't have to.' She gets to her feet and pushes her chair across the space between us, coming to sit by my side. I feel empty, wrung dry, battered, bruised, but right now, with her by my side, I don't feel alone. Marie's right – again. No one can do it alone. They shouldn't have to.

There were so many Christmases that I spent in my room, plucking up the courage to force myself to go and be with people who were essentially strangers to me. There were others, where I felt part of something for a moment, but then I was moved on to the next thing.

This isn't a pop-in, pop-out situation…

Theo's words hurtle through my mind. I know my uncle Bob showing up doesn't change the fact that this gig is important to Theo, to Church Street… to *me*. I know that the least I can do for them all is pick myself up and try again.

'So, you went on a something-like-a-date with Theo?' Marie asks, eyebrow raised.

'Not like that.' Obviously. I'm still in love with George. Otherwise, why would I be here? 'We were just talking about the gig and stuff,' I say, not knowing why I feel accused, or even caught out. 'You will be there tomorrow, right? I don't think I can do it alone.'

'Yes, you can.' she smiles, holding my hand in hers, as warm and maternal and present as the night we first met. 'But you shouldn't have to. I'll be there.'

Holding onto Marie for a moment too long as we say goodbye, I try to imbibe her confidence. I'm going to need it. It's only one day until Church Street can add 'gig venue' to its multifaceted accolades. Only one day until I have to watch my undeniably ex-boyfriend doing the thing he loves most, perhaps even in front of a girl he's starting to love more. And only one day until I hope we finally secure enough volunteers to open at Christmas. Now that my Cotswolds dreams have come crashing down, I might have nowhere better to be. As I take the final steps across the churchyard and into the building, I know I could do a lot worse.

Taking a deep breath before heading inside, I prepare myself to see Bob again. What will I even say if he's there? Why didn't you try harder? To keep me, to find me, to even *try*?

As I emerge into the crowded space, I try to remind myself of Marie's assurance that it takes bravery to try. That it may take bravery to try to understand. Scanning around the room, I notice all the familiar faces, bar one: Bob is nowhere to be seen. I breathe a sigh of relief before I see Roger, not on his usual sofa, but walking towards me with some kind of hacksaw. *What the hell?* My pulse picks up pace, as I bridge the gap between us. Maybe Molly Mathers was right to be scared of this place?

'Roger, what are you doing?' I say, quickly looking from his almost deranged-looking smile to the saw held in his grubby fingers.

'Cupcake.' He smiles back at me and I remember how frosty he'd been when I first met him, how conversation after conversation I'd watched him soften and thaw. 'I'm heading outside to help Theo with the Christmas tree.'

'The Christmas tree?' I ask. I didn't know we *had* a Christmas tree but at least that explains the hacksaw. Roger just smiles, a big gummy grin. He looks like he's going to hurt me or hug me, but I know that despite his current serial-killer appearance, he's much more likely to do the latter.

'Three days sober,' he grins. Theo wouldn't let him use a hacksaw otherwise.

'Roger, that's amazing…'

'Don't tell anyone, I don't want no fuss…' Roger shakes his head. 'Follow me.'

Walking in Roger's shadow, past the smiling visitors, all busy and hanging up Christmas decorations, I can tell that something has changed here. There's an urgency, a purpose. Some get-up-and-go. If I hadn't found that message from George's new woman, this would have been the perfect piece to complete the purposeful, passionate Poppy-puzzle. It's just a shame that he didn't want to play that game in the first place. I shake away the thought, letting the sight of the visitors laughing and joking and getting into the Christmas spirit soothe me. The real reason for this gig might be redundant now, but it's definitely not for nothing.

'Here he is!' Roger says, pointing with the hacksaw still in his hand. It's enough to get my heartrate soaring and then I see Theo.

He's dragging a tree twice the size of him across the grass-covered space outside the church, his muscular arms exposed in a once-plain white T-shirt, now marked with mud – as is his angular face, which is now beaming back at me. With the fleece and flannel shirts long gone, he looks like a flipping thirst trap.

'I got hot,' he stands up straight to look at me. *Yes, you did.* He reaches to pick up his fleece, discarded to one side.

'You got a tree?'

'I was thinking about what you said, about why we don't hang decorations here – even if we don't get the volunteers we need on the big day itself…' Theo goes on, walking the few short paces between us. He's the one with his arms out in mid-winter and yet somehow, *I'm* the one who feels exposed. 'It's no reason not to invest in them now, to enjoy the build-up... after all, the "big day" itself is "overrated" right?'

I never actually said that. Just that I preferred Christmas Eve. But I don't want to tell him why. I nod, my words still held hostage in his sweat-glistening arms. Damn it, Poppy. Remember why you're here. Except, George isn't the reason anymore, is he? It's these people, the volunteers, Theo, the gig.

'Roger, I think it just needs about three inches taking off the bottom.' Theo hasn't forgotten the task in hand. Roger nods, and as much as I don't want to be anywhere near him hacking those three inches away, I do want to make myself useful now that I'm here.

'I could help,' I begin before Theo starts shaking his head at speed.

'No, no,' he says quickly, looking from the saw to me with a smile as I remember how he had wanted to keep me away from the visitors, in the back office, for as long as he could until he started to trust that I wasn't going to leave them all high and dry. Well, I'm not anymore. 'I've got a special job for you. How do you feel about heights?'

'Not great,' I say, now my turn to shake my head.

'In that case...' Theo grins again. 'How do you feel about holding ladders?'

I follow him around the side of the church building, to find a rickety old ladder and a tangled bunch of Christmas lights resting against the old stone wall.

'Theo, do you not think this is overkill?' I say the words I never expected to say when it comes to anything Christmassy. Although enough has happened over the past three weeks to put me off Christmas for life.

'I thought it would make the building more visible for tomorrow,' Theo says, as he lengthens the ladder and props it against the building. It does *not* look safe. 'And you know, more Instagrammable.'

'Since when did you care about Instagram?' I laugh back up at him, holding the ladder tightly in my hands as it wiggles with his weight. I hand the string of lights to him when he's halfway up and our fingers brush as he takes them from me.

'Since it started bringing more volunteers inside,' Theo says, looking down at me before turning to hang the first of the lights. 'You've made a real difference here, Poppy.'

'I can't take all the credit,' I say, as he steps back down and we move the ladder along to the next spot. 'You've stopped staring people down when they arrive as well….'

'Yeah, as I said…' Theo starts to ascend the ladder again and I hang onto his words: 'You've made a real difference…'

He climbs back down the ladder and we move it along the wall together until we're back around the front of the church.

'I mean… just look at that noticeboard now,' he says, climbing the ladder once more. I try not to get distracted from the task in hand, the *ladder* in hand. Not by the noticeboard. Not by Theo's backside, moving further and further up the ladder before shimmying down again.

'At first, I thought you were just coming here to prove a point, to look good in front of your ex-boyfriend or something,' Theo says, as we repeat our climb-and-hang routine. I had thought so too. 'But now I can see that you genuinely care about this place.'

I watch as he takes each step with care, holding onto the ladder before me tightly as it shakes under his weight, trying not to think about how close to home his observations are; things have changed now. Then, on the second-to-last step, he stumbles, coming crashing into my body as I try to catch him, or steady him, or *something*, in my arms.

'Good save,' Theo says, his face just inches from mine, my arms holding him tight.

'It's pretty nice to feel like the hero for once,' I whisper. Not the victim, or the left-behind one, or the one trying to hold it all together, but the one with enough strength to catch someone else when they fall. Theo leans in closer to me, his breath heavy on my lips.

'Poppy?'

Theo and I turn, still holding one another. I take a step back. Because standing there, smiling back at me, in exactly the same place he found me three weeks ago is George.

Chapter Twenty-One

'George?' I let go of Theo to take a step towards him. I know Theo's still lingering to my side, the same way he did when the three of us had our first run-in three weeks ago. Back when Theo was just some random stranger, but one I was pretty sure was looking out for me even then.

'Poppy, Dee said you might be here,' he says, smiling, moving a step further in my direction. Theo takes another step back. *Dee? What's Dee got to do with any of this?* I study George's figure, puffed up in a similar black jacket to the one I'm wearing. We bought them together. His and hers. He's standing near the noticeboard, as gorgeous as the first time I met him, looking a little like a mirage. I can read the words I hung up behind him: *You Belong Here.* But George doesn't, does he? He wouldn't *want* to. So, what is he doing here?

'Are you here to check out the venue?' I ask. Of course, that's what he'd be doing, even when we're just propping a few amps up in the church, always such a professional.

'Oh no, I'm not actually…' He speaks quickly, eyes oscillating from Theo to me. How much did he just see? Us laughing together, chatting? Or holding each other, very nearly… well, whatever was about to happen? 'I'm here to talk to you, actually.'

'Oh?' It's all I can think to say, especially with Theo by my side.

'Yeah, like, I spoke to Dee and she told me the *real* reason you are here…'

I hold my breath, feeling my cheeks flush red.

'All the lengths you've been going to, to show me that we're good together…' George goes on and I can sense Theo's every motion beside me. 'Like the nine-track mixtape and our seven minutes in heaven…' George turns the volume of his voice down, but I know Theo can hear every single word. I hate that he can. And I don't know why. 'And you volunteering here, even working here, I know it's an act – that you're acting up… for me.'

I risk a glance to Theo, feeling his eyes burning on my neck, my face burning too. I want to run to him, to tell him that my connection to this place may have started like that but has absolutely one hundred per cent turned into something else, something more.

'Poppy,' George takes another step forward until he's standing right in front of me and I can smell the familiar scent of his after-shave. He smells like home. Out of the corner of my eye, I can see Theo gathering the rest of the lights together, pretending to look busy. 'You can stop pretending now…'

'But I…' I begin, but George's eyes on mine steal the end of my sentence.

'Dee also told me that you saw that message. After we spent the night together…'

I give George my blankest expression. Not because I can't remember every single second, but because it took place after my something-like-a-date with Theo. It shouldn't matter, but…

'On Monday night?' George goes on. I wish he would stop, because what is he even saying? It's over now. Why can't George just play this gig and leave me to start over? Again.

'You spent Monday night together?' Theo says from behind me, quietly, slowly, like he's just understanding the words. Yes, we did. Like we have so many times before.

So why do I feel so guilty?

'Yes,' George says to Theo, reaching a hand to my arm. Theo flinches. So do I. Why is he here if not to check the venue? To deliver the final blow of our break-up. I get it. I'm moving out. I don't have anywhere else to go. But can't he just leave me to invest in a place that might be able to pick me up when I fall on those hard times? *Even harder times.*

'Poppy, that message you saw meant nothing,' George says, looking down at me intensely. It's the same intensity that brimmed between Theo and me just moments ago.

'It didn't look like nothing.' I wish I didn't sound like a child. The same child that objected to our break-up sat crossed-legged in a Christmas jumper in the first place. 'You bought her a coffee maker.' *That sodding coffee maker. That stupid upgrade.*

Out of the corner of my eye, I can see Theo shift. This sounds like a lovers' tiff. But it's not a tiff, it's a rift. One that George has made abundantly clear no amount of planning or scheming can plaster over.

'I did,' George says, his broad shoulders slumping. 'But it was a mistake. Honestly, Poppy, you're not the only one who has been acting out of character to work out whether this break-up is what we want…' His hand is firmly on my side now. Theo is edging further and further to the entrance into the church. Seeking sanctuary or some space away from me.

'I went out with another girl a few times, tried to throw myself into it, because you went on a date the weekend after our break-up.' George squeezes my arm tighter, not letting me go. *My date with Aran? I didn't even think he'd noticed.*

'I was trying to work out whether I could see myself with anyone other than you.' George is so close now. 'I can't, Poppy. I can't.' He envelopes me in a hug, one that I find impossible to shrug off. This is George. *George.* The first person to see me as something other than the broken foster kid from a broken home.

'So, you can give up the act now,' he goes on, looking past Theo to the church behind him. 'I know you've been doing this all for me and I really, really appreciate it.' Before I know it, he is tilting my chin up to him and kissing me, softly at first but harder and harder, with more and more urgency, as if we don't have any more time to waste.

As I pull away, I glance behind me to see the back of Theo, walking into the church. For some reason, the sight sends a searing pain through my stomach.

'Poppy, I'm so sorry.' George says all the things I've been longing to hear. I push my fingers into his outstretched arm as if to check that he is real. 'I've been a complete moron, just wrapped up in the band and everything. Please give me another chance.'

'Is that what you really want?' I say, held hostage in his amber eyes.

'More than anything,' he says, smiling back at me. 'For a couple of days, I thought I had done the right thing, but then I remembered all the things I love about you. I remembered all those amazing dates we spent together, axe-throwing and dancing on tables; that you say yes to anything even when it pushes you out of your comfort zone or into very *very* cold water.' He breaks off to smile at the memory.

'I remember that you support my dreams better than anyone I know, that even when you're getting stuck into something yourself, like your time at this place, you're always thinking of how to bring me and the band into it, how to share it with me.' He breaks off to breathe deeply, pulling me closer still. 'And I remembered our chemistry, that even when I'm trying to move on, you keep pulling me back in, that we're drawn to each other like magnets. Didn't you feel it too when we were stuck in the closet? When I kissed you goodnight on the forehead? I thought I was giving you all the signs?'

'I thought I was giving you all the signs too.'

'I definitely clocked the strawberry bikini,' he says, a smirk around his mouth that I promptly kiss off. 'I've been such an idiot and I don't know how you're ever going to forgive me,' he goes on, but I feel like I already have. I don't want to remember idiot George, making me feel less-than George. I just want to remember the George who is here right now. Holding me. Choosing me. 'But I've got you a pretty big present to get started.'

'Oh?' I say, still holding him close. It feels familiar, what I've always known. Or at least, what I've taught myself was my day one, forcing myself to forget all that came before.

'I know we have the trip in the Cotswolds with everyone…'

I had almost got used to the fact that I wasn't going. Passed on all the details to Dee. Told Theo that I may be around to be one of his eleven volunteers. But at least tomorrow's gig should get him a few more sign-ups, make up for my loss.

'…but I've booked us into a spa hotel for the weekend before they arrive.'

'You've booked us in?' I repeat. So, there was no doubt in George's mind that I'd say yes? That we were always going to be spending Christmas together. 'That's this weekend!'

'Tomorrow,' George beams back at me, as I wrap my coat around me, suddenly cold.

'The gig is tomorrow.'

'Of course,' he says hurriedly now, reaching a hand to his chin. 'I think with the short notice… And the panic of losing you… I kind of just… I've not been thinking straight. The band could still play without me?'

'Yeah…' I begin, before realising George is the frontman. 'Will they be able to carry a show without you?'

'Well…' He hesitates for just a second too long. If Theo was here, he'd roll his eyes. But Theo *isn't* here. He's inside, with the people he cares about, thinking that I don't care at all. 'Yes, yes, I'm sure they'll be able to. They'll do a great job.'

'But…' I hesitate. '…I think they're pretty excited about seeing the *whole* band play, including their lead singer. Can we not just go on Saturday?'

'I've already paid for the spa,' George says, concern clinging to his brow. It wouldn't be the first time he'd double-booked us, I was always the organised one of the two.

'But we can lose a little bit of…?'

'Poppy, I'm kind of putting it all on the line here…' A dart of insecurity flashes across his face. 'What are you saying? Do you not want to spend Christmas together?'

Thoughts of Theo and Avery and Roger and *Bob* fill my mind. These guys have become my family these past three weeks but it's like Theo says, 'Come as you are, don't stay as you are' – and I can't settle here at Church Street forever. But I can settle with George and have the life and the future I always hoped for.

'Of course, I do,' I soften. *Of course, I do.* 'I just don't want to let anyone down.'

'I know, Pops. I'm sorry,' George looks genuinely regretful. 'Perhaps we can find another lead singer to step in and play with the band?' he adds with an encouraging smile, eyes begging me to accept. 'To make up for me not being there?'

'For tomorrow? But it's such short notice…'

'Giving back is the new going out,' George parrots and I remember that stupid headline from the magazine I was reading, just before he broke up with me. He's clearly been into our room and found the exact same article. 'And with our contacts?' he grins and I hate the fact that I hear Theo's voice in my mind telling me that followers aren't the same as friends. 'We'll find someone in no time. We were planning to play lots of Christmassy covers anyway. But no pressure, the guys will be fine either way.'

'Are you sure?' I ask, willing him to have all the answers for me again.

'As sure as I still love you.'

I look back to him, inches from my face, pushing Theo and this place and the service users from my mind. This is everything I've ever wanted. All I've been fighting for these last few weeks.

'I still love you too,' I whisper, pushing all thoughts of tomorrow from my mind.

Chapter Twenty-Two

Friday, 17 December

The heat wakes me up. Which is saying something seeing as it must be about minus two degrees outside. I kick off the covers to find something solid by my side, the world's largest hot water bottle. George. Exactly where he's supposed to be.

With eyes still closed, he reaches a large arm across my torso, drawing me closer into his sweat-glistened side. It's only been three nights since we slept together like this, when I thought our nights of sleeping apart were finally over, written off as a wobble. Now here we are, back to being 'George and Poppy' again. So, why is my mind forcing thoughts of Church Street and Theo and Bob between us?

'Morning, gorgeous,' George whispers, holding himself up so that his body is leaning lightly along mine and I can feel his breath on my skin.

'Morning…' I whisper back, before he kisses anything else I have to say away, a welcome interruption. George's arms wrap around me, his fingers tracing their way through my hair as I settle into his kiss. This is nothing like the kisses of the past few months, short and functional, like a routine or an obligation. If those kisses were full stops, these kisses are ellipses, encouraging me on and on. And yet, my thoughts race along too. Annoying stupid thoughts. Like, has he been doing this to that other girl?

'George, I…' I say, breaking away and scrambling for breath. I don't know why I can't just sink into this, or what's holding me back. And then I remember. 'It's Friday.'

'I know.' His eyes are scanning from my eyes to my lips, moving lower and lower. 'Today's the day…' Of the gig. The one everyone at Church Street is looking forward to. The one that everyone at Church Street deserves. '…that our Christmas truly begins.'

I look back at him, George, *my* George. Attentive and available and in awe of me again. I deserve this too, don't I? The visitors may deserve to be invested in, but George and I have been investing in us, in our future, for five years and I'd be a fool to let this go now. And I've finally shown him that he was a fool to let us go in the first place.

'So, why don't we start now?' His eyes light up. We've got a lot of time to catch up on. Even before our break-up our sex life had stalled, I just hadn't wanted to admit it. But now, now George is here before me, looking like there's nowhere else he'd rather be. He belongs here. We belong here. *You belong here…*

'But we need to try and find a replacement singer for Church Street.'

'Poppy, you've already done enough for that place…' He kisses me again.

'I know, but…' I begin.

'Okay, okay,' George breaks off his kisses to look at me, his eyes wide with affection.

'Let's try our best to find a replacement lead singer but then you need to give yourself a break, Pops. After everything we've been through over the past few weeks…' Everything *he's* been through? 'I think we deserve to run away together for a few days.'

I know he means running away from London, escaping to the Cotswolds, but for some reason I can't help Marie's words from running through my mind: *do you know how brave it is to even stay and try to fix something?* But she was talking about me and George. My true love. Even so, I feel like I should try to fix things for Church Street.

'But don't you feel a bit like we're letting them down by not being there?' I ask again. George is getting out of bed now. Damn it, I should have just gone with it – I've put too much effort into keeping him close to push him away now.

'The band is still going to be there,' he smiles across at me, willing me to just stop worrying. 'Plus, the gig was a favour, no contractual obligations for us to technically break.'

This is why it's so hard for Theo to find his volunteers, to *keep* his volunteers. There's nothing tying them to the place other than a favour. And then their lives move on. *Like mine.*

'Okay, I just feel a bit, I don't know, guilty… about not being there.'

'Pops, I promise you,' George says, pulling on his jeans before coming over to kiss me on the forehead, the way he did when I got in from my drinks with Avery, 'you've already done more than enough. I've got some work to sort before I log off for Christmas, but you okay to set off in a few hours? Try and miss the rush-hour traffic?'

I reach for my phone, expecting to find a string of messages from Theo asking what the plan is now. And how could I? And was my caring about that place all just an act? But there's nothing. And it's gone ten. Theo will have been up for hours by now.

The thought of him hating me makes me feel sick. But George is back now. He's all the family I needed before. Still, I've got hours until the gig is supposed to start. And I know I need to at least do *something* to fix this.

George heads into the living room, leaving the door wide open before him. There's no his and hers spaces now, this place is ours again. And I need to pack for the weekend, for the five nights after in the Cotswolds to come, and then, how about after that? What happens then?

'George,' I say and he looks up from his laptop. 'Are we going to your parents for Christmas Day, you know, after we say goodbye to the others?' The others, the couples, who have rarely been in touch with me over the past few weeks.

'Yes, definitely.' He beams back at me. 'I thought that was a given?'

Yes, I thought so too.

'Have you confirmed with your mum yet, though?' I ask and he looks noncommittal, just like he did when she called us about it after our seven minutes in heaven.

'She knows,' he says with a grin. But that doesn't technically answer my question. George does this a lot. Just assumes that people know what he's thinking – what he's feeling. Sometimes it doesn't hurt to say it out loud. 'Where else would we be on Christmas Day than back with the fam?'

Back with the fam. *His family.* For a moment, I feel annoyed that he never asks after mine, until I realise that I've made it abundantly clear over the past five years that I didn't want to talk about them. I *didn't* want to talk about them. But then, thanks to Bob's rogue appearance down on Church Street, my family are becoming much harder to ignore.

'I figured now that we were back on track that this Christmas would look a lot like last year?' George leaves his laptop to one side and comes to stand in front of me, and it's the display of where his priorities lie that I've been looking for. Right here with me. Standing in the exact same spot where he told me the opposite. 'Do you know, I think maybe I didn't tell my parents about us breaking up because I didn't think it would stick, you know?'

'Yes,' I say, looking up at him. 'I thought that too.' It's day ten of my twelve days of crossing paths with George here in our apartment, here in our home. And I've done it. I've fixed this, *us.* Now, we're going to spend day eleven in some health spa and day twelve in the Cotswolds. Five full days, four couples, three day trips, two hot tubs, one wonderfully wintery getaway… Finally, the numbers make sense. 'Christmas with the family sounds good.'

The next three hours pass in a blur. George on his laptop, working on spreadsheets and balance sheets. George on his phone to the band, confirming all the details for the Church Street gig. And me, sat beside him, trying to find them a singer as some sort of compensation.

I message Molly Mathers, begging her to still show up, but without *someone like her* going, I know her answer is going to be no. Turns out my message doesn't even warrant a reply. I message some other singers that have been on the gig circuit with George, but to no avail. The people at Church Street will talk about the gig for weeks, years even. It would make their whole bloody Christmas; any band would be lucky to play for them.

'Don't worry, Pops,' George says, reaching a hand to squeeze my knee as I sit beside him on the sofa. 'The gig is still going ahead and it's not all your responsibility, remember? You've done such fantastic things for that place already.'

'It is kind of my job,' I say, feeling the panic rise inside of me. I never used to care about things that George didn't care about, our interests and passions were so in sync. I made sure of it. I look down at the social media account but can't stomach their smiling faces.

'Yeah, and the coffee shop?' he says, a teasing look in his eye. 'Dee told me that bit too.'

I feel my cheeks pinken, but why? There's nothing wrong with working in a coffee shop and at least I got paid for this part.

'Honestly, Poppy,' he reaches an arm around me, holding me closer. 'The efforts you went to for me, for *us*, it means the world. I love you so much.'

I force myself to smile back at him, reminding myself of the thousands of reasons I love him, the thousands of reasons I love our life together. I'll start feeling like myself soon, just as soon as this gig has come and gone, and I'm wrapped up in blissfully wintery fun.

'You made me a breakfast lasagne, you swam in freezing water... what else did you do to prove me wrong?' George smiles, bending to place a light kiss on my shoulder.

'I joined a choir,' I mumble as his laugh fills the room. I love that laugh, my favourite sound in the world. Except, maybe, the sound of thirteen random voices singing songs together and somehow sounding like a symphony.

'You joined a choir?!' George laughs louder now and I remind myself that it sounds warm. That he's not laughing *at* me, he's laughing *with* me. At how foolish we've both been to think that we could spend our Christmases anywhere but with each other.

'I actually made some good friends there,' I object, giving his chest a push. I hope it comes off as playful. Something inside me feels the need to defend them. I guess it's because I've never had friends that he didn't introduce me to.

'Really?' he says, glancing from me to his laptop, drawing him back in.

'Yes, there's Marie,' I begin, unable to stop a smile from spreading across my face when thinking about her. Between George showing up at Church Street and us heading home together, hand in hand, I haven't had a chance to tell her that our plan, *the plan*, actually worked. 'And then there's Aran, he's the one I went on a date with…'

'So, not that Theo guy?' George prickles, his jealousy palpable. But then, he did try to make me feel jealous with that girl he was messaging, even buying gifts for.

'No.' I push the thought of George's other lover away, not knowing why Theo kind of feels like mine. 'You'd like Aran, he's a musician like you.'

'Really? That's cool. Maybe you can introduce me some time?' He smiles and it's only then that I realise that Aran may just be the answer to my frontman problems.

*

'Popstar!' Aran picks up the phone almost as soon as I've dialled his number. I hate that my new nickname has made its way into this friendship group too, hate how much it hurts to hear it now. 'What can I do you for?' He might not remember but they're the exact same words he said to Marie the first time we met, before I knew how special they'd both become to me. For a time. Because I didn't have anyone else. I didn't have George.

'What are you doing tonight?' I ask, pacing our living room carpet at speed.

'Not going on a date with you, if that's what you're asking,' he laughs.

'It's not,' I say, whilst looking at George. He keeps looking up from his laptop to the sound of my laughter like he doesn't know what to make of it.

'I'm going to the gig at Church Street,' Aran says, like this is what I wanted to hear. Marie must have told him and the other choir members that it was happening by now.

'Good,' I say slowly. 'How do you feel about being bumped from audience member to centre stage?'

George looks up, indicating his crossed fingers for me.

'Erm… I was kind of looking forward to being part of the crowd.'

This is what makes Aran so awesome; that he's content to bring people into whatever he's doing, whether that be arranging the music for a choir or cheering them on through the post break-up mess. He doesn't need things to be all about him to enjoy them.

'Something's come up and we can't be there…' That 'we' again. The one I missed. The one I had *worked* for. 'Well, George and I can't be there. Can you step in, sing a few Christmas tunes with Side Hustle? We want to make sure it's a really good show and it'll mean so much to Church Street and—'

'You won't be there?' Aran's tone is stuck between confusion and concern.

'George is taking me away for the weekend.'

'I thought you were heading to the Cotswolds on Monday?'

'We're going early,' I say, as George looks up at me and smiles. 'Just the two of us.'

'Okay, well…'

I can hear the uncertainty in Aran's voice; he doesn't sound too happy about it. But I suppose I am bailing out last minute, putting him on the spot.

'Sure.'

'You're a life-saver. George will put you in touch with the band and I'll let Theo know about the change in line-up now…'

'Great, but… we'll see you in the Cotswolds?' Aran goes on. 'For *our* performance?'

'Well…' I begin. George has just closed his laptop and is getting to his feet. The choir was only meant to be a temporary thing. Another new thing to show George that I was the kind of woman he wanted to be with, but they've come to mean so much more. 'I…' Thoughts of the Cotswolds gang watching me rush through my mind again and I'm not sure I can stand them; not sure I can step out of line and do something differently from them when I've orchestrated our week away together to keep us all in sync. 'I hope so.'

'Good,' Aran says after a long pause. 'We'll miss you if not.'

They may miss the Poppy they knew, the broken and love-bruised girl who needed them, but I don't need to be that girl now. I can be the girl I've always wanted to be again.

'All sorted?' George wraps his arms around my waist from behind. No, not really. I have to tell Theo that Aran will be there; I have to tell Marie that I won't be. 'Ready to go?'

'I thought you needed to work for a while longer?' I whip around to face him.

'Yeah, but it's the last working day before Christmas,' he says, smiling warmly. Is he really going to put me before work, before his band, before a gig? This is like old times, except possibly even better, like my plan has got all of George's priorities back on track. 'And I can't stop thinking about getting you in that spa…' He bends to kiss me on the neck. 'Especially in that strawberry bikini,' he grins again. 'Will it take you long to pack?' He moves his head to kiss me on the other side of my neck.

'No, it shouldn't…' I begin. 'And don't worry, I'll pack toothpaste and moisturiser and all the shared bits you usually forget about, too.'

George laughs, bending to kiss me on the cheek.

'What would I do without you?' He smiles, before placing his lips on mine.

It takes less than half an hour to pack for the spa, the trip and for Christmas with George's family, the family he's always been so willing to share with me. I pack each of the presents I've carefully selected for them, every one tied in a bow, complete with hand-written tag to let them know they are from 'Poppy *and* George'. I pack all of the outfits that I have modelled for Dee, all of the cashmere jumpers that she said made me look like Cameron Diaz in *The Holiday*, but I decide to leave the comedy couples' jumper at home – it doesn't feel that funny anymore.

I know I need to talk to Theo, to talk to Marie about the choir too, but George keeps rushing me, eager to get away. It's like ever since I talked to Aran, ever since I mentioned speaking to Theo, every chance to actually tell him has been swept up in George's excitement to get up and get going on our getaway.

'I just need to make a phone call…' I say, as I walk out of the bedroom with my luggage to find George photographing a bird's eye view of his Patagonia weekend bag. He's got another suitcase as well, but something tells me travelling light looks better for the 'Gram.

'Great, can you ring them from the car?' He hurries over to help me with my stuff and I see his muscles strain as he carries all our baggage out of the door.

'Sure,' I say, not wanting to make a fuss. This is already going to be one of the most awkward phone calls of my life. Now I have to make it in front of him.

As soon as we set off, I know that George was right to hit the road before the rush-hour traffic begins. It already takes us far too long to get out of the city, the slow churn of cars along the road not giving me nearly enough distraction to drown out my thoughts of London or leave the memory of Church Street behind.

The familiar sound of indie rock fills the silence between us as we trundle along. I haven't missed this music, the monotony, listening and doing the same things all over again. George was right: new things, taking risks, has been good for me.

It takes us over an hour to get out of London, but I know it's going to take me longer to shake the thought of the gig and Church

Street and *Theo*, if I don't just call him and get this awful conversation over with. As if the sight of his fallen face wasn't hard enough to deal with, now I'm going to have to listen to him letting me know how much I've let them all down, that because of me they won't be able to open on Christmas Day. But that's not true, is it? I've not left them any worse off than when I found them.

Hovering over Theo's number in my phone, I steal a glance at George: how much did he see yesterday? Before he interrupted whatever was about to happen with Theo. That's *if* anything was about to happen because, let's face it, I haven't been that good at reading signals lately. I thought things with George and I were finally over. I look to him now, eyes fixed forward, driving us to our country retreat, his hand warming the same spot on my knee. I'm good now, I'm protected now. With George by my side, there's nothing Theo could say to hurt me.

I pull my phone to my ear, George's hand still cemented to my skin, holding me steady. I hear the dial tone ring once, twice, three times and I can imagine Theo's chiselled face looking down at my name on the screen.

It rings four times, five, six and I start to wonder whether he's ignoring it, whether he's giving me the silent treatment. *Seven, eight, nine*, I count the rings, remembering how Theo isn't one to play games or manipulate magic moments. *Ten, eleven…* he's the kind of person to throw his all into something and commit to it one hundred per cent. He's not there looking at his phone. It'll be stashed on silent in his back pocket as he chats to the visitors as they all get excited for the gig tonight, the gig that I helped to make happen.

Twelve... I hear Theo's voice telling me that he can't come to the phone right now and just the sound of it makes me want to cry. I bite back the tears, risking a glance to George, before trying to find the right words to fix this.

'Hey, it's me. Look, I just wanted to say I'm so sorry for yesterday, for being all over the place this week. It's just, with planning the gig and everything, George and I got to spend some more time together...' I break off; this isn't technically true. It's the *not* spending time together that made the difference. Potentially, it was me spending so much time with Theo.

'We've decided to give it another go and so our Christmas plans, yeah... they're back on. But I was calling about *your* Christmas plans, the gig. Side Hustle are going to be there, they're so excited to play... and I've got a replacement sorted for George. Aran Tooley, he's a wonderful acoustic singer-songwriter and the visitors will just love...' A tear trickles down my cheek and I chase it away before George can see it.

'And I've got everything crossed that you'll get enough people in to secure your volunteers...' Theo and I both know that he's at least one volunteer down now that George and I are on the up. And, without Molly Mathers there to promote the place to all her followers, I'm not quite sure the event will get us, well, *Theo*, over the line.

'I really wish I could be in more than one place at the same time but...' The lump in my throat causes my voice to crack. What I really wish is that I could be two different *Poppys* at the same time. 'Yeah, so... I'll miss you... all.'

Hanging up, I bite back the tears, forcing my face towards the window, forcing my mind to concentrate on the steady back and forth of George's hand stroking my leg. With the city now behind us, the countryside shoots past at speed and it finally feels like we're flying forward. That the future that I'd always dreamed of for myself is now back in reach.

Rain hammers hard on the glass rooftop of the orangery as George and I sit across from one another at breakfast the next day. So much for a white Christmas.

'Orange juice?' he offers, already pouring the vibrant yellow drink into my glass as his bare feet find mine under the table. *At least our robes are white*, I think as I wrap my dressing gown further around me. This place is amazing, with tall ceilings and ornate photo frames hanging from every wall and tastefully decorated trees standing tall in every corner of every room. I never got to see how Theo and the others decorated their tree or whether Roger managed to hack it to a suitable height without losing an arm. I can only imagine the box of tacky tinsel that I saw waiting in one corner of the church hall wouldn't be welcome in here.

'What are you smiling at?' George asks, grinning back at me.

I didn't realise I was.

'What do you think?' I shake away all thoughts of Church Street and force my mind back into the room, to the aroma of the fresh pastries before me and the sound of a distant piano playing carols and the feel of George's feet playing footsie with mine.

'This morning?' He smiles broadly now, remembering how we made love in a luxurious four-poster bed when only days ago I was sure we'd spent our last night together.

George reaches for my hand across the table and begins making circles on the back of it. In our silence, I can hear the notes from the piano filling the space between us, just wishing that they could drown out the space in my mind that is still thinking about Church Street's gig, wondering how many people showed up, whether it all went well. George says the band enjoyed it, but I'm more concerned about the visitors: did *they* enjoy it, did *they* feel invested in, did *they* feel special? I've messaged Aran and Marie and Theo too, but none of them have replied. I can't even bring myself to message Avery. What kind of role model just ups and leaves for a man? But then, I didn't leave for a man. I left for a family, the only one I've ever known, the one that has welcomed me in for the last five years and made me feel like one of their own. I'm sure she would understand that that's something to fight for.

I look across the table at George, who is busy looking down at his phone. I follow suit, my fingers moving automatically to Church Street's social media account. There's nothing on there about the gig. But why? Was it a success? Something to be proud of?

A waiter brings out our cooked breakfasts, but I don't feel hungry. I swipe through my newsfeed, looking for answers. Then I see George's most recent post, the one he took just before we left our apartment yesterday: *Ready for Christmas with the missus. We've been looking forward to this all week!* I read the caption and then look up to George before me, biting into his bacon. That's not technically true, is it? I spent Monday night planning a gig to win him back, the early hours of Tuesday crawling into bed with him, the next day devastated, Wednesday wondering what the hell would happen next, never dreaming it would be *Bob*. Thursday, hanging decorations with Theo, saving him in my arms. And yet, to the outside world, it looks like we've been counting down the days together all week.

I scroll down George's posts and there's no trace of anything out of the ordinary all month. To the outside world our break-up didn't happen, nothing has changed. But what if *I* have? My phone vibrates in my hand and I read Marie's name on my screen.

I spoke to Aran. He says you're a 'maybe' for our performance... I read her words as soon as they dart into my phone, fearful of what might come next. *Aren't you in Broadway in the Cotswolds anyway?* I look from George, tucking into his toast, and back to my full plate, my stomach swimming with confusion. Why can't I just *trust* that everything's good now, that the ground I once thought was steady has stopped shaking once again?

Yes, but it's back on with George!! I don't know why I feel like I'm forcing the excitement. *I'm not sure I can just ditch him and our friends that easily.*

Marie: But wouldn't he want to come and support you? As soon as I've read Marie's latest message, I remember George's face when I told him I had joined the choir. Even Marie knows that joining the choir was just a part of my plan to win him back.

I hope I can be there, I'm going to try my best to be there, but we've got loads planned. But the twelve days of Christmas thing worked!

Thank you so much for suggesting it. Very soon, the messages between us are coming thick and fast.

Marie: I didn't suggest this exactly, Poppy. Not all of it.

Poppy: But you started it. Planted the idea to show George.

Marie: I thought he'd take a little nudge, a little shock. Not the whole song and dance.

Poppy: You said it was brave to stay, to try.

Marie: Yes, for the right things.

Poppy: This is the right thing.

Marie: Great, I'm happy for you, Poppy. I really am…

Why do I already feel like there's a 'but' coming?

Marie: I just thought you'd sound happier about it? x

I turn my phone face down on the table, stung by her words. She's just saying that because there's a chance I'm bailing on the choir. Because my true love worked out and hers fell at the first hurdle. I feel rage bubbling through my body. This was her plan to begin with, not the nine-track mixtape or the crazy workout or locking my boyfriend in a cupboard but… it worked; I've got my old life back. I just need to get my mind off my new one. Which is pretty impossible to do whilst I'm still checking the account every two minutes.

Taking one last look at Church Street's Instagram page, I marvel at the following, how it's now shy of the ten thousand they need to be able to swipe up on their stories to link to pages and advertisements, pages like Church Street's 'Find Out How to Volunteer' page on their website. There's a number of direct messages, waiting to be read. But I know I need to empower Theo to take over this for the account to be able to grow sustainably, to move with the times whilst I allow myself to move on, move forward with George.

I go to the account setting and log out of the page. That's step one.

Then, I message Theo, resisting the urge to scroll through all our messages before. *Hey, hope it went well last night. I thought I should hand the social media over to you now, don't forget to check the messages…* I write, knowing that he's unlikely to reply. Not after how we left things. I hand over the account passwords, everything he needs. Then, I look back to George. Everything I need, right in front of me. He smiles as my phone buzzes.

Theo: Thanks, but I'll probably just leave it…

I read the start of his message, heart in my throat, and open it to read the rest.

Theo: We don't want to attract people who are only trying to look good anyway.

Chapter Twenty-Three

Monday, 20 December

George leans over to kiss me as soon as we've parked up in the driveway, reaching a hand to my cheek as he does. I savour the warmth of his skin, reminding myself for the millionth time since he whisked me out of London that there's no place I'd rather be.

Pulling away from him and pushing the car door open, I step out to see the Cotswolds cottage in front of me, every inch as picturesque as the photographs I looked at back in the summer when I first found this place. My eyes scan from the thatch roof to the wreath on the front door, and although it's rained on and off all weekend, I swear I can glimpse the first sight of frost sprinkled on top of it. I never doubted whether I'd be here back when I booked this holiday. Now, it feels crazy that George or I ever doubted us at all.

Taking my hand in his, we walk down the pristine stone pathway, through the ivy arch towering across it and towards the front door, passing Charlie's car as we do. Clearly, we're not the first to arrive here but that doesn't matter; we've already had plenty of time to catch up alone, thanks to George's surprise spa weekend. Theo's frozen expression when George first showed up at the community centre darts across my mind before I can force it back out again. I'm here now. With *George* now.

Pushing the front door open, we walk into the hall – which, like the rest of the cottage, manages to look both quaint and spacious – and hear chatter coming from the kitchen-dining room coming off it. Dee and Charlie are standing either side of a large marble island in the middle of the room, squabbling over something that I can't quite make out. George coughs. They swing around.

'You're here!' Dee thrusts her arms open to engulf me in a hug. Is she really that surprised? This time last week she didn't even know George and I had broken up. She releases me and switches places with Charlie, who throws his big rugby-boy arms around me. Evidently, they're not going to say anything about our break-up and in exchange we're going to pretend that we didn't just walk in on them having a domestic.

'Champagne?' Dee moves around the kitchen as if she owns the place, pulling a magnum of Moët out of a hidden fridge-freezer. How much must that have cost? And there are *five* of them in there. One for each of the nights we're going to be staying here. Dee thrusts a glass in my hand and I feel my stomach sinking as I watch the bubbles rise. My biological family could have sold one of these magnums to finance their whole Christmas.

'Cheers!' Charlie thrusts his own flute into the air, spilling some as he does. Dee and George follow suit and then three sets of eyes turn to me, wondering what's taking me so long to get into the Christmas spirit. It's what I've been wondering for the last two days too. For days, weeks, *months*, my mind has been set on this, counting down the days. But now that we're here, I can't help but be distracted, Theo's damn message about just *trying to look good* seeming to bubble over, spilling into the room, just like Charlie's champagne.

'Charlie, careful!' Dee barks at her boyfriend, the tension between them palpable.

'Yes, *Mum*,' Charlie says, rolling his eyes and fixing them on George, and he laughs too as I look around the room to find a dishcloth to mop up his mess.

'Shall we have a look around the gaff?' George says back to Charlie. The gaff? He never talks like that when he's just with me. In any case, the 'gaff' looks great. The hosts have decorated the whole country cottage – if you can call a place this big a cottage – for Christmas so decadently they could open to the public. We look around each of the rooms in turn, claiming the best bedrooms before the other four can arrive.

As our tour comes to a close and we settle down in the living room, it doesn't take long for Charlie and George to start playing with the fire, stacking up the wood even though they have no idea *how* to make a fire. For some reason the thought of Roger with that hacksaw comes flying back into my mind.

'Party people!' The door into the increasingly smoky living room flings open and we look up to see the modelesque figure of Frankie striding into the room. She's wearing a pair of skintight leather leggings that look as out of place with the country-manor décor as Jesse's light denim jacket. He must be *freezing*.

'Yay!' Dee jumps up to throw her arms around Frankie.

'I'll get you some drinks,' I say, rushing to the kitchen, feeling in need of space. I've spent so much of the past few weeks in a church hall packed to the rafters with people and yet somehow adding a third couple to a cottage that is bigger than the community centre itself feels too crowded, claustrophobic. But as I get to the kitchen, I find Becca and Andy unloading box after box of goodies from the back of their boot and into the room.

'Poppy!' Becca says my name with the same squeals that I've just left in the living room. 'You're here!' Did she ever think I wouldn't be? I look to Andy, the band's bassist, with suspicion. Did he know about coffee girl too? About George supposedly trying to work out if he could imagine his life with anyone other than me?

'How many people are we feeding here?' There're no fewer than six Waitrose bags stacked to one side. 'I thought we were heading to the markets today?'

'Just some nibbles,' Becca beams back at me. 'Don't want us to go hungry!'

I watch as Becca tops her champagne flute up and head into the living room to see the others. This group of people wouldn't know hungry, or what it means to go without, if I hit them with it.

'Shrek! It's Shrek!' Dee is practically jumping up and down as Charlie holds his hands out before him to signal that whatever he's acting out is actually a book. George catches my eye from across the room and I smile back at him. We're miles ahead in this game of charades, but then, after two years of living together, we know how to guess the other's next move. I'm not sure what Charlie and Dee's excuse is.

'It's a book, you idiot!' Charlie shouts back at her and everyone laughs.

'Well, why didn't you say so?' Dee looks around for support.

'You do know what charades is, don't you, Dee?' Andy laughs at her expense. We've been playing so-called 'parlour' games for two hours now and I'm itching to get to the local Christmas markets, to immerse myself in the twinkly lights and finally start to feel festive.

'Shall we get going?' I ask into the room, but no one is really listening. But we didn't come all this way just to drink and eat and do exactly what we do in London, anyway.

'One more round?' Andy asks and I don't know whether he means of the game or the drinks. I forgot how much we used to drink together. I look down at my third glass of Moët, as Roger's tear-marked face comes into my mind. I'd also forgotten that sometimes it was too much of something and not too little that could bring you down, until I'd spent time with him.

'Or we could go in the hot tub?' Charlie says and Dee instantly shakes her head.

'Be careful, mate,' George pipes up. 'You know not to mess with Poppy's plan.' Everyone laughs and I force myself to join in, feeling more and more like a fraud. Part of me still wants to steal away to sing in the choir but I'm not sure how to weave this into my carefully planned agenda without my friends feeling like I've lost myself completely. 'But, Andy, if you want one more round, Pops and I love to win.' George winks in my direction, as if everything is exactly as it's meant to be, like nothing out of the ordinary has happened between us. *Pops and I love to win.* Has this whole last month just been a game to him?

Two hours and three more drinks later, we eventually make it out of the cottage and into the village centre of Broadway, which is already bustling with activity.

'Is it everything you dreamed it would be?' George loops his arms either side of me as I look across the Christmas market. Stone buildings are lit up with warm-white fairy lights and unlike the South Bank markets, everything is tasteful and quaint. No tacky tinsel here.

'Yes,' I turn around to face him, standing on my tiptoes to give him a brief kiss. And it is. It's luxurious and neat and as carefully curated as our couples' retreat itself. A million miles away from the multi-coloured mess of Church Street, a far cry from the haphazard hecticness of a place for people who have fallen on hard times. A million miles away from the kind of Christmas I imagine my own biological family would have shared before everything started to fall apart for them. I move forward, holding George's hand tighter still. I've spent a long time leaving the girl I was behind, fighting to be *me* again. So, I don't know why I don't feel more myself. Why I somehow feel out of sync with the very people I've *designed* myself to fit in with. It's like Church Street has changed me somehow.

'Smile,' George says as we come to stand in front of another large Christmas tree, decorated to perfection, every ornament placed with precision. I didn't realise I wasn't smiling in the first place. I turn around to see that he's holding his phone in the air, that the mirror image on his screen is capturing my fallen face. I correct it quickly, beaming back at our reflections. George captures the photo. We look perfect together.

Holding my hand in his, we weave through the streets, passing rosy face after rosy face, looking every inch like we've fallen into one of the Christmas cards that is standing on the mantelpiece in our apartment back home.

'What are we going to do about the apartment?' I forget my filter for a moment.

'What do you mean?' George says, steering us to the next stall, showing an array of handcrafted Christmas ornaments, wooden carvings of perfect cottages and perfect families.

'We were going to stay until the end of the year and then… then what?'

'Well, now that we're… well, *us* again…' George smiles, looking back at me, wrapped up warm in my puffer jacket, the *Missus* to his *Mr.* 'I assumed we'd stay?'

That damn word again. I *assumed* a lot of things. How come every time George assumes something he's right and yet when I assume something, I end up feeling like a fool?

'Unless you don't want to?' he says, a look of insecurity flashing across his face, an expression that looks so very foreign on him. 'You're happy there, aren't you?'

I look from George's gorgeous face to the happy people around us, settling into their Christmases without a care in the world. I wasn't happy when I lost my job or when I spent days in the flat trying to find a new one, trying to convince myself that I could build a network for myself, when it was taking everything in me to make sure my connection with George stayed strong. But I was happy because *George* was happy.

'Poppy?' George is standing still now, holding my body against his, his hands holding my hips, fingers hooking into my back pocket. Then my phone buzzes. We both feel it. Breaking apart, I reach for my phone. A small part of me hopes that it's Theo. I don't know why, probably just because I know I've hurt him, and I have an insatiable need to please.

'Who is it?' George looks down at me now, but his voice feels distant, like it can't quite reach me. I look at the sentence, lighting up my screen.

Hi Poppy. I hope you don't mind me emailing. Theo from Church Street gave me your details. I've been meaning to get in touch for quite some time...

That's all I can see but I know it's from him, Bob. *My Uncle Bob.* My heart beats faster, my hands start to shake, but I can't open it here. Not in front of George. Not without opening the 'I'm not who you think I am' can of worms. Not that George has really tried to open that can in the whole time we've been together. No, he took me at face value. That's part of the reason why I fell in love with him in the first place.

'It's no one,' I say, smiling up at him, pulling him in for a quick kiss.

'I thought I saw Theo's name...' George says, evidently having looked at my screen from his six-foot-something vantage point.

'Yeah, it's... yeah... just a Church Street mailing list...'

'Oh, those damn mailing lists follow you around forever,' George says, resuming his composure, broadening out his shoulders. 'I can help you unsubscribe if you like?'

'Yeah, I...' I look around me, trying to find a way out, a way to read Bob's message, even though I'm dreading what it might say.

'Bought anything?' Dee materialises from nowhere and I instantly think of Avery, how she seemed to just appear everywhere.

And now, as far as she's concerned, I've disappeared off the face of the earth. But I learned from the best. I feel Bob's message weigh in my pocket, unable to ignore it.

'Not yet,' I grin back at her, my best friend in the group. She clearly said the right thing to George to make him see sense, whether accidentally or on purpose. I owe her for that. 'But I think I'm going to go and get one of those proper hot chocolates.' I nod to a busy stall in the middle distance, lovers and friends gathering in tight-knit groups around it.

'Ew, Poppy,' Dee begins, a hand on her hip. 'Do you know how many calories…?'

It was a safe bet. I need to get away.

'I'll be back soon,' I say to George, breaking away, knowing not to look back. Walking across the market, everything blurs into one: the sights, the sounds, the smells; it all seems like Christmas, but I don't feel Christmassy at all. No, I feel like my Christmas pasts and Christmas presents are colliding in a way that will screw up my future royally.

Joining the back of the queue for hot chocolate, I look around – not a single one of my friends in sight – and reach for my phone, opening the one message that I feel like I've been waiting for my whole life, until George came along and fooled me into feeling complete.

Hi Poppy. I hope you don't mind me emailing. Theo from Church Street gave me your details. I've been meaning to get in touch for quite some time…

I reread the part that George must have seen before forcing myself to read on.

I was hoping we might run into each other this Christmas at Church Street, but Theo said you have stopped volunteering there so I feel like I may have lost my chance.

I read the words, rage rising inside me. Yes, he's lost his chance. That whole damn family has lost their chance. I tried to find them, tried to be available to them. For years. But no one wanted to know. So, I changed. I changed myself into someone worthy of knowing.

I know this message is long overdue, that it might all be too little, too late, but I wanted you to know that deep down, I've always wanted to know you but if I'm honest, I thought you might not want to know me, that you might be better off without me. That everyone might be better off without me.

Truth is, I've made some bad choices in my time – ones that have lost me my whole family, our whole family. I first visited Church Street around five years ago, when I had nothing left to give, no one else to turn to and I've spent the years since then trying to get a job, get a house, get my act together to the point where I felt able to maybe, somehow, help somebody else. I never thought when I followed Church Street's account that I would see you. Someone who looks so much like my sister it's scary. I'm afraid I lost touch with your mum, probably around the time she was your age, and I know it's too late and you probably don't want anything to do with me. I'm going to take a step back, won't randomly show up at Church Street, give you your space, but I wanted you to know that if you ever wanted to talk, find out a bit more about your past or anything, then I'm here. Bob x

I read the words again, and then a second time, and then a third, sure that I'm making them up, that they can't be happening. Teardrops fall onto the screen as I study every last line, every single character.

This is from my Uncle Bob. The man from the photograph I have hidden in a box in our apartment. The man from the photograph of people who have come and gone from Church Street. The man who walked back in there, looking for *me*.

The tears come quicker and thicker, as the people around me fade into the background. The cheer and chatter tune out completely until all I can hear is my hurried thoughts. I don't know what to do. Who to tell. Who to talk to. Theo. Marie. Aran. Just someone who knows I'm so far from the perfect Poppy I've been trying to be. Someone who knows that the designer-wearing, confident, fun-loving persona I've built for myself is only half the story. That there's a whole history book that I've buried deep inside me.

I've burnt my bridges with Theo. The thought makes me cry harder. But Marie, maybe Marie will be willing to find a messy girl in the markets all over again.

Marie, can you talk? I send the words with shaking hands and wait for her reply.

Hey Poppy. Just buying last-minute Christmas presents. Some of us from the choir have decided to come over on Wednesday to spend the day in Broadway and check out where we'll be performing, so maybe see you then if it fits in with your plans. Everything okay?

No. I don't know… I begin to type, tears falling onto my screen as I do.

'Everything okay?' I stop still, hearing George echo Marie's words behind me. I wipe my face, willing my make-up to be expensive enough to cover my breakdown and turn around to see George smiling down at me, reaching a hand up to the top of my arm. It used to feel strong enough to hold me up, to hold me together, but what about now? Is he strong enough to handle this? Are we? When I've tried so hard to hide the past away from him?

'It is,' I turn to face him, pulling myself together for what feels like the thousandth time, hiding my hurt within me and my phone in my pocket. 'Now that you're here.'

Chapter Twenty-Four

Wednesday, 22 December

'I think I'm going to get one of those hot chocolates Porge got the other day,' Charlie says, his broad shoulders and confident swagger cutting seamlessly through the crowds of the Broadway Christmas market. It's every bit as magical as it was on Monday. Well, on paper. The thought of Bob's email and what the hell I'm going to say back is not just taking up space in my mind but erecting a whole bloody building in there.

'Like hell you are,' Dee says, scurrying into step by his side. 'And stop calling them Porge, you know they don't like that.'

George and I walk in their two-person slipstream, brushing shoulders with strangers on either side. I don't mind 'Porge'. Sure, it's not the best couples' name but I liked the way it made me feel a part of something. George reaches for my hand.

'Let's get smoothies.' Dee ushers our couples' walking train in the direction of her dietary requirements.

'There is *nothing* Christmassy about a smoothie.' Charlie comes to a standstill as George and I practically walk into his built-like-abrickhouse back and Frankie and Jesse and Becca and Andy bunch up behind us. 'How about mulled wine?'

'Not *everything* has to be Christmassy,' Dee says, her voice low and clipped but her frustration evident for even the man serving hot chocolate – now regretfully far away – to see. Dee may be looking at her boyfriend, but her frustration feels directed at me. Ever since I got that message from Bob, I have been on a one-woman mission to save this trip. And it's not like I haven't had practice, it's what I've been doing all month.

From the second I stashed my phone, and the message, deep in my pocket and plastered on a smile, I've been trying to tell myself it belongs here – the smile, that is. I told myself as George paid for our hot chocolates and proceeded to kiss the whipped cream moustache it left on my face. I told myself as we bought even more Christmas decorations and filled every corner of our country cottage with classy yuletide touches. When we took a trip to the neighbouring town of Chipping Campden and I suggested everyone play Christmas games on the way. When I suggested we bake Christmas biscuits. When I forced George to play Christmas songs on his guitar to get us all in the mood. Even when George was in the mood for something else and we started kissing, I rushed to my bag to pull out a sprig of fake mistletoe that I'd forgotten I'd bought to hang up in the house somewhere.

'Okay, Pops. We get it, it's Christmas,' George had said, but he doesn't get it. He doesn't get that I've had so many bad Christmases, disjointed Christmases, fragmented Christmases, that I thought that my first Christmas with George was a signal, a *promise* that there were no bad Christmases left to come. Even the good Christmases with the good foster families, the kind foster families, were always temporary, a present I had to give back.

'Strawberry and banana.' Dee thrusts a smoothie in my face. What kind of Christmas market does smoothies? Still, I smile. She knows it's my favourite. I savour my first sip. I guess this Christmas isn't *bad*, it just tastes different to how I imagined.

'Thanks,' I say, as Dee hooks an arm through mine and we walk side by side through the throngs of people and I try my best to sink into that magical-market vibe. This one has everything you could ever want. It's *perfect*. Except for some reason my mind keeps harping back to the haphazard imperfection of ruddy Church Street. I shake the thought away.

'Charlie is doing my head in,' Dee whispers, as we walk past a food stall selling steaming hot jacket potatoes and for a moment, I'm right back with Avery serving the visitors lunch, side by side. But no, I'm here. Right where I'm meant to be. 'You know what I think, though? Poppy, are you even listening?'

'Huh? Sorry,' I say, forcing my face back to her. 'I thought I just saw someone I…'

'I think Charlie is being annoying on purpose, throwing me off the scent,' Dee says, thrusting her gloved hand into the air and wiggling her ring-less fingers.

Well, I think Dee is deluded. But then, didn't I want to believe that lie too?

'It would be the perfect Christmas surprise,' she whispers quickly, her eyes alive with promise as the boys come back to join us, smoothies obediently in hand. I know George would have preferred a coffee. Probably out of some fancy cafetière. No. No, I won't go there. Won't let my mind sabotage what I've been building back together again. We're only halfway through our trip and we still have so many fun surprises to come. Well, surprises for them; it's hard to be surprised when you're the one orchestrating said surprises.

'Poppy!' I hear my name from behind me and instantly flinch. George, Dee and Charlie stop to follow the sound of the voice, our other four friends following suit. Slowly, I turn to see a bright flash of red hair bounding towards me and before I know it, my face is being pressed against a familiar chest.

I pull away to see Marie's face beaming back at me and for a moment, I have to bite back the tears. Last time I spoke to her, she was asking pointed questions, pressing into the places of me that hurt. But now she is looking at me like I'm every bit as loveable as the first time we met. Somehow it doesn't feel fake; it feels like even when probing and pointing out the flaws in my plans, she might have been loving me all along.

'Marie?' I manage to choke, her hands still holding the tops of my arms.

'Is that her *mum*?' I hear Becca whisper somewhere in the near distance and it reminds me that no less than seven sets of eyes are staring at us.

'No, I…' George says slowly, as I force my gaze to remain on Marie even though I can hear his mumbled words loud and clear; it's like I have a radar, some sort of super listening powers, when it comes to him. 'I don't know much about her mum at all.'

It's a good job Marie is still holding my arms as George's words make my legs want to buckle beneath me as for the very first time, I realise that I want him to know about my mum, about why she's not around, when until a few weeks ago I dreaded him finding out the truth. Now I think I want to find out more too. I only have a handful of early photos to go on. But Bob, Bob might know what she...

'Honey? Are you okay?' Marie echoes her very first words back to me, back when she had to rescue me from crying in the happiest place in the world the first time. But I don't need rescuing now. I'm with George now. I'm happy now.

'What are you doing here already?' I muster some enthusiasm, as I hear Frankie echo 'honey?' to one of the others. Suddenly, I see Marie through their eyes. A woman twice our age, curvy and vivacious and wearing more colours than the rest of us put together. My blushing cheeks add another hue into the mix.

'I told you we'd be here,' Marie says, her face falling a little as she notices that my friends are eyeing her suspiciously. She takes a small step back. 'Didn't I?'

'You did, I replied...' I begin before I realise I didn't. I was about to, about to tell her that I wasn't okay at all, that the Bob-story had hurtled into a whole new chapter. But then, George showed up. 'Oh, I thought I did... I must have got distracted.' I force a smile and the fact that Marie mirrors this back to me tells me she thinks I've been having loads of fun. I *have* been having loads of fun, I just haven't quite got that elusive festive *feeling* yet.

'We're all here!' Marie says and I look around her to strain to see the others but all I see is a sea of my unfriendly-looking friends, unable to hide their confusion as to why a colourfully dressed stranger has just crashed our couples' trip. Wait until they find out she's single. That'll get her pushed out of our loved-up octagon in no time.

She may be single but she's certainly not *alone*.

'Popstar!' Aran jostles his way towards us, his smile falling somewhat as he sees my six friends and one boyfriend looking him up and down. At least Aran is age-appropriate for them, though he's unknowingly committed the crime of being cooler than the other guys. Why aren't they being more welcoming? Although, I guess I never welcomed them into *this*, my life with George, the perfectly paired-off trip that could so easily be thrown off-balance.

'The whole choir is here early,' Aran says, throwing his thick denim-clad arms around me, his large scarf making up for his too-cool-for-winter attire. He pulls away, lingering for a second. He smells great. In another non-broken-hearted life I can see he'd be the kind of guy that would make anyone happy. But I am happy.

I am. I am. *I am*.

'Choir?' Frankie echoes back to one of the others again, like one of those hype-men repeating the last thing their fellow rapper has just said. *Why won't they just move on?*

'Are you still joining us for the performance?' Aran asks as I begin to hear the muffled sound of giggles in the background. I turn to see Frankie and Dee trying not to laugh, George looking smug like he's just let them in on some sort of secret. My stomach drops.

'I'm…' I begin, their laughter getting louder. It's the kind of sound that goes through me, like nails on a chalkboard, reminding me of all the times I've been on the outside of the laughter before. 'I'm not sure I'll have the time to sneak away.' I glance towards the women in our group. We're all in our mid-twenties now but I'm sure this must be how Avery felt when those five mean girls from her school showed up at the centre.

Meat Girls. Theo's mistake cuts through the noise in my mind, the one that highlights that he's so out of the mainstream that he's lacking half of the cultural references a man of his age should have. A true outlier. But *I'm* not an outsider anymore. I'm on the inside again, with George again. And after all I've been through, I deserve to feel some sort of safety in numbers. I deserve to feel on the inside of this joke.

'We've got some cool stuff planned.' The excuse comes out harsher than I mean it to.

'But…' Aran looks genuinely taken aback. I instantly want to apologise. And yet, George has taken a step closer to my side. So have the others. Like I'm one of their own. 'But you've been practising for this performance for the past three weeks…'

Marie takes a step back to stand beside Aran. I want to stand there too. But then George moves his body next to me, looping his fingers around mine. I need to stay here.

'Yeah, sorry.' I want the ground to swallow me. 'It was only a short-term thing…'

'Sure,' Aran says, more disappointed in me still. 'But we thought that your friends could spare you for a couple of hours.' He musters a smile, encouraging me to just say 'yes'. They know how much coaxing it took for me to sign up to join the choir in the first place, for me to find my confidence, find my voice. And now they're trying to do it again.

'Look, mate, Poppy doesn't want to sing in the choir anymore,' George says, finding my voice for me. I wouldn't have said the words so flippantly. But it's not like I've told him that it means – no, *meant* – something to me, something more than just winning him back.

'Can Poppy tell me that for herself?' Aran says, squaring up to him. Oh God, no. They can't be about to have a fight. Not in the happiest place in the world. Well, *my* happy place. George is looking at me now and I feel torn.

On the one hand, Aran and Marie have shown me so much kindness since I met them, have become proper friends to me – even for the shortest amount of time. On the other hand, if it wasn't for George taking a chance on me when he did, investing in our relationship for the past five years, maybe I wouldn't be the kind of girl they'd *want* to be friends with. The kind of *woman*. I grew up with George. Finally found my feet with George.

'She can,' I say, as George goes to stand with the others. Aran and Marie stare back at me, willing me to be *their* Poppy again, the fragile thing that needed them to pick me up. But I'm not that Poppy. I'm the strong, go-getting, tries new things, takes risks Poppy that George fell in love with. 'I don't want to… to erm… sing in the choir… anymore.'

Somewhere behind me, I hear that damn girlie giggle again and then George whisper: 'She only joined for me, to show me she had a busy social life or something…'

'Call singing in a community choir a social life?'

I don't know which one of them said it, but I heard it. Aran and Marie heard it too.

'Well, I guess we'd better leave you to it,' Aran says, shoulders still broad. Not intimidated by a group of twenty-five going on fifteen-year-olds. Unlike me.

'Wait, I…' I begin, literally caught between two people I like and seven people I've been trying to *be* like for so long that I'm scared I won't ever fit in anywhere else.

'Yes?' Aran looks down at me. I shrink completely. Marie offers me a sad smile and I force myself to look happier than I feel. Being with Marie and Aran reminds me of the girl I used to be, but she wasn't happy. She was drifting until she found someone strong and solid to hold on to. Marie gives me one last smile, before turning to walk away. My Ghost of Christmas Future with her mission accomplished. My Christmas has been fixed, restored, put back together again. So why doesn't it feel like all my Christmases have come at once?

'Did the gig go okay?' I ask Aran, tilting my chin upward to stop the tears falling. 'Did people show up?' I can tell the others are still listening and I don't know whether that's a good or a bad thing. I've always wanted them to gather around me like this, make me an insider. But making Aran feel like an outsider isn't making me feel good. Not one bit.

'Yeah,' Aran says, bruised by my words but not beaten, eyes shifting to George like he just needs me to say the word and he'd swoop in to protect me. But I don't need to be protected from George, I've always been protected *by* George. 'Not as many as if Side Hustle had *all* performed, mind.' He says this loud enough for George to hear. I know he's appeasing his ego, but that there's some truth to his words. 'We're going to donate a portion of the money we raise at our performance on Friday to the community centre...'

'Do you think Theo will have enough volunteers to open on—'

'We're getting a bit cold waiting, Pops,' George says, smiling softly. I look from George to Aran, who shakes his head slowly, unable to hide his sadness as he turns to walk away from me and towards the remaining members of the choir. George slides his fingers through mine again and we begin to walk further into the market, but I can't leave the thought of Aran shaking his head behind. What does that mean?

They're definitely not getting cold in their North Face jackets.

I can't believe how unfriendly your so-called friends are.

No, I don't think Theo will have enough volunteers to open on Christmas Day…

As George wraps a protective arm around me, a sinking feeling tells me it's all three.

'Is this your choir, Poppy?' Frankie says, feigning interest as we come to a sandwich board standing in the middle of a square, advertising their performance on Christmas Eve.

'Yes,' I nod, remembering again how Theo had first convinced me to join. Theo, who spends his life building others up. Theo, who I have just let down royally. 'Well, not *mine*.'

'I didn't even know you can sing!' Dee chips in. There's a lot she doesn't know.

'We all know she joined for me,' George says, a genuine smile covering his face as he holds me closer. For someone who once said he didn't want my life to revolve around him, he sure seems to like being the centre of attention. I know he's missed having mine.

'We're going though, right?' Charlie says, a cheeky smile on his face.

'Oh, for sure!' Dee beams back at him.

'That way we can imagine our little Popstar centre stage,' Andy teases as the rest of them giggle and George gives me a tender squeeze. The pet name doesn't feel nice when Andy says it. It feels like he's mocking the choir, mocking my friends. It feels like he's mocking me. And I'm not his little Popstar, I'm Theo's. No, no, I didn't mean that. I meant *George's*. I have to be. Because I've only ever belonged with George.

Haven't I?

Chapter Twenty-Five

Friday, 24 December

'It's today.'

I feel George's whisper on my eyelashes and open my heavy lids to find his face just inches from my own. The sun is streaming into the room through the gaps in our curtains. We must have slept in. Still, everything in me wants to roll over and go back to sleep. George's hand smooths across the sheets and slides under my bare back, pulling my body towards him as I feel his solid frame against my own. Very solid. At least one of us is up. George's lips linger just above mine and I bridge the gap between us until he eclipses everything else.

'It's today,' he repeats again as he pulls away.

'What's today?'

'Christmas Eve.'

I snort between us. George looks surprised.

'What's so funny?' He looks uncertain, cautious. Like me, George hates not being in on a joke. Unlike me, he hasn't spent the last day feeling like the joke.

'What's today? Today? Why, Christmas Day!' I quote *A Christmas Carol* back to George, who doesn't look amused – or aroused –

anymore. 'It's Charles Dickens…' I say, but his blank expression tells me he's either none the wiser or simply doesn't care.

'Why's that funny?' he says, rolling over onto his back, the moment gone.

'It's just Marie and I…' I stop myself. George doesn't know Marie or the role she played in our getting back together. He doesn't know that in holding *us* close I've chipped away at our short-lived friendship to the point where I'm not sure it's still standing anymore.

'But it's Christmas *Eve*.' George is still confused. Confused by my run-in with Marie and Aran in the market. Confused as to why Theo's name keeps popping up in conversation.

'It doesn't matter,' I say, shaking my head with a smile.

'I thought it was your favourite day of the year?'

Oh, I meant the book thing.

'Yes,' I say and George kisses me softly. 'It is.' I've been counting down the days to this one since early November. How could I have forgotten that now? Between Marie and Aran and thoughts of Theo and Church Street it's proving hard to just be *present*.

'I've got a present for you,' George says, smile resumed. This makes it easier.

'For today?' I beam, pushing myself up to sitting, pulling the sheets close around me.

'Well, I know that tomorrow we'll have all the family around…' All his family. Bob pushes his way into my mind for the thousandth time since he walked into the centre. What will he be doing tomorrow? Serving at Church Street, or sat eating alone? 'So, I wanted to get you something special to open whilst it's just us two. Close your eyes…'

I do as I'm told, as anticipation races through me. There's that feeling. The Christmassy rush of warmth and magic. I savour the moment. In bed with my naked boyfriend, who is rummaging in a bag to find a special present just for me. It's perfect again. This is what I worked for. For the kind of Christmas little girls dream of.

'Now, open them.'

I feel the weight of something in my hands, small and soft, and open my eyes to see a tiny velvet box, the kind that George's mum suspected he might be buying for me this year.

Oh shit, he can't have. We're not there yet, are we? I mean, we *were*. But then the break-up happened. The choir happened. Church Street happened.

Slowly, I prise the box open to see a sparkly diamond staring back at me. Two of them. Earrings. And just like that I'm laughing. Shoulder-shaking, audibly chuckling, into my ring-less hands. And there is nothing I can do to stop.

George looks at me like I'm certifiably crazy.

'I love them,' I say, remembering again how Theo and I had joked about the very many people who would be hoping for rings and landed with earrings this Christmas. I'm one of those people. I'm just like them. Except, I feel more like Theo, on the outside looking in.

'Are you sure?' George eyes my laughter lines with suspicion, far from convinced.

'So sure,' I say, stifling my laughter. I can't wait to tell Theo about this. Except, I won't get a chance, will I? *We don't want to attract people who are only trying to look good anyway.* I remember his last words. Suddenly things don't feel that funny anymore.

'I can erm… take them back if you want to…'

'No, no,' I say, holding the box in one hand and drawing George in with the other. 'They're absolutely gorgeous. They're perfect.' He's gorgeous. He's perfect.

'Phew!' George says, kissing me again. 'Because I pride myself on my gift giving.'

Something twists in my stomach as I remember the coffee maker. *Last night was fun, baby. Thanks for the espresso machine. It's the perfect gift…*

I push the thought away, willing myself to stay in this moment. This picture-perfect moment. But untamed thoughts and unanswered questions are bubbling to the surface. George had brushed this girl off as an experiment, a chance to see whether he could fall for anyone but me. But *which* day of my twelve-day plan finally made him see everything we had was already good enough? When did he end it, or…?

'Did you end it?' I blurt the words before I can stop myself.

'End what?' George says, reaching my hand to kiss it. We can both feel it shaking and like that, any romantic tension, excited tension, turns into tension-tension – the bad kind.

'When you were dating that girl…'

'Like you were dating that guy?' George raises his eyebrows. *This isn't a game.*

'George, I'm serious. Did you end it or did she?'

'There was nothing to end,' he says, shaking the thought away. That didn't really answer my question.

'You bought her a gift,' I object.

'I buy everyone gifts.' Way to undermine my earrings. 'But yes, I ended it,' he softens and I feel my tension soothing too. I should be content with this. Stop asking questions. Just be thankful. Thankful for my present. But…

'Why?'

'Poppy, why do you think?' George smiles, kissing me on the back of the hand again, the back of my hand he knows so well. Just like I know his. 'Because I know there's nothing you wouldn't do for me… and well, we're a good fit. We're "George and Poppy" in the same way that Charlie and Dee are "Charlie and Dee".'

'Yeah, but not *exactly* like them.' I can't help but widen my eyes at the thought of their constant bickering, never quite seeing eye to eye but somehow forming a united front.

'Yes, we are!' George says this like it's a good thing. 'They're perfect together.'

'No, they *look* perfect together. On social media. It's not the same thing.'

'They're *Charlie and Dee*,' he says this again like they're small-town celebrities, but there's nothing small about London. It's full of young professionals just like us, investing in their side hustle because one honest hustle doesn't always *feel* like enough. 'They're flipping Charles and Diana,' he accentuates their full names. 'Prince and Princess Perfect. They're meant to be,' George grins before adding, 'And so are we.'

Clearly, he doesn't know that *The Crown* suggested that Charles and Diana were famously far from perfect behind closed doors; that their whole relationship was for show. But it's not George's fault that he only sees what's on the surface. I've also been pretending there's nothing underneath.

Christmas Eve, The Best Day of the Year, is exactly how I imagined it to be. From presents in bed with George to Buck's Fizz over breakfast with the gang and an excess of food and drinks and games and banter. An excess of everything, really.

The girls swooned over my earrings from George but now that I've had them in for five hours, the weight of them is beginning to hurt. And the champagne tasted better alone, too expensive to be watered down with even the best orange juice. The food tastes too rich. Everything is perfect but nothing feels right. And for once, I don't know how to fix it.

'We should get going or we're going to miss it,' Frankie says, looking down at her vintage Rolex and back up at Jesse. The price of that watch could feed everyone on Church Street. Or employ a permanent member of staff for a year so that they wouldn't have to rely on volunteers. The centre will be open today but I'm almost convinced it won't be tomorrow.

'Miss what?' George says, coming to put a hand on my shoulder. Right now, with my mind full of Church Street, it feels as heavy as his earrings. If I thought deleting their social media account from my phone would delete that place from my mind, I thought wrong.

'The big show,' Frankie chips in.

'I didn't know you had a gig?' I look to George and he smiles sympathetically. It's the very face I've never wanted to see from him. He's looking at me like I'm a charity case.

'They mean the choir concert,' George says, trying to stifle his smile again. That's the last place I want to be. Watching Marie and Aran bob up and down to the 'Twelve Days of Christmas' even though last time, that song had the power to pick me up.

'I don't really feel like going…' I begin, heart hammering harder. They've been laughing about the fact that I joined a choir for over twenty-four hours now. Saying things like 'I didn't know you were into that' and 'I didn't think you were the type' as if there is a particular 'type' among the twelve brilliant, generous individuals I've got to know a bit this month.

'Tough,' Becca says, standing up. 'We're going. It'll be fun!'

Yes, but for whom? Not for Marie and Aran whilst Becca and Frankie laugh at their expense. Not for me, stood on the sidelines, not strong enough to run to their defence.

'It does sound pretty Christmassy, Poppy,' George says, using my kryptonite against me in a way that only those closest to you can.

Considering that I practically had to drag them out to the Broadway Christmas markets on our first day in the Cotswolds, the six of us arrive at the market in record time. Each one of them has donned a comedy Christmas jumper. Given what happened the last time I wore such a jumper, it feels like more salt in the wound.

As we weave our way past a row of stalls and into the makeshift square in the middle of them, I see the twelve choir members huddled around, going through their set list as the last of the winter sunshine begins to dip below the horizon. As it does, their figures are silhouetted and I will my own body to evaporate into the crowd. I should be with them. I hate to let them down. But I hate to let George down more. Against the increasingly dark night sky, the lights of the Christmas market shine in all their glory as more and more people huddle together around the area marked out as a stage.

'Anyone fancy a turkey sandwich?' Charlie asks our group.

'You've *literally* been eating all day,' Dee snaps back as George's words about them being the perfect couple circle around my mind.

'Fine,' Charlie says shortly. 'Shall we get a bit further forward?'

'I'm okay here,' I say, snuggling into George, who is wrapping his arms around me from behind. I want to morph into him, to hide away in the shadows so the choir doesn't see.

'I for one want to be in the cheese zone.' Charlie sounds more laddish still.

'What did I just say about eating all day?' Dee throws hands to bony hips.

'It was a joke,' he says, rolling his eyes. 'I mean, like the splash zone.'

Without waiting for a response, Charlie begins to navigate his way through the crowds and one by one, Dee then Becca, then Frankie and the boys follow. I'm the only one left behind and nothing in me wants to go and watch the space where I *should* have been.

'Coming, Pops?' George turns to holler back at me. And I remind myself again and again that this is where I *am* meant to be, that it's just taking a while for my old life to feel like mine again. Well, my old-new life. Singing in this choir, being at Church Street, made the veil between where I am now and where I came from feel uncomfortably thin.

I nestle in next to George, hoping to hide under his wing as the choir starts to sing 'Do They Know It's Christmas?' They're performing acapella. No music to hide behind. Just their voices. They're not the best voices in the world but together they sound sweet.

I look to my left to see Frankie and Becca sniggering; on my right I see Charlie holding up his phone to take a photograph, not of the choir but of himself and Dee. Even by my side I can see George scrolling through his phone. But before me? Before me I see Aran and Marie, Rosie, Kimmy and the other choir members singing earnestly and yet still not taking themselves as seriously as my so-called friends. No, no, they are my friends. I'm standing on this side of the 'stage' for a reason. It's just that right now, as the choir sing about feeding the world whilst I'm standing with a group of people only interested in feeding themselves, I couldn't feel further away from the Poppy I have been trying to be: George's Poppy.

As the notes rise, I find my legs moving further forward, leaving George on his phone a metre or so behind. This is wrong. All of it. I thought I belonged with George but right now, I don't feel like I belong anywhere. And it's a feeling so familiar – I thought I'd run through my fair share of not-belonging by now.

From my new position in the crowd, Marie catches my eye and it's enough to make the tears begin to gather and my throat grow hoarse. I couldn't sing a note if I tried.

'Fancy going up there, Pops?' Andy says. I see the others have jostled forward too.

'Nope.' I bite back the tears. I won't cry here. Not in a Christmas market. Not again.

'I really can't see you up there,' Dee says, hooking her arm through mine.

'You've not really got that charity shop chic they've got going on,' Frankie adds.

'Did you really just join for George?' It's Becca's turn to pipe up. 'That's so romantic.' Yes, yes, I did just join for George. In the beginning. But then it became a bit more about me. And, well… I look to Aran and Marie before me as they finish one song and prepare to start another. It became about *them*.

The realisation hits me like a tonne of bricks. George may have thought my life revolved around him, but it didn't, it revolved around *me*. A 'me' trying to build a life for myself that I never had before, one I felt I deserved. But what if I didn't deserve anything? The good or the bad. The clients on Church Street certainly didn't deserve the hands they've been dealt – the thought of Stanley and Linda playing cards back at the centre runs through my mind. Avery didn't deserve to be bullied, didn't deserve to have her friends bail on her – I can't help but look around me at mine and wonder where they were when George and I first broke up. George didn't deserve to be born into a happy family when mine didn't want me.

The tears are falling now, faster than I can wipe them away. Theo didn't deserve to have a dad who is an alcoholic. Maybe none of us deserve anything. Maybe we just have to do the best with what we have. Treat life like a gift. Any life. No re-gifting, no receipts.

'On the first day of Christmas…' The choir begin to sing.

'Come on, Popstar,' Frankie jokes again. I want to say she's never been this bitchy, but I know she has. That her insecurity can morph into a meanness, pushing people away before they can do the same to her. I think of how I acted to Aran and Marie on Wednesday and know I've done that too. 'Sure, you don't fancy joining them?' she teases once more.

'On the second day of Christmas…' The choir sings on. I can see Aran looking back at me, concerned. It's as if he's seen my tears even though the people standing close-up haven't. But then, sometimes you have to stand back to get some perspective.

'My true love gave to me…'

I didn't want to stand back from my life with George. I knew what life was like before him. But our break forced me to. I stood out. Stood back. Stood on my own two feet. But I didn't do it alone. I did it as part of a community. In the choir. Down on Church Street.

'Gave to me…'

The same lyric jumps out at me; I hadn't thought about that part of the song before.

I'd thought about the countdown. About the gifts. I thought about the true love – a lot. But the next line? So little you could miss it. I hadn't really *heard* it until now.

True love *gives*. But not like this song, not just gifts. But time and energy. Our full messy selves. And love gives freely – not to get, not to manipulate – but simply for the joy of giving. Because they know generosity won't run out but will grow and change and expand.

Aran smiles at me, Marie does too, and I begin to clap, cheering them on. Frankie looks at me like I've gone insane. But it's not enough. Love doesn't cheer from the sidelines.

I take another step forward, willing my legs to join them, but something holds me back. I've been holding back this whole time, holding parts of myself down. Not like the clients on Church Street who give their whole selves to each other, not like…

Theo? From across the opening where the choir are standing, I can see him singing along as part of the crowd, gathering around the twelve choir members, in a semi-circle; his strawberry-blond mop bobs up and down as he does, his pink cheeks as rosy as ever. What's he doing here? The sinking feeling in my stomach tells me everything I need to know. Church Street Community Centre is closed for Christmas.

'That guy looks so young, though,' Becca says to someone close to my side. They must be talking about Aran, but I can't draw my eyes away from Theo's place in the crowd to look. 'Surely, he's the kind of person to have something better to do on Christmas Eve?'

Then, Theo spots me from across the open space, forcing a sad smile as he does. Here I am, enjoying my couples' Christmas exactly as planned. I want to tell him that I didn't use him; that it may have started that way, but a part of me is still with Church Street. Except, it's not. I'm done being a fraction, leaving parts of myself scattered in the past. I'm a whole damn woman. And the whole of me now knows that actions speak a lot louder than words.

'On the twelve day of Christmas my true love gave to me...'

I take a step forward into the space between the choir and the crowd until I'm standing in the way. I breathe deeply, legs trembling beneath me as everybody watches on. I can take a step back, stand alongside George and Charlie and Dee again. Or I can take another step forward, joining the choir in the not-so-unlucky thirteenth spot made for me.

'What are you doing?' I can hear George hiss from behind me, but I'm already too far forward to go back now. I fall in line beside Marie, who swings an arm around me before forcing my shoulders down to join in the bobbing. Oh God, I hate the bobbing. Still, I laugh. Dee, Frankie and the others are laughing at me too. But as I sing the words louder and louder, I feel my limbs relax, my heart and mind let go, and I feel that feeling, that Christmassy magic feeling, and know it's not something I ever had to chase. It was inside me all along.

Chapter Twenty-Six

'I *knew* you wanted to sing with us!' Aran throws his arms around me as soon as the choir has finished their final song – *our* final song. His bearded face is beaming and it feels infinitely better than his disappointed expression staring back at me only two days ago.

'Did you?' I ask, still a bit shell-shocked. 'Because I didn't.'

'We saw the performer in you from day one.' Aran's smiling, but with my friends looking across at me like they don't know who the woman that has left their side to go and sing in some random choir is, his words take on more weight than he means for them to.

Being up there felt exhilarating. I can see why George loves the stage. Although this performance technically didn't have a stage. And it felt a lot more like being part of something rather than having the limelight all on you. I look across to Dee, Charlie and the others and it kind of feels like I'm under the spotlight now. Marie must have seen them looking over before she comes to stand beside me, putting a hand on my shoulder. It feels maternal, somehow.

'Poppy,' she says, smiling kindly. 'Your friends… They're a bit—'

'I know,' I say, cutting her off before she can say something like 'cold' or 'rude' or 'cliquey'. 'They have their moments.' I look across to them, chatting and joking and taking smiling pictures of one another. 'But they have their good moments too.'

I'm defending them though no one asked me to. It's just they're different from Marie and Aran, they've made that abundantly clear, but different people can have a lot in common. I don't want to build barriers anymore. From across the smattering of people, I see George walking over, bridging the gap between us. But then, another familiar face fills it instead.

'Hey,' Theo says, smiling down at me, folding his arms against his trademark fleece.

'Hey,' I echo after the longest time, hoping the smallest of words can make up for so much. Why is he here? Standing right in front of me now? I try to slow my quickening heart.

'You were good up there.' He looks to the space where I've just been singing before glancing to Marie and Aran, who both seem to take a step back. He lets out a heavy sigh and in our shared silence, my mind scrambles to work out what to say next.

'Thanks.' It's a start. I want to thank him for a lot of things. Thanks for inviting me into Church Street, no matter how reluctantly. Thanks for opening my eyes to the fact that my past is nothing to be ashamed of. Thanks for passing on my email address to Bob, even though I'm not really sure what I want to do about it yet.

I watch as Theo brushes his big, rough hands through his floppy hair. Nothing like the smooth skin that George had moved over me this morning. Out of the corner of my eye, I can see George lingering beside us, arms folded before him. Theo's eyes remain on me and the intensity of the moment freezes me to the spot.

'What are you doing here?'

'Aran invited me,' Theo says, taking a step closer towards me. I see George take a step forward too. 'When he performed at the fundraiser, we kind of hit it off...'

'Asked him on a second date yet?'

'Have you?' Theo says, wiping the smirk off my face. I love that they're friends now. Hate the fact that they've swapped notes on me. That by now Theo knows that I used him, I used the centre, I used Aran and everyone else to get what I wanted. And now what I wanted is standing right beside us, arms folded, trying to find a way to bring this conversation with Theo to a close. But I have so much left to ask. And this might be my last chance.

'But why are you here? Why aren't you at Church Street?'

'After Aran stepped in like that to support us, the least I can do is support him too.'

True love gives. And receives. And gives again. And receives again. Never entitled. Never expecting. But never ending. *Every moment, every move, with you ever more.* The lyrics George penned for me force their way into my mind as George himself forces his way forward. But true love shouldn't be forceful, or pushy or impatient, should it?

'Did the gig go okay? I've been dying to ask...' I rattle off my questions at speed before George can interrupt to tell me that our friends are ready to go home.

'Yeah, it did go okay.' But I wasn't there. 'Aran and the band were great, but we didn't get the volunteer numbers we need for tomorrow,' Theo says, the sadness evident in his voice.

'I'm so sorry that I wasn't there, if I did anything to—'

'No, Poppy.' Theo shakes his head. 'You helped, you really did. I'm sorry for what I said in my message. The marketing stuff, the social media, *that* noticeboard,' he breaks off to laugh. 'We should have done it all sooner, should have invested in the commercial stuff a long time ago. The visitors are too important not to.'

'I know, but it didn't work…'

'But that's okay. We tried our best. That's all we can do.'

'Is it, though?' I know he's right, but maybe in this case, there's another way.

'What do you mean?'

'Well, is it really over? Has the moment passed to get your eleven volunteers? Has the moment passed to tell the service users that you'll be open tomorrow?'

'Yes and no,' Theo says slowly. How can both be true? *How can I be on and at somewhere at the same time?* One of my first sassy questions to Theo runs through my mind. I suppose sometimes seemingly impossible things can become a reality. 'No, the moment hasn't passed to tell the volunteers. We could open up tomorrow morning and the visitors would be there waiting. It may surprise you, Poppy, but lots of them aren't all that diarised.'

I laugh, hard. I know Theo is imagining Roger with a Filofax or something too. Just a metre or so away, I see George puff up his chest beside me, looking Theo up and down. Then Theo's face falls; mine follows suit. If the centre doesn't open, some visitors may still be outside, waiting to get in, with nowhere else to go.

'How many volunteers are signed up now?' I ask, as George closes in.

'Poppy, everyone's going…' he says. I turn to raise my hands, giving him the 'five more minutes' sign, but I may as well have flipped him the bird. He looks furious.

'Some signed up, some dropped out…' Theo goes on unsurely, like he doesn't know whether to let me go. 'So, we're still at eight. We need three more to get the ratios we need.'

'Have you checked your DMs?'

'My what?' Seriously. I'd think this guy lives under a rock if I didn't know where he spends most of his time.

'Poppy?' George says again, increasingly urgent. Increasingly pissed off.

'Your direct messages. On the Instagram account.'

'I know what DMs are, Poppy. I was joking…' With George increasingly agitated beside us, the joke doesn't really land. And I can tell from Theo's face that he hasn't checked.

'There were a few messages when I logged out the last time.' When I handed over the account and Theo said the words that stung the most. 'You should check them. You never know, there may be a Christmas miracle or three among them.'

'Thanks,' Theo smiles.

'Poppy, I'm freezing my bollocks off here!'

I wince, embarrassed by his behaviour, by his lack of willingness to wait for me.

'I'm going home. Are you coming with?'

I look to George, urgent and angry, and I know part of me doesn't want to, wants to stay here with Theo. But *all* of me needs to go somewhere and I think it's time that George got to see it, to see the sides of me I've been hiding for too long. I owe him that.

'Check the messages,' I turn back to Theo, willing him to keep fighting for this.

'I will,' he nods, looking from George to me, that same sadness weighing on his features. It's like he's giving up on something else, but I'm not sure I want him to.

'It's so good to see you,' I whisper, not meaning my voice to crack as I do.

'All part of the plan,' Theo says. What? No, it wasn't. Not *my* plan. 'Aran told me you would be here. I hoped I'd run into you so I could say sorry and…'

'And what?' I say, the hue of his deep green eyes looking back at me.

'Yes, and what?' George says, but his voice feels so distant now. Theo looks between the two of us and nods, making a silent decision with himself before he turns to leave me with three little words.

'Merry Christmas, Poppy.'

Chapter Twenty-Seven

We walk back to the country cottage in silence, using our phones as torches as we navigate the early evening darkness. I'm with my favourite person on my favourite day of the year but this doesn't feel like a moment we'll want to remember. I bet we will, though. Because I'm learning that turning points in your journey rarely stay in your past.

I look to George now, to his statuesque frame as he pushes the door into our Christmas cottage open. It looks every inch like the picture but it *feels* nothing like I imagined. Instead, it feels like another turning point. Which is fitting really, seeing as meeting George was the last major turning point I can remember. That is, before he broke up with me.

'Well, that was rude,' George says, as soon as he's closed the door to our bedroom.

'I was going to say the same.'

He steps back like I've just hit him. He's not used to me standing up to him. Well, except when it comes to forcing him to lighten up. Little does he know that every attempt to keep things light, frivolous, has been another way of keeping the heaviness of my childhood hidden safely in the past.

'Honestly, Pop-py.' He separates the syllables of my name in a way that tells me that if I went by a nickname, he'd be calling me by my full name right now. 'Do you know how humiliating it is to stand there on the sidelines whilst you laugh and joke with some guy you've been talking about for weeks?'

George looks across at me accusatorily. I didn't see it at first, but it wasn't the mixtape or the lasagne or the seven minutes in heaven that won him over in the end, it was jealousy. It was me revolving around something else other than him. Looking at his stone-cold expression, I'm not sure he'd appreciate the irony right now.

'Yes, I do,' I say the words I imagined one day I'd be saying to him, although in a totally different context: I do. *I do. I do.* I'll do whatever you want me to. 'I've been watching you from the sidelines for years.' Every gig, every venue, every tween-scattered crowd, I've been standing there on the sidelines cheering him on. Scared that if I wasn't, he'd find someone else to cheer for him. Like I was replaceable. Temporary. Because my childhood taught me that I was.

'You love me, right?'

Oh, so he just gets to come out and ask these questions without sounding desperate or deluded. Like somehow from a man this sounds like emotional maturity but from a woman it sounds like emotional instability.

'I do.' There it is again. And I do. With all my heart. But he doesn't love all of me. He's never had the chance to.

'Then why did you spend so long flirting with this Theo guy?'

'I wasn't flirting.' I actually wasn't. I care about him, sure. But it's more than that. We care about things together. Other people. Other causes. George sighs deeply, as I brace myself for what comes next. But the worst has already happened, hasn't it? Exactly a month ago today the man I thought was propping my whole life up broke up with me. And I didn't crumble completely. Well, not with the help of others lifting me back up.

'What do you have in common with these people, anyway?'

There it is. The opener I've absolutely not been waiting for, but which has brought matters to a head, nonetheless. I look at him, looking back at me, inches away from leaning back on the far wall of our bedroom, like he couldn't be further away if he tried.

'These people?' I ask, giving George the benefit of the doubt. I sit on the edge of our bed, knowing that any kisses or advances between us have seen their last. The thought stops all others. Is this the end? It *can't* be. I feel the inevitable washing over us, all the times we've plastered our way over open wounds, because I've let it be this way.

'The church gang, the Christians?'

My jaw drops by an inch. Maybe two.

'You think caring about people is about religion?'

'Maybe? I don't know. They seem like a bunch of do-gooders.'

'That doesn't make them religious, it means they do good things. And just because you say they're something, doesn't mean they are.'

I look to George now, cowering in the corner of the room. He's all I've ever wanted to love and be loved by. But is it really enough if I'm only being a fraction of myself?

'I do have a lot in common with them, though,' I go on and ever so slowly, George comes to join me in the middle of the room. He doesn't know it yet, but this move means a lot. It means that the person I've spent my past five years with isn't so unreachable that he'd stay on the far side of the room. 'Do you ever wonder why we don't talk about my family?'

'Because you don't want to?' George says, now sitting on the far edge of the bed. He's right, I didn't want to talk about it. But he also didn't keep asking. I don't know whether to feel mad at him or compassionate towards him. Maybe both. Maybe human emotion can't be encapsulated into the neat boxes I've been trying to put us both in. That he's been trying to squeeze us both into as well.

'Yes,' I begin, everything inside me wanting to say 'stop'. Wanting me to just be content with George, content with the life we've built together. But what is a life if it's missing half of yourself? 'But I want to now.' To George's credit, he simply nods.

'My mum had me when she was fifteen…'

Now it's George's turn for his jaw to drop.

'She couldn't cope with me…' I say the truest fact of all, the fact that has taken root and told me that I'm fundamentally too much, that no one in their right mind could ever cope with all of me. But she was only a girl.

'So, I was taken off her… or given away from her… or something, when I was two.' George just looks on, stunned. 'From there, I went into foster care, shifted from one family to the next, taking all my baggage with me but trying to fit into whatever space could be made for me in some other family… But I don't know… maybe I wasn't enough? Or was too much?' I go on, once again looking to George for answers. I know now that he doesn't have them. 'I think now… maybe, I don't know… that maybe my birth family wanted something to do with me…' I instantly think of Bob. 'And that's why the fostering was so transient, because someone, somewhere was still holding out hope that our family could be restored somehow, but I turned eighteen and was done with it. I knew I could make a fresh start.'

I look towards George, perched on the end of the bed. He so often had the answers but now he doesn't. I bet he has a thousand questions swimming around his head.

'I tried telling the truth about my past, my story, for a couple of years,' I go on and I'm not sure when tears started tracking down my cheeks. I'm not sure it matters. Like me and George sitting here at a stalemate, or every client who has ever set foot in Church Street, I'm not sure the 'why the hell are we here?' matters as much as the 'well, what are we going to do next?'

'And if I'm honest, I even tried to find my family for a bit longer, keep an ear to the ground, but nothing. And sharing my full story with the new people I was meeting didn't buy me any favours either. I saw enough good guys fancy me and then instantly *not* fancy me once I'd told them my history to learn that it is a turn-off.' *A turn-off. A dead end. A taboo.*

George sighs, his annoyance evaporating, his curiosity mounting.

'Then I met you,' I say and the fact he's buoyed by this tells me a lot.

He may have thought my life revolves around him, but his life revolves around him too. Maybe his parents are to blame? Maybe it's him. Maybe again, the 'why?' matters less than 'well, what are we going to do next?'

'And I didn't tell you who I was,' I continue. 'I started from scratch. And I liked it.'

'I liked it too…'

'Well, what about now?' I ask, now that he knows the full story. Well, as much as I can know it until… maybe I meet Bob and we start to fill in some of the gaps we left open.

'You lied to me,' George says and it's the truth, I lied by omission.

'Would you have given me a chance if I didn't?' I ask, not wanting to jump to conclusions. No one can be put in a box, Church Street taught me that. 'If I had told you that my mother was a teenager and ever since then I'd been shifted from home to home?'

'I, err…' The fact George needs to hesitate tells me that this is so far out of his wheelhouse that he can't say for sure what he would have done, whether he would have claimed we were just too different, from two different worlds. 'This is a lot.'

'Yeah, it is,' I say and it feels good to call a spade a spade for once rather than use all my strength to fabricate it into something more palatable. 'George, you're wonderful.' He smiles again and suddenly I'm the one who's empathetic, who wonders whether he's been so built up by his parents that without constant praise, he's the one whose world would crumble. I guess all upbringings have the power to shape us or screw us up.

'But the second I stopped being the woman you fell in love with, the second I stopped being enthusiastic and perky and purposeful, the second I started wondering what I want from my life independently from you, you broke up with me.'

'I know, I…' George begins and then shakes the thought away. I encourage him to go on. 'I guess when we started going out, you just fitted into my life so well. It just flowed. You never held me or my dreams back, never got in the way of what I wanted…'

Yes, because I made sure that all I wanted was him.

'But then things happened with your job and you started to question and well… everything kind of unravelled with you… slowed down with you…'

'Maybe I needed to just stop and rest for a bit before I had the energy to work out what I wanted next?' As soon as I've said the words, I know they are true. I've never had a stable enough foundation from which to dream about anything other than having a home. Then, when I started to trust my foundation with George and I stopped to work out what I wanted other than him, it threw our balance, our whole life, off-kilter completely.

'I thought you were putting too much pressure on me,' George says, his voice heavy with emotion. 'But it's only because you've been everything I've needed you to be for the past five years. I've not had to compromise once…'

Looking at him now, I can't help but remember jumper-gate. That he finally put it on. At least that was one compromise he made before deciding we weren't right together.

'It only took one out-of-character move to throw us off-balance,' George says. 'Well, what I thought was out of character. Did you ever feel like yourself with me?'

'Yes,' I say, my tears falling freely now, grabbing my hand in his. 'In some ways I felt more myself than I'd ever felt before with you. I am who I am because of you, but…' I look to him now and we both know where this is heading, that too much has happened for us to go back to what we were now. 'But also, I am who I am because of my family, my upbringing, all of my experiences, the good, the bad and the ugly.'

'We all are,' George says, nodding his head slowly as if working out something for the first time. 'I mean, look at me… I've gone from having my mum do everything for me to depending on you to make my life easier.'

'Maybe,' I say, with a slight grin, remembering all the little things I've done so that he can keep his big dreams alive. 'I think I need to spend some time reconnecting with my past, making my peace with it, owning it.' I smile and George does too. A sadness brims between us but there's love there too, hope for what could lie ahead, for both of us. 'I'm not sure I can do that at the same time as being one half of Poppy and George…'

'George and Poppy,' George corrects before I can hit him in the rib.

'You wanker…' I say, laughing through the tears.

'I think you're right,' he says, bringing me in for a big bear hug. I know we'll have to sort out logistics soon, talk about what happens tomorrow and every day after that until we go our separate ways. But for now, we both cling on to this moment, feeling closer somehow now that we know we're going to part.

'I'll always love a piece of you, Poppy,' George says and I know he means it. I also know it's not enough. That we shouldn't be content to love pieces of each other. That we don't need to *like* every bit of the other, but we should fall in love with the whole damn thing.

Chapter Twenty-Eight

'Are you sure you're okay with this?' George turns to me, his hand resting on the door handle as he prepares to leave the bedroom and head down to join the others.

'I will be.' I smile back up at him, still perched on the edge of the bed we slept in together just last night. No one likes a break-up. But somehow, having had a trial run this past month, I think we both feel a bit more prepared. At least I know what *not* to do now.

'I'll stall things whilst you pack and then we can tell them, together,' George says with a kind smile. Now that things are over between us, now that the games are over, it feels like we're on the same side again. No winners. No losers. Just two people who have helped each other in some ways, hindered one another in others.

'Sounds good.' I watch as he leaves the room. Tell our friends about our break-up on Christmas Eve? Let them know that I'm leaving? It doesn't sound good at all. But I know it's the right thing, it's what we need to do next.

George said he was happy to spend the holidays together, for us to postpone our break-up until the end of the month, for me to play happy families with him and his parents tomorrow but I'm done pretending. Even the wrench of pulling away from his family doesn't feel as bad as trying to be something I'm not for one more second. I know I'll always love them like I'll always love George, shooting up a 'thank you' every time I think of them, grateful for the times we've shared and the memories we've made. But I also know I need to pack up my things now – the jumpers I bought, not because I liked them but because George would like me in them – and follow him into the living room. Then we'll tell our friends the truth together and I'll book an Uber to the station, because everyone is already too many drinks down to drive. Plus, I don't own a car. Like most things in my life recently, that belongs to George. But all that is about to change. Everything is about to change. Turns out change is the one thing you can depend on. Well, one of the things.

After planning this trip meticulously, slowly, savouring every detail, I pack everything away at speed, throwing things into my weekend bag haphazardly. Now that I know my time here has come to an end, I just want to get back to London. It's like every minute to be enjoyed is now just another minute until my train leaves the station. For all the anticipation I've tried to muster for this day, it turns out sometimes counting down can ruin the present. I zip up the bag and take one last deep breath, savouring the lingering scent of George's aftershave mingling with the perfume I've just sprayed. The smell of 'Poppy and George' – or 'George and Poppy' – depending on who you ask.

'Poppy! Your performance… just wow,' Frankie says, as soon as I've entered the room. The others clap, expressions ranging from a little impressed to full-on sarcastic. Maybe this trip won't be that hard to leave early, after all. One by one, I look between their increasingly merry faces. I have memories to treasure with each of them individually but en masse, they are hard to handle, like each of us is so scared of being on the outside that we have to become louder, more boisterous, meaner, or risk being the odd one out. George comes to stand by my side, putting an arm around me.

'Guys, we've got something to tell you…' he says into the room and all eyes turn to him. He's got a beer in his hands. Already getting back into the Christmas spirit. I know he's going to be okay as I leave him behind. More than okay.

'Omigod, you're engaged!' Dee says, a glimmer of genuine affection in her eyes. Nice to know that despite her own unmet desires, she'd still be happy for me.

'No, we…' George objects, holding me tighter, propping me up. He's not going to be able to do that anymore. But I need more than one person to prop me up, so does he. They say it takes a village to raise a child, maybe it takes a village to help us navigate adulthood too. Perhaps it takes a whole bloody community.

'You're pregnant!' Frankie says, as I resist the urge to suck in my stomach. Dee shifts in her seat uncomfortably.

'No, we…' George tries to object again, but for all his showmanship his voice keeps fading into the noise.

'They can't be. George is drinking!' Charlie says, his lame joke showing us he's clearly drunk enough for all of us.

'Are you kidding me right now?' Dee snaps at his sloppiness and I smile. I don't want to be in a relationship if the reins on who you are and what you say have to be that tight.

'We're breaking up,' I say, as six sets of eyes look back at us, stunned.

'As in… breaking up to look for something?' Becca asks, trying to make sense of this.

'Kind of,' I say, looking up to George.

'But you're perfect together,' Frankie says. 'I wish we could be like you half the time,' she adds, her honesty feeling like the most refreshing thing she's shared all week. Maybe that's why she gives me such a hard time. She's jealous. Of a lie – or a half-truth.

'We're not,' I assure her. 'In fact, we broke up this time last month too.'

'Is this because of Chloe?' Charlie throws another grenade into the group. *Oh, so she has a name?* I look to George, who looks caught in the act, but it doesn't matter anymore. We've both done our fair share of acting this past month, these past years.

'No, it's not,' George finally finds his voice. 'It's not to do with anyone else.'

I nod, backing him up. But it feels like another half-truth too. Another yes-but-no situation. It was to do with me and George. But it was also to do with Marie. And Aran. And Avery. And Roger. And Bob. And Theo…

'But it's Christmas!' Dee objects. She knows how much I love this time of year. Now, at least. She has no idea why I didn't love it before. 'You're not leaving now, are you?' She eyes my travel bag. It feels like a giveaway. 'You can't spend tomorrow alone.'

'I've actually spent Christmas alone before,' I say and she looks more concerned still. 'Millions of people do. But I won't be alone this time…' I smile. George knows this too. 'My Uber is on its way,' I go on and she looks genuinely sad.

'Cancel it.' Dee is getting to her feet now. Is she going to bar-ricade the door?

'I've really got to go,' I say, shaking my head as she comes to stand before me.

'I know,' she says. 'I'm driving you to the station.' She has the keys in her hands.

'But haven't you been drinking?' I say and Dee shakes her head quickly, silencing my next line of questioning nervously.

It looks like I'm not the only one who has been hiding something.

Rain hammers down the car windows as Dee pulls away from the dream cottage and my dream life. It takes all my strength not to press my face to the glass so that my tears can't be seen, like some cheesy ballad music video. When George and I first moved in together, I thought I'd finally found a permanent base. That I'd said goodbye to saying goodbye.

'I'm so sorry, Poppy.' Dee breaks the silence between us.

'Me too,' I say, savouring the warmth of my last hug from George. 'But it's for the best. It's the right thing for both of us. What about you? Are you okay? Are you—?'

'How do you know?' Dee interrupts and I feel the panic in her voice.

'I don't, but you haven't been drinking and I just thought…'

'I mean, how do you know it's the right thing for sure?' She changes the subject.

'Well, I guess I don't know for *sure*,' I say, turning to her, her face fixed forward. 'But it's a risk I'm ready to take now.' *Take risks, try new things.* 'I think I'm strong enough to handle it. And you're—'

'I know you are,' Dee interrupts again and in the darkness, I can see there's tears falling down her cheeks too. 'You've always been so strong, so together.'

'Oh, babe.' Of all the 'babes' we've said to one another before, this one feels the most honest. 'I am so not together it hurts. I don't know my family. I've got *massive* attachment issues. I have been lying to everyone about my childhood for years now... I'm a mess.'

'Why didn't you tell me?' Dee says, her face falling further now.

'I didn't think you'd understand.'

'I would have tried.'

'But even when I told you about me and George breaking up the first time all you could talk about is you and Charlie, about finally getting that ring. Do you ever wonder whether all we have in common is the boys?' It feels harsh but then, after today, who knows when I might see her again? 'I've been obsessed with George, with keeping him happy and all you seem to care about is you and Charlie.'

'And the baby,' she whispers, tears falling freely now, her eyes still fixed on the road.

Oh crap, she's actually pregnant?

'Why didn't you tell me?' I echo her last question to me, word for word.

'I've not told anyone yet, not even...' Dee begins, and like a tap that has rusted over, her words splutter then flow like water. 'I'm scared that Charlie won't want it, that he's not ready, that it'll ruin everything with the band...'

'That sodding band.' The further away from George we drive, the clearer I can see things for what they are. Side Hustle are great, stand a good chance at making it, but it's still just a chance. And we've invested in a future that might not even happen at the expense of our present. Love gives, but nor should the recipient just take, take, take.

'That's why I've been so obsessed with "finally getting that ring",' Dee mirrors my words and the coarseness of them makes me wince. We never know what's going on below the surface. 'I want to know he's ready to commit to *me*, not just because of...'

I watch Dee move one hand across her stomach, tender and kind, as the station comes into view.

'You have to tell him,' I say, putting a hand on hers as she pulls into the drop-off bay.

'But what if...?'

'I promise you, secrets don't stay secrets forever,' I say, knowing that I never could have hidden the truth of who I was from George – or myself – forever. The light exposes the dark places eventually. 'And babies have a tendency to grow.'

Dee buries her face in her hands, but I can tell she's laughing at my final words, at the absurdity of trying to keep a pregnancy a secret for longer than a few months.

'Everything is going to change now, isn't it?' She turns to me.

'I think it already has.'

'Maybe once you've moved out of your place and things settle down a bit...' Dee doesn't need to finish her sentence for me to know what she's about to say.

'Yeah, maybe,' I say, as she smiles back at me.

'I'd like to get to know the real you.'

'Yeah,' I smile. 'Me too.'

Dee throws her arms around me and I give her a big hug. I thought that our boyfriends were the only thing holding us together. But as I think of the little life held somewhere in the middle of our hug, I know we've been sharing a lot – fear about the future, about imperfection, fear about losing the people we love most – we just didn't let our friendship go deep enough to see the hidden threads weaving us together.

'Are you sure you've got plans tomorrow?' Dee calls out of the open driver's window as I come to stand just in front of the door into the station. Plans? Not exactly. But I'm sure I know who I'll be spending Christmas with. I nod and wave at Dee, before watching her car pull away. I really hope Theo's offer to spend the day together still stands.

The train carriage is basically empty as I clamber on board. But then, people don't usually *leave* the Cotswolds for Christmas. Especially this late in the day. The train pulls away from the station. There's no going back now. Only forward. I dial his number.

'Poppy?' Theo picks up instantly. No waiting, no power-play. 'Everything okay?'

'I wanted to check you've followed up with the DMs,' I say – it's part of the reason I'm calling him now anyway.

'Yeah,' he says slowly, jarring against my intensity. 'I did.'

'And?'

'One more volunteer,' he says, forcing the positivity in his voice. Any volunteer help at Church Street is a plus but without more, it doesn't help him out tomorrow.

'So, you've got nine?' I say, heart feeling heavy. Part of me hoped that once I tell Theo what I'm about to tell him, we'd have the eleven we need to open tomorrow. But even with my help, we'd only have ten volunteers and as much as I've tried to get Theo to bend the rules, he knows it's not worth risking getting a fine or being shut down by the authorities. I know by now that he has to do everything by the book.

'Well, actually…' Theo says, as I look out at the twinkly town-houses passing by at speed. 'Avery's dad had to cancel on her…' Ouch, I know what that's like. My heart aches for her. For every child that ever gets cancelled on without cause. 'So, we have ten.'

'No,' I say, pain for Avery and a rising excitement swirling in my chest; it turns out both can exist without cancelling each other out. 'You have eleven.'

I wait for Theo's reply, anticipating his questions, anticipating his own excitement. But there's nothing. Nothing at all. I look outside and it's pitch-black. Damn tunnel. All I can do is wait until my signal returns and tell him again. You have eleven. *We* have eleven.

The tunnel seems to go on forever, as one minute without signal stretches to two. Eventually the twinkly lights of the streets and houses passing by reappear and my phone jumps to life. Theo is calling me back. He must think I hung up on him. He must have been trying to call me back this whole time.

'Sorry, I was in a tunnel,' Theo says as soon as I've picked up the phone.

'*You* were in a tunnel?' I don't mean to sound so accusatory.

'Well, technically the train was in the tunnel.'

'And you're on the train?' I say, heart throbbing in my chest.

'That's how it works,' he says like I've gone certifiably insane. 'Poppy, are you okay? What were you about to tell me?'

'You're on the train to Paddington?' I ignore his question completely. If he's where I think he is then I won't need to tell him like this.

'Yeah… I thought you knew I was just in Broadway for the day?'

'Which carriage are you in?' I say, standing up.

'C. I'm heading back to London for Christmas.'

I'm in B. Could it be that I've been just one carriage away from him all this time? Or have we literally just missed each other?

I walk past empty seat after empty seat as fast as my legs can carry me. And then I see a messy mop of strawberry-blond hair, a phone pulled up to his ear and my heart stills.

'Poppy, is everything okay? What were you calling to tell me?'

I hang up the call. The line goes dead.

'Shit.' Theo looks down at his phone, then out of the window. There's no tunnel.

'You have eleven volunteers,' I say, my phone now stashed in my pocket.

Theo's entire body freezes for a second. Then slowly, so slowly, he turns around.

'Hey,' I say, standing there before him, my weekend bag by my side.

'Hey,' he grins back at me. 'What the…? What are you doing here?'

'You know how you said that if my Cotswolds trip didn't go to plan, that I could always spend Christmas Day with you?'

Theo nods, a huge smile on his face. 'I do,' he says, brushing a hand through his messy hair.

'Does the offer still stand?'

'It does.' Theo comes to stand before me and for a moment, I think he's going to kiss me, but he just stands there and smiles. 'But I might be spending the day with my friends *at* Church Street *on* Church Street,' he beams back at me.

'It sounds perfect,' I say, so pleased to be standing here now, all my baggage in tow.

'It won't be,' he laughs and I know it's going to be rough and ready and real.

'That sounds even better, actually.'

Chapter Twenty-Nine

Christmas Day

'Ouch,' I say, looking down at the minuscule nick the wrapping paper has just given me. I'm on my hands and knees, adding the last ribbon to the gifts we've wrapped for the service users who signed up for lunch today before we knew whether it could even happen.

Theo swings around from his position perched on the third step of the old rickety ladder as he replaces the latest dead bulb in the world's shabbiest Christmas lights.

'Everything okay?' he asks, looking down at me.

'Paper cut,' I say, looking back up at him. Even with the barely-there brightness of the string of lights, they seem to make his eyes shine brighter.

'From the cards?'

It was Avery who thought to buy Stanley and Linda a new pack of playing cards. Avery who bought a fresh box of cupcakes for Roger. Avery who silently never stopped believing we'd be able to open the community centre today, buying the most personal presents and putting them away for everyone throughout the course of the year.

'Wrapping paper,' I say back to him, my knees still curled up beneath me on the grubby wooden floor. 'That's the last of them wrapped now,' I add as Theo walks down the ladder to stand before me. Half of me is waiting for him to stumble on the last step, tripping into my arms again. But he doesn't need me to save him. He reaches down to take my hand in his, studying the paper cut before releasing my hand. He doesn't need to save me either.

'Well, don't cut yourself on this...' Theo says, reaching into his pocket and pulling out an unpeeled sticker. I already know what the scribbles say on top. Sure enough, he reaches down to put the sticker to my chest, every bit as awkward as the first time he did, back when I was boxing up food parcels and wondering how the hell I could win back my life with George. Now, electricity tingles through me as I surrender to whatever comes next. Theo reaches for my hand, pulling me to my feet and holding me close and then...

'Everything's set!'

We break eye contact to find Avery, beaming from ear to ear. The fact she's still managing to pop up from nowhere doesn't feel startling anymore, it feels comforting. As does the fact that Lily – one fifth of the mean girls and Avery's old but new-again friend – is standing there beside her. They've been busy in the kitchen preparing the dinner trimmings for a couple of hours now, along with several other members of our team.

'Time to open the doors?' Lily asks, looking from Theo to Avery. It's not even ten in the morning, but we know that the visitors coming here today will have nowhere else to go. We posted our plans to open on social media yesterday but know that most of our regulars don't need a prompt to turn up here.

'Let's do it!' Theo says and I watch Lily glow. Sweet seventeen with a starry-eyed crush. I remember what it's like to dream like that, to fabricate how fabulous a life with someone would be. I only stopped doing it yesterday. Theo leads the way and Lily follows.

'Avery?' I ask. She swings around. We've not had a second to speak just the two of us since I told Theo I was available to volunteer, available in more ways than one, last night. 'I heard about your dad...' I say slowly. Until recently, I'd never be the one to bring up family matters, too cautious that the conversation would turn back around to mine. 'Are you okay?'

'It's okay, I'm used to it...' Avery says, her usually shiny face falling for a second. Before I can stop myself, I grab her in a massive hug, holding her head to my chest.

'Just because you're used to it doesn't make it okay,' I whisper.

'I know, I just keep going over what I could have done differently, I...'

'No,' I say, breaking off the hug to tell her what I wish someone had been around to tell me when I was her age. 'It's not your fault. These things sometimes just... happen.'

Life happens. At the wrong times. In the wrong circumstances. When we're not ready for it. I think of Bob's email, the one I hid away from George in the Christmas market. I haven't replied, haven't found the words to say, but I might. And I'm going to chat to Theo about him, tell him everything about my past, ask him all about Bob. But not today. Today, Theo's waited far too long to enjoy the people who are here, now. In the *present*.

One by one, service users come through the open doors; familiar faces smile, Stanley waves, Roger comes over to me and Avery to give us each a massive hug. I can smell alcohol on his breath and it still breaks my heart that he can't break that habit, that he's seemingly relapsed again, but that doesn't mean he's not welcome here, it doesn't mean he can't belong. There are other people too, people I don't recognise, that I haven't seen before.

'There's loads of them,' I whisper, as soon as Theo is back by my side.

'I knew there would be,' he says, turning to me as I try to work out his expression, which is teetering somewhere between satisfaction and sadness. Satisfaction, because he knows he's making a difference. Sadness, because he wishes he didn't have to.

'That's why we needed at least eleven volunteers,' he goes on. 'I knew if we opened, and word got around that there would be more visitors here than we expected. No one likes to be alone on Christmas Day.'

I know that. I know it first-hand. I can't help but wonder how Bob, my Uncle Bob, is spending his day. After leaving his email unanswered, part of me doesn't want to ask. I also know what it's like to be rejected by those who are meant to love you most.

'It's nice to be able to do something special for them.' Theo smiles across the bustling hall, filled with colour and cheer and *tonnes* of tacky tinsel.

'This whole place is something special…' I say, feeling Theo's body so close beside me, his opening palm hanging dangerously close to mine. '…because of you.'

At just that moment, a football that some of the children have started playing with flies across the room, hitting the section of lights that Theo was fixing less than an hour ago. They flicker for a moment and then go out.

'No, no,' Theo says, shaking his head but unable to stash his smile. 'You can't pin this place on me,' he laughs. 'I'm just a normal guy…'

'A Normal Larry,' I say, a glimmer of mischief in my eyes. As if Theo has *facials*.

'A normal *guy*,' he reiterates again, glaring back at me. 'Trying to make a bit of difference in the world.'

One by one, the light bulbs hung painstakingly across the room seem to flicker and fail, like the children's game has caused some kind of unfortunate chain reaction. I wait for Theo to be irritated or annoyed that his work has gone to waste but he just smiles, shakes his head again, and goes to retrieve the football, kicking it back to them across the room. I feel something flicker inside me, and for just a moment, I think of George. He's wonderful and I want him to be happy but for now, it feels refreshing not to be tied to someone chasing the limelight and instead to be around people who don't need bulbs to light up a room.

'Dinner is served!' Avery says, throwing her arms wide as if she's revealing something when really, it's taken all our strength to keep some of the visitors away from digging into the food as soon as the volunteering team place it on the table. I know for a fact that Stanley has stashed three pigs-in-blankets in his coat pocket already.

The tables look wonderful, two long rows now set for forty-two, with fold-out chairs pulled close around every edge. One by one, visitors and volunteers make their way to the seats. Although we needed a specific number of volunteers to be able to open today, there's no 'us' and 'them' here, especially when it comes to food.

'Mind if I take this seat?' Theo says, pulling out the chair beside me, just in time for Roger to plonk himself onto it. There was once a time when Roger didn't want to sit with anyone. 'Even better,' Theo says to no one in particular as he takes the seat next to him.

I marvel at the spread before us. In reality, it's not much – just a bunch of Christmas dinner rolls and pigs-in-blankets and bowls of crisps piled high – but considering that we've pretty much thrown it together in the past twenty-four hours, it's a mini festive miracle.

My mind jolts to Marie, to our own Christmas miracle, almost exactly a month ago. It may not have worked out how we had planned it, but looking around now, this doesn't feel like an accident.

'We've not said grace.' I hear one mother slap a sandwich out of her son's hands just as he's about to take a massive bite out of it. She needn't worry, Roger's almost finished his.

'Who's Grace?' Stanley pipes up from far down the line of people. The mother bristles like she's about to say something back, when Theo lets out a little cough. That's the trouble with bringing a bunch of people who have different views and opinions and beliefs together; there's always the risk of conflict bubbling under the surface.

'Right!' Theo stands and everyone freezes, no fewer than four arms poised and reaching for their second helpings. 'Everybody hold hands.' There's an audible groan but the mother and her four children reach out their hands instantly, as do a smattering of others.

I feel Roger reach for my hand and I hold his rough fingers in my own; he feels like a friend. 'I'm going to say a quick prayer…'

'Amen!' one service user shouts.

'That wasn't it...' another whispers back to him.

'I don't have anything to do with religion, not even the traditions...' yet another says.

'What about Christmas?'

'Oh yeah... well... that's different...'

'Quiet!' Avery says, popping up to stand by her brother again.

'Thank you.' Theo smiles at her sister as the rest of the mumblers obediently hold hands. Theo takes a dramatic breath and I wait for the solemn prayer to come next.

'God,' Theo says loudly, authoritatively, and I have to force myself to keep my eyes closed. 'Bless this bunch whilst they munch their lunch!'

And that's it. He sits back down again. But it must have done the job because laughter spreads around the table like wildfire and the children who were waiting get the nod to eat.

Afterwards, when all that is left on the table are crisp crumbs and crackers that have been pulled in half, some of the volunteers walk over to the Christmas tree and hand out gifts to each of the people sat around the table. I sit and watch as the paper I so lovingly wrapped around them gets ripped off and even flung around the room in the melee of present opening. My hands may be empty, but my heart is full – not to mention my stomach.

'That was *amazing*,' I say to Roger and Theo, a hand over my bulging belly. I think of Dee and wonder whether she's said anything to Charlie yet. I may not be the praying type, but I find myself shooting off something like a blessing for that bump. And one for Marie and Aran, even though I've already exchanged messages with them today. And one for Uncle Bob and the rest of my family and the many foster families I've spent my Christmases with before. The good but gone too soon. The bad but not forgotten. The ugly I'd *like* to forget.

'Cupcake?' Roger grumbles, having just opened his box of six creamy cakes.

'I would literally explode,' I reply, bringing my attention back into the room.

'Please don't,' Theo says across Roger. 'I'll have to clear it up and…' he hesitates for a moment, a seriousness washing over his face. 'I wanted to give you this.'

Across Roger, Theo gives me a small, wrapped present, complete with red bow on top. I take it and feel the small box in my hands, unwrapping it to find a velvet jewellery box.

'Bloody hell!' Roger says. It's what I was thinking exactly.

'Roger… do you mind if…'

'Cupcake?' Roger pushes the box towards Theo. I know he's being facetious now.

'Can we swap places?' Theo finishes his sentence.

I know this is the last thing Theo wants, metaphorically, that he never wants to drink too much, that he never wants to be in the same position as his dad. Just like I never want to repeat the story of my own childhood. But physically? Physically, I want nothing more than to be sitting closer to Theo, whilst I open this unexpected, uninvited, unreciprocated gift.

Slowly, ever so slowly, I prise open the box to find a coupon for a free coffee at Church Street. My laugh echoes across the room.

'Sorry, but I didn't have long to prepare.'

'Just what I wanted!' I throw my hands together and swoon sarcastically.

'Now that you don't work here…' Theo begins. 'You don't work here anymore, right?'

I guess my scrappy attendance and disappearing for a week may have told him that. But it's not like I have anything else lined up. Except, maybe now that I'm not shadowing George around the gig circuit I may actually be able to get some freelance work promoting things I'm passionate about. I know it's worth another shot.

'No, I'll volunteer though,' I say, knowing I'll have to get some work soon if I'm going to be able to afford a room in a house-share. But I know that I'll be able to, that when I put my mind to something, wholeheartedly, I can make it happen. 'And I'd like to keep helping grow your social media account, if you'll let me…'

'Please!' Theo says, like he's had about enough of it after answering one message. 'And maybe one day, when you're ready…' he says reluctantly now, his eyes searching mine. 'Would you like to go out for a drink with me? A proper one.'

'Like a date?' I ask, smiling; who knew Theo would thaw into such a charmer?

'Exactly like a date,' he grins back at me. 'If you'd like to,' he adds quickly.

'I'd like to,' I say, beaming back at him, a surge of emotion, of *joy*, rushing through my veins. 'A lot, but…' Theo's face falls for a moment at the word 'but' – the word I never wanted from George, until I let it lead us somewhere better, somewhere more real. 'But that'll have to be my gift to you,' I say, feeling a bit guilty. 'I've not got you anything… I didn't even think…'

'You being here is more than enough.' Theo's eyes look across the table, at families and friends chatting and laughing across the room.

'I guess I'm your lucky eleventh volunteer…'

'You're the twelfth actually,' Theo says, now his turn to look guilty as his eyes dart across to the main doors into the halls, to the broad figure that has just walked in. The broad figure from the photograph under the angel and my old family photograph: *Bob*.

Chapter Thirty

'I hope you don't mind,' Theo whispers quickly, his head oscillating between me and Bob as he makes his way across the room towards us. 'He told me that your paths have crossed before, that he is an old friend of your mum's and he really wanted to see you, and I thought that maybe…'

'He was more than a friend to my mum,' I say and Theo's jaw drops an inch, looking like he's definitely done the wrong thing in telling Bob that I'd be here today after all. 'He's my uncle,' I add, reaching a hand towards Theo and resting it lightly on his shoulder.

'That's where I recognised…' Theo says, looking like some kind of penny has just dropped. 'Sorry… I mean… you have the same eyes… you looked at me and instantly reminded me of someone I used to know here. It was *him*.' Theo's smile fades. 'Oh, Poppy, I'm so sorry. I shouldn't have just got him to show up unannounced. I didn't know.'

'It's okay,' I say, my heart running a mile a minute but my legs standing slowly. 'He emailed me…'

'I'm the one who gave him your address through,' Theo says, still not sure whether he's in the doghouse. He may have overstepped the mark, meddled in my mess, but isn't that what family does? Because isn't that what everyone is here at Church Street, a ragtag bunch of randoms with a thousand different opinions and beliefs who all make time and space for one another to be accepted exactly how they are?

'You just saved me having to email him back,' I say with a smile before turning away from him and walking the few short steps left between me and Bob.

'Poppy?' he says awkwardly, shifting his weight from foot to foot. 'You don't know me, but I emailed you and I'm not sure if you got it and if you want me to leave that's absolutely okay and—'

'It's okay,' I say. Bob exhales, his cheeks flushing red as he does. 'I got it and I was going to reply, I've just had… a lot going on.'

'You don't need to explain,' he says, looking around the room. 'If anyone's got any explaining to do, it's me.'

'Bob, isn't it?' I say, offering him my open palm. He takes it in his and shakes, a gesture too formal for family but evidentially warmer than he was expecting.

'Yes,' he nods. 'I can't believe how grown-up you look,' his voice quivers slightly.

'It's what tends to happen after twenty or so years,' I laugh. 'I can't believe you're actually *here*. Do you…?' I begin to say but Bob chatters on nervously.

'Yes, I still live locally – share a house with some friends. I know it's not the coolest thing for a grown man to do but it feels like a mansion compared to…' Bob is speaking so quickly that he seems to lose his train of thought. After so much silence there's not enough time to say everything we want to.

'I was actually going to ask whether you wanted some lunch? There's loads left.'

'Oh, I…' Bob begins before a smile spreads across his face. 'I'd love to.'

Theo stands up to embrace Bob as soon as we've retraced my steps back to where I left him. His eyes meet mine, widening as if to ask whether everything is okay; I nod back to him. I know he has so many questions, about my past, about why I don't seem to know my own uncle. I have questions too. So many questions. About Bob, his life. About my mum and hers, about why I never heard from her again, why she never tried to find me. But he's here now, living locally, and for the first time in a long while, I feel like I have time to take things slowly.

'I've got so much to tell you,' Bob says, taking a seat beside me.

'I want to hear it all,' I say, never meaning anything more. I'm done running from the truth. 'I'm not going anywhere.'

'Nor am I,' he smiles, holding my gaze fast. There's no twelve-day countdown to force a relationship into being what I want it to be. There's just hours and days and weeks and months to let things simply unfold. To let the chips fall where they may.

'Who's up for poker?' Stanley shouts from the far end of the leftovers-scattered table, his own pack of brand-new playing cards held in his hands.

'I don't gamble,' Bob says, turning to look at me apologetically. 'Any more.' Our eye contact stretches for a second and I wonder whether this is one of the many mistakes he referred to in his email. I remind myself that I don't need all the answers this instant. That after years of questioning my past, I'm surprised to find I'm more interested in getting to know the man sat beside me now. The man who Church Street helped get back on his feet again. The man who came as he was but didn't stay as he was.

'How about Articulate?' I shout back down the table before smiling at Bob. For some reason, getting the group to shift gears from gambling to a game feels like I'm protecting him. Perhaps at one stage this protection was meant to be the other way around, but I know now that true love doesn't wait to receive before it gives. Theo and this place taught me that.

'And to think less than three weeks ago you didn't know what Articulate was,' Theo says, settling in beside me. 'Shotgun on your team.'

'Shotgun on *anyone* but Linda's team,' I whisper under my breath, recalling the erotic bird flamingo scenario all over again.

'Same,' Bob says and I remember again that he used to be a visitor here. 'I'll have to tell you about the time she fell out with me over Uno.' His laugh is loud and warm.

'Now *that*, I have to hear,' I say back to him, smiling broader still. That and everything else I feel pretty confident we'll make time for. 'But she's *not* good at Articulate.'

'I could tell you over dinner sometime?' he asks, cautiously. 'Or a coffee... whatever you feel comfortable with,' he adds, knowing to take this slow.

'Dinner,' I say, smiling back at him, feeling braver now. 'Dinner sounds good.'

'I'll go first!' Avery pops up from her seat, interrupting the moment. Of course, she pops up. 'Okay, okay... you can push it, or you can sit on it... you cut the grass with it...'

'Scissors!' Linda shouts back at her.

'A lawnmower!' Another voice guesses the right answer.

'Bloody hell, Linda! How long does it take you to cut the grass?' another shouts.

'I'm next!' Stanley gets to his feet. I know by now that turn-taking here isn't a thing, it's more a case of who can jostle their way to the front. There's something refreshing about the honesty of that.

'Okay, this is easy…' he begins as Theo reaches to pour himself a glass of water, preparing to guess. Stanley is gesturing with his hands, creating a ring with one hand and forcing a finger through it with his other. It looks hugely suggestive – *erotic*, even – and I have to bite back my giggles as others around the table scream at Stanley to stop acting and describe what's on the card out loud. 'It's *Lord of the Rings*.'

Theo spills his water across the table. I let out a big belly laugh, complete with snort.

'How did no one get that?' Stanley throws his arms wide in disbelief.

Theo looks to me, but I can't control my giggles. Bob seems to be enjoying this too, standing to go and join some of the faces he seems to recognise from his time spent here all those years ago. As the next person begins to describe the word on their card, Theo leans in closer towards me.

'Do you still think Christmas Day is overrated, Popstar?' he asks as Avery comes to stand beside us. I scooch up so that she can perch on one side of my chair.

'I never actually said that…' I object, brushing a stray tear of laughter from my cheek. 'Just that I've always preferred Christmas Eve.'

'Why?' Avery says, looking up at the game descending into chatter and chaos.

'Honestly?' I say, looking from Avery to her stupidly handsome big brother.

'Of course,' Theo smiles and under the table, he reaches for my hand.

'Well, if I'm really honest…' I begin, lacing my finger through his; this feels like a secret, but I know nothing stays hidden for long.

'Christmas Eve has always felt like a time for friends, when everyone goes to the pub and has a good time, and then, well, Christmas Day, everyone is with their family…' My voice breaks and Theo squeezes my hand a little tighter.

'And I've never really had a family…' I say, my sentence trailing off as I look to Bob laughing with Roger, Linda squabbling with Stanley, and Ruth sipping her fifth cup of coffee next to him, a bunch of children scattered randomly by their feet. Avery wraps her arm around me and Theo grins, holding my hand in his, and I can't help but think *until now*.

I've never really had a family until now.

A Letter from Elizabeth

Dear Reader,

I want to say a huge thank you for choosing to read *Twelve Days to Save Christmas*. If you did enjoy it, and want to keep up to date with all my latest releases, just sign up at the following link. Your email address will never be shared and you can unsubscribe at any time.

www.bookouture.com/elizabeth-neep

It feels both minutes and decades since I was writing a letter to lovely readers like you in the back of *The New Me* (isn't it strange what a global pandemic can do to our concept of time?!). In that letter I explained that all my book ideas to date had been sparked by something ridiculous happening to either me or my friends in real life (that my imagination then took *way* out of hand). And yet, thanks to the pandemic putting a pause on many nights out, dates, spontaneous run-ins and chance happenings, the story behind this book is a little different.

It was my agent who first emailed me to ask whether I'd ever had any ideas for a Christmas book. Initially, I said no (because I hadn't and I'm a terrible fibber) but that I'd take some time to think about it. Turns out I didn't need very long. Moments after sending my reply, I went for a run around Central London and very soon Poppy's story was materialising in my mind. As I ran through Borough Market, I imagined it lit up with Christmas lights; through the winding streets behind London Bridge station, I dreamt of Poppy and George's picture-perfect life hidden away in the aspirational apartments. And, passing a crowded community centre, I stumbled upon the idea of Poppy finding herself inside there, physically *and* metaphorically.

For me, one of my favourite moments in Poppy's story is when she stops trying to muster her festive spirit and realises 'it's not something [she] ever had to chase. It was inside [her] all along'. And in many ways, I feel like Poppy's story was always somewhere in me too; a creative combination of consuming countless rom-coms, volunteering through my local church and my love for Christmas, which (like all great loves) has evolved throughout the years.

To say I was excited about Christmas as a child would be an understatement. In fact, my parents had to invoke a rule in our house that I wasn't allowed to talk about it before the October half-term (ha!). From writing my letter to Santa to leaving a carrot out for his reindeer, I loved it all. But then, as I got older the magic started to wear off. The truth is, there was still a whole lot of wonder in my adulthood Christmases, from time spent with friends and family (all the more precious when you're working most of the year) and great gifts – often smaller, more thoughtful, personally picked-out – to champagne and cheese and *The Big Fat Quiz of the Year*. And yet, I've always been someone who finds transitions quite hard, reminiscing about the rose-tinted past, clinging to an idea of how I want things to be but struggling to relax into the joy of the reality. The good news is – a little like Poppy – I always get there in the end.

This book, like *The Spare Bedroom*, *Never Say No* and *The New Me* before it, is about embracing life in all its multifaceted glory – the good bits, the hard bits (often at the same time) and letting go enough to enjoy the ride. For me, personally, I've found my Christian faith really important in that process of surrendering and choosing to be thankful in all seasons – and if you can't be thankful at Christmas, when can you be?

Whether you're reading this on the night before Christmas or picking it up in the middle of July (which is coincidentally when I'm writing this), whether your family celebrate Christmas or you just fancied a wintery read, thank you so much for choosing Poppy's story.

I hope you loved *Twelve Days to Save Christmas* and if you did, I would be very grateful if you could write a review. I'd love to hear what you think and it makes such a difference helping new readers to discover one of my books for the first time.

I love hearing from my readers – you can get in touch on my Facebook page, through Instagram, Twitter, Goodreads or my website.

Thanks,
Elizabeth x

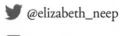 @elizabeth_neep

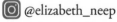 @elizabeth_neep

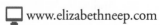 www.elizabethneep.com

Acknowledgements

As a young (and strangely ambitious) child, I used to dream about writing acknowledgements pages – but the reality is I find them pretty tricky. There are so many snippets of the people I have met and the conversations I have shared that have shaped this story into what it is that it's impossible to name everyone here. If you know me and you recognise some of yourself in these pages, consider yourself seen and loved and thanked.

Huge thanks must go to Rebecca Hilsdon and my lovely literary agent Sallyanne Sweeney for even putting the idea of writing a Christmas book on my radar; I'm so pleased I have been able to submerge myself in the most joyful time of year (even when it's been thirty degrees outside!) Thanks also to Cara Chimirri, Therese Keating and the entire team at Bookouture for taking this book on and helping me shape and mould it into the story you are holding in your hands today. And to every book blogger, Netgalley reviewer and reader, thank you so much for choosing to journey with Poppy during this magical season.

When I started writing this story, I knew I wanted to name Theo after the kindest boy I know, so big thanks to my three-year-old godson, Theo Nelson, for being the cutest and to Becky and Jonny Nelson for choosing me to be your Fairy Godmother.

Though this book is a lockdown baby, thank you to the friends who kept me sane throughout with phone calls, long walks and socially distanced coffees. And to the people who do the emotional heavy lifting when I'm knee-deep in editing: Nick (aka the real

Normal Larry) and Mango (who won't read this, because she's a cat), thank you for filling our lockdown bubble with talks, cuddles and belly strokes (attribute these to Nick and Mango as you will). And to Mum, Dad, Tom and Rachel, thank you for being the best.

My final thanks are always to God; for helping me bumble through this life with purpose, for loving me when I fail and picking me up when I fall – oh, and for Christmas!

Made in United States
Troutdale, OR
11/12/2023